"You want to pair **[barcode: D0631611]**

"Sort of..." With a bashful grimace, Mia took Julian by one arm and led him to the tarp. "I also want to taste you."

"Taste me?"

"To see if I've gotten the flavors of the body paints right."

"And how will we test that?" He moved in to kiss her, but Mia stuck a brush between them, making a broad swipe of glistening red paint across his chest. Then she layered a stripe of warm midnight-dark liquid next to it.

"Bittersweet chocolate and strawberry. Always a good combination." She plopped another full load of the paint onto his chest, watching with an almost scientific interest as a rivulet ran across his stomach to pool at his navel just inside the waistband of his shorts.

"Maybe you should take them off." Her round cheeks pinkened. "In the name of science."

"Maybe *you* should take them off," he replied. His voice dropped, grating in his tight throat. "In the name of *sex*."

Blaze™

Dear Reader,

You might be wondering about the title of this book. *Taste Me*. Rather provocative, isn't it? Try being the author who must answer *"Taste Me"* when asked about her next title! Blaze leads me down some very interesting paths....

Just as Mia does to Julian in *Taste Me*. She's an outlandish creative type and he's the conservative CEO who's ready to follow her anywhere—even to the world of edible body painting. No slouch as a Blaze heroine, Mia's thrilled to experiment on the man who's been named one of the country's hottest bachelors. This book is a continuation of my SEX & CANDY miniseries (with all new characters), so you know the fun doesn't stop there.

Mmm. Taste me.

That's the book talking—I swear!

Carrie Alexander

P.S. Look for my next Blaze SEX & CANDY book, *Unwrapped,* in December, and go online to www.carriealexander.com to enter my contests and subscribe to the Get Carried Away e-newsletter.

Books by Carrie Alexander

HARLEQUIN BLAZE
20—PLAYING WITH FIRE
114—STROKE OF MIDNIGHT "Enticing"

HARLEQUIN TEMPTATION
925—THE CHOCOLATE SEDUCTION*
929—SINFULLY SWEET*

HARLEQUIN SUPERROMANCE
1102—NORTH COUNTRY MAN
1186—THREE LITTLE WORDS

*Sex & Candy

TASTE ME

Carrie Alexander

HARLEQUIN®

TORONTO • NEW YORK • LONDON
AMSTERDAM • PARIS • SYDNEY • HAMBURG
STOCKHOLM • ATHENS • TOKYO • MILAN • MADRID
PRAGUE • WARSAW • BUDAPEST • AUCKLAND

ISBN 0-373-79151-8

TASTE ME

Copyright © 2004 by Carrie Antilla.

All rights reserved. Except for use in any review, the reproduction or utilization of this work in whole or in part in any form by any electronic, mechanical or other means, now known or hereafter invented, including xerography, photocopying and recording, or in any information storage or retrieval system, is forbidden without the written permission of the publisher, Harlequin Enterprises Limited, 225 Duncan Mill Road, Don Mills, Ontario, Canada M3B 3K9.

All characters in this book have no existence outside the imagination of the author and have no relation whatsoever to anyone bearing the same name or names. They are not even distantly inspired by any individual known or unknown to the author, and all incidents are pure invention.

This edition published by arrangement with Harlequin Books S.A.

® and TM are trademarks of the publisher. Trademarks indicated with ® are registered in the United States Patent and Trademark Office, the Canadian Trade Marks Office and in other countries.

www.eHarlequin.com

Printed in U.S.A.

1

THE WET PAINTBRUSH hovered above the woman's bare breast, then dabbed down, adding another coating of goop to her perky nipple so it looked like a shiny red cherry. A glistening globule broke free and rolled along the curve of the most perfectly shaped breast Julian Silk had ever seen. He could hardly believe his eyes.

"Damn!" The artist pressed her finger to the painted breast to stop the runaway drip, making the woman's flesh jiggle slightly. Stretched out on her side, the model didn't move, except to stifle a yawn.

One of the assistants darted in with a handful of Q-tips to repair the mistake.

"Cress!" the artist called. She removed her finger and stepped back, giving the model an evaluating stare. She held an open palm under the gooey paintbrush. "I need more cornstarch in the cherry paint, Cress. It's too thin. Angelika's thighs are streaking."

Julian looked. The model's thighs were also perfect. Not as perfect as the breasts, because Julian was a breast man, but perfect enough to make him want to wrap his hands around them and lick from stem to stern. That the thighs happened to be painted with candy-cane stripes had nothing to do with it.

He couldn't say the same about the words *TASTE ME*,

which were written out in silver nonpareils that framed the perfect little belly button on her tight, flat tummy.

Julian shoved his hands into the pockets of his trousers, giving himself a little more room down there. So this was why the X chromosomes on the *Hard Candy* staff had staged a Nerf ball tournament to decide who got to "supervise" the December cover shoot.

Victor Noone, the magazine's advertising sales director, looked up from a consultation with a contingent from Sugar High, the up-and-coming candy company that was buying heavily into the gala holiday issue. "Julian! Please join us."

At the sound of his name, a female head snapped to. Petra Lombardi, the *Hard Candy* art director, hurried over. "I didn't know you planned to be here, Julian." Her voice was like sliding silk, her heels staccato spikes. Silver-blond hair and milky skin looked an even whiter shade of pale against a black leather suit with dainty silver buckles. Petra was a woman of sharp contrasts and biting smiles. Attractive, but potentially poisonous. After a short-term exposure, Julian had developed a resistance.

"You must say hello to the Sugar High executives." She took his arm. "And our creative team, of course."

Julian cast another lingering look at the photo set before letting Petra tug him away. The reclining model was arranged on a satin-draped tabletop. Every inch of her skin had been coated in glorious color—edible paint, he'd been told. A team of black-clad assistants, wielding paper cones of frosting as glue, rapidly affixed assorted hard candies to her body, decorating her in stripes, scallops and swirls. Even the model's hair was transformed, pulled back into a knot, sprayed white and strung with strings of candy dots.

The woman with the paintbrush hovered over a long table set to one side, out of the heat of the lights. The surface was chockablock with painting implements and small buckets of the sugary concoctions in a rainbow of hues. A young black man with sunglasses perched atop his shaved head was shaking a box of cornstarch into a plastic bucket.

The artist stirred the red syrup, lifted a long-handled spoon high to test the thickness, then licked a dab off her pinkie. She nodded at her cohort. "Thanks, Cress. That's better."

He cocked an eyebrow. "We can't have streaky thighs."

"Julian?" purred Petra. She squeezed his arm, her sharp burgundy nails narrowly missing skin as they bit into his rolled-up cuff.

"Coming," he said, without moving.

The artist glanced at him. Not a startled look, nor an eager one. She merely glanced once and looked away without reaction, as if he were just another boring plebeian she had to put up with while creating her masterpiece.

Julian forgot about the nude model. "Who is that?" he asked Petra.

"The body painter. Mia Somebody."

Some body, indeed. Even though she was clad in a pair of shapeless overalls and high-top red sneakers, it was obvious that Mia the body painter was her own work of art. Her face was button-cute and topped by a mop of black ringlets. She was short, but her legs went all the way up to a pert bottom. The bib of her overalls bagged over a baby-doll undershirt that clung to breasts that might have been as bodacious as the model's if he could get a really good look at them.

While Mia may have been aware of Julian's interest, she wasn't standing still for a leisurely inspection. Now that the cherry paint had been adjusted to her taste, she flitted between the model and the paint table, making adjustments and adding color, perfecting every splotch and candy dot of her creation while the bald assistant followed, spraying the model's completed parts until she was as lacquered and shining as a French glycée tart.

And all the while, Mia Some Body continued to show no interest whatsoever in the presence of Julian Silk, CEO of Silk Publications and such a dashing, sought-after playboy that he'd recently been named one of *Celebrity Gossip* magazine's Hottest Bachelors of the Year.

Not that he cared for that tripe. The publicity was mildly annoying and even embarrassing, particularly when it led to dazzled young women stopping him on the street to take photos or to have him autograph their bras. He didn't want to be a sex symbol celebrity, even for fifteen minutes of fame. His conservative board of directors had let it be known they felt the same.

On the other hand, Mia's complete disregard was humbling. And rather inspiring.

For the first time in months, Julian was roused to prove to a woman just how irresistible he could be.

"THE UMBRELLA over that strobe should be adjusted." Mia Kerrigan gnawed her knuckle as she watched the photographer direct his assistants as they finished lighting the cover shot. "There's too much shine coming off the paint."

"Out of your hands, sweetheart," Cress said. Even though they were standing off the set and out of the glare, he slid his Gucci aviator sunglasses into place. He claimed the bright lights hurt his eyes. Mia thought he just wanted to look cool for Angelika, a top model they'd worked with before, but who was too pricey to be one of Mia's regulars.

"I want this to be perfect." Mia was used to photographing her own artwork when she staged body-painting sessions in her home studio. But the money she got for freelance jobs was so attractive that she'd resigned herself to giving up creative control of the end product.

With a sigh, she reminded herself that Phil Shavers, the photographer the magazine had chosen, was one of the hottest in the business. Angelika would look gorgeous on the cover of *Hard Candy*, the sexy new men's lifestyle magazine. A truly edible feast. If the glazed eyes and openmouthed expressions of the spectators were typical, the magazine's young, buff, upwardly mobile readers would want to ravish the model like a pack of hungry wolves.

"It's perfect," Cress said, being completely sincere, unlike the toadies who'd gathered around. Cress's taste was impeccable...for a raging heterosexual.

Reminded of why she hired the photo stylist whenever it was financially viable, and relied on him as a friend the rest of the time, Mia stood on her toes to throw an arm around Cress's thin shoulders. She gave him a sloppy kiss on the cheek. "Thanks."

"Ugh. You're all sticky."

She licked his jaw. Sugar granules melted on her tongue. "So are you."

He gave her a squeeze. "Let's go shower off."

"Not until the shoot is over. We might need to do touch-ups if Angelika starts to melt. Her butt is already looking globby."

Cress managed an obvious leer from behind the sunglasses. "Says you."

"Get her number yet?"

"She slipped me her card."

"Before or after you gave her the Brazilian?" Mia needed her models to be as slick as porpoises from head to toe. Cress had developed a magic touch with the hot wax—one of his many skills.

"Models appreciate a man with gentle hands," he gloated.

"Uh-huh. Nothing says you're special like ripping out stray pubic hairs."

Satisfied that the shoot was under control for the moment, Mia turned away to sort out her table of supplies. There were paints in every flavor—cherry, lime, grape, orange, three shades of chocolate. She was fully stocked with penny candy, as well. Sugar High, the candy company that was underwriting the cover as a heavy advertiser, had sent over a box of product for her use. To be doubly sure she'd have every color and shape under the sun, Mia had sent Cress out for an even larger variety. He'd gone wild at Sweet Something, a popular candy store in the Village, and come back with enough hard candy to decorate a hundred models plus their agents.

The unusually large amount of ingredients and supplies had maxed out Mia's credit card, but she'd get the cost back a hundredfold when the check from the magazine was cut. If she was lucky, there'd be enough to pay her rent for a couple of months and still put a good chunk aside for the complicated multimodel tableau she'd already sketched out for the International Body Painting Expo coming up in a couple of months. With an attention-grabbing *Hard Candy* cover on the horizon, a good showing at the expo would shoot Mia to stardom in the body-painting community.

Big frog in a small pond, her father would say, *if you can be satisfied with that.* Pastor Robert Kerrigan ran his church and congregation like a Fortune 500 company. He believed in sticking to the rules and striving for the highest level of success, in any field.

Mia believed in breaking the rules and playing her life by ear. "Happy frog," she mumbled.

"What?" Cress said, appearing at her elbow.

She gave him her biggest grin. "Can I book you now for the expo? It's the first week in October. I must assemble the best team possible to have a chance at the gold medal in the group category."

Cress sniffed. "I'll have to check my schedule. I'm much in demand these days."

"Oh."

"Yeah, right, *Vogue* called and I forgot to tell you." He slid his sunglasses down his nose and looked at Mia over the frames. "Of course I'll do it. You're my homie."

Mia flicked a paintbrush at him. Cressley Godwin IV was from a family as well-off as her own. They'd met years ago in private school, two misfits more interested in the arts and independence than shopping for designer labels on Daddy's dime and doing Ecstasy at dance clubs. Cress talking 'hood style was like Mia trying to carry on a coherent conversation with her mother's French classics book club.

Cress frowned at the lime flecks on his champagne-colored raw silk shirt. "You got paint on me. The sugar will spot."

Mia handed him a sponge. "Send me the dry-cleaning bill, homie."

"Oh, don't worry, I will."

"Touch-ups!" screeched the photographer.

Mia grabbed the bucket of cherry paint and the air brush. "Bring the vanilla paint and the gelatin glaze. We need to layer another coat on Angelika's southern hemisphere."

"Have glaze, will travel to uncharted territories," Cress muttered as he followed her to the set. "Just like Lewis and Clark."

Mia began to spray the model's striped thighs. "Or Stanley and Livingstone."

"Livingstone got lost in the jungle. I've never met a thicket I couldn't conquer." Cress smiled at the model. "Isn't that right, my angel?"

Angelika giggled. Most models giggled around Cress, who first made them his friends and then got them to take him home. He claimed that once they were in bed together, the typical supermodel soon forgot that they had six inches of height on him. His prowess supposedly dazzled them. Mia believed that his girlfriends had a shortage of brain cells to start with.

"Mmm-hmm." Mia pointed the nozzle of her spray gun at the twenty-one-year-old's plucked pubis and squeezed the trigger. Usually, the models wore tiny unobtrusive thongs no bigger than an eye patch, but going without produced a cleaner look.

When a model was willing to pose sans thong, Mia was careful to shoot only tastefully arranged poses. While she had much appreciation for the sensual aspects of body painting, gratuitous salaciousness frosted her cookies. Her art came first, not *Hard Candy*'s horn-dog target audience.

She shot a glare at the gaggle of onlookers. *Huh.* Several were edging closer, wanting a better look at the tempting display. Mia turned her backside to them while she worked, deliberately blocking their view of Angelika. She wasn't in the mood to deal with the sniggers and bawdy comments that were typical of a nonprofessional audience.

"Okay, looks like we're good," she said a few moments later, after Cress had made a final pass with the protective gelatin glazing medium.

The photographer darted in and adjusted a peppermint-swirl candy by an infinitesimal degree. "Now we're good. Clear set!"

Mia rolled her eyes at Cress as she backed away. She bumped into one of the spectators, who put his hand on her butt and said, "Careful, sweet cheeks."

Gross. Pretending to be startled, Mia whirled around and let go with a spurt of the cherry-flavored paint. It sprayed across the starched shirtfront and loosened tie of a tall, dark-haired man, barely missing another of the onlookers when he lunged out of the way.

"Hey!" the lunger said. He brushed at the sleeve of an expensive suit. "Watch what you're doing. You might have stained my Hugo Boss."

Although she'd been on the verge of a smart retort, Mia snapped her mouth shut. She recognized the voice of the man she'd missed as the one who'd made the "sweet cheeks" comment and had assumed he was also the ass-patter. Wrong.

She aimed an apologetic shrug at the man she'd sprayed and was startled to recognize him. He was the guy who'd arrived late and stared so intently that he'd broken her concentration. Quite an achievement. Typically, she lost herself in the artwork and had to be snapped out of her trance by Cress or an extremely fatigued model.

"Uh," she said. "Sorry about that."

"Me, too," he replied. "I didn't mean to grab your butt. I was just trying to stop you from backing into me."

She felt less sorry, but he was smiling at her, and his smile was pretty damn charming, so she wasn't mad, either. His voice was nicer than the other guy's, too. Deep, rich and smooth, like buttered rum. There was something familiar about his face. Maybe she'd run into him at another shoot?

Even so, he was only a suit. Albeit a cherry-flavored suit.

"I've wrecked your shirt." Mia reached for his arm. "Come over here, we'll get you cleaned up."

"Shouldn't I lick myself clean, like a cat?" the man said, letting her lead him to her table. He lifted the end of his tie to his mouth and took an experimental taste. His mouth puckered. "Uh, maybe not. I thought the paint's supposed to be edible."

"Technically it is," Mia said. "But I wouldn't want to eat it with a spoon." She squeezed out one of the soapy sponges they kept on hand. "We're more concerned with looks and application than the actual taste."

"So it's not a good idea if I set the Sugar High execs loose on—" the man nodded toward Angelika "—our holiday treat?"

Mia glanced sharply at him while she dabbed at his tie. "That would be in bad taste all the way around."

"I was kidding."

"Of course you were." She tossed the tails of the tie over his shoulder, trying not to notice how wide and square it was. She normally wasn't attracted to the men who huddled in conference at photo shoots, even when they were distractingly gorgeous. But this one had more than a thoroughbred body and a handsome face. He possessed black-licorice eyes struck with starbursts of good humor and the male version of a Mona Lisa smile. He was self-aware, not merely self-involved like the usual suit.

Then he ruined it by saying, "I'm Julian Silk," as if she should be impressed.

Julian Silk? Uh-oh. She'd spray-attacked the man who'd be signing her current paycheck.

Never mind, she told herself, remembering that she wasn't impressed with either power or money. She'd decided *that* nine years ago when she'd chosen art school instead of the Ivy League, despite her parents' protests. She'd been on her own ever since.

"Hey, wow," she said. "Congratulations."

Mr. Silk gave a surprised half laugh. "Congratulations for what?"

"The stork must have loved you." Mia tilted her head. "Being born into the Silk family is a little like winning the lottery, don't you think? If I'm impressed, it's only by your luck."

"That's one way of looking at it, I suppose."

She plucked at his shirtfront to hold it away from his body while she scrubbed at the stain. Mr. Silk stood quite still, but not tense, nor embarrassed. Perfectly casual and unconcerned, as if he were used to being attended to. Which, of course, he was. The man was so sharp and well put together that there had to be a team of tailors, barbers, workout gurus and maybe even plastic surgeons at his behest.

He made a motion, lifting his hand to his lips and then flinging it away.

She squinted an eye at him. "What are you doing?"

"Taking the silver spoon out of my mouth so you'll talk to me."

Behind her, Mia heard Cress smother a laugh. "It would be extremely idiotic of me to be rude to the man who can have me hired and fired," she said.

"Then you know who I am."

She sighed. "Now I do."

"After I told you." He ruminated on that, lifting one corner of lips so handsomely carved they belonged in the Louvre. "Dumb move. I was enjoying the anonymity."

"Uh-huh." But he'd just had to pull the I'm-rich-and-in-charge card. She suppressed another eye roll and redirected her attention to getting the stains off his shirt. They'd faded to pink.

Unfortunately, when his mouth was distracting her, she'd dabbed with too much force and had dampened the fabric to the point where it was almost see-through. The wet cotton clung to his abdomen. She had to scrape the material off with her fingers, pressing them into a slab of corrugated muscle that made her temperature rise beyond acceptable core-activity levels.

"What does 'uh-huh' mean?" Mr. Smooth-as-Silk asked, still completely oblivious to the potentially intimate situation. He probably thought of her like the tailor who measured his inseam and asked if he dressed to the right or left.

But he *had* cupped her ass.

"It means that you're one of those types," she said. *Scrub, scrub.* Her knuckles rubbed his abs. "The ones who are just so, you know, sick of being catered to, kowtowed to and sucked up to. You want to be one of the guys. A regular Joe." But not *really*. "And as for women—"

She stopped, reminding herself to breathe, then forgetting to as soon as Julian Silk looked down at her. His black-as-sin eyes gleamed. "Please continue. What about the women? They want me only for my money?"

"Hardly." Mia gave one final swipe of the sponge. "They want you for your money, your social standing *and* your looks. Which means that, as the proverbial total package, you can't pin down your dissatisfaction so easily. But you're bored with high-maintenance socialites and ambitious starlets. You're restless. You need more. Suddenly, you're thinking it's time to taste the earthy flavors of a working-class girl."

Mia patted his abdominals regretfully. They were lovely.

He drew in a noticeable breath. "Hmm. Interesting analysis. Are you offering?"

"Not me. But I'm sure you'll have no trouble finding willing prospects, Mr. Silk. Perhaps even in this room." Mia turned away from his intent stare, more flustered than she wanted him to see. Cress was stirring a cup of the chocolate paint, watching her with more than idle curiosity.

Oh damn. She'd been a smart-ass. When would she learn to keep her head down and her mouth shut?

"Call me Julian." He slipped his tie off his shoulder, sliding his hand along the silk length in a way that made her wonder what he'd be like in bed, running his hands over her thighs.

"Sure."

"Or maybe not." His tone was dry. "I wouldn't want you to think I'm too egalitarian."

She shrugged, feeling the warm pink in her cheeks.

Julian gave her a long look, then turned and took several steps before stopping to glance back at her. He cocked an eyebrow. "Oh yes, I almost forgot. You're fired."

2

THE ROUND-BOTTOMED pixie's mouth dropped open. Twin sparks appeared in her vivid peacock-blue eyes. Julian almost smiled. He'd shocked her, as intended.

"Unless you tell me your name," he added. His palm went automatically to his wet shirtfront, as if that would quell the interesting sensations she'd set off inside him with her diligent scrubbing.

"Or I could just call you the laundry maid," he said to provoke her further. There was a bit of the devil in him today—and she'd put it there. Before her, he'd been coasting on boredom, having everything in his empire but his crazy sisters under control.

With her tart tongue, quick mind and ripe figure, Mia Some Body was an intriguing prospect. Soon to be a satisfying conquest, when she'd received a full blast of his charm-her-pants-off charisma. He supposed that was conceited, but false modesty was a waste of time when the truth was that he hadn't met a woman yet who could resist, as Mia had said, the full Julian Silk package.

Ahem. He'd better get his mind off full packages before his own became blatantly apparent.

"I'm no servant," Mia said. She looked as if she might be grinding her teeth.

"Naturally. But I *can* hire and fire your delectable ass. You said so yourself."

She blinked hard, widening her eyes to half-dollar size. "I don't recall discussing delectable asses."

He stepped closer and lowered his voice. "An oversight on my part."

"Are you trying to be funny?"

"Do you see me laughing?"

Mia glanced at her cohort, the lithe young man she'd called Cress. He'd slid the sunglasses off his nose and was watching them with astonishment, the earpieces dangling down so the glasses hung under his chin like a chrome beard.

Mia motioned to the man. "Start packing up. Looks like the shoot is almost over."

Julian cleared his throat.

"Right," she said, in a way that meant "Oh yeah. *You.*" She tossed her head, regarding him with a smile gone smug. "Lucky for me, this job is over. I don't have to take your orders, Mr. Silk."

The little minx. "So you won't tell me your name?"

She stepped behind the table and made herself busy, gathering a fistful of gloppy paintbrushes. He could tell the sudden activity was so she didn't have to look at him, and that gave him some satisfaction. Not much, granted, but she was proving to be more of an elusive target than he'd expected.

"I'd be happy to," she said. "If you ask nicely."

"I was only teasing you about the firing thing. You're not fired. In fact, I'm actually tremendously impressed by your work, Miss…" He gave her his warmest look, the one he used on orphans, harried secretaries and his sister Nikki when she broke up with another boyfriend.

"Kerrigan. Mia Kerrigan."

"And please call me Julian."

Her head tilted. "Not Mr. Silk?"

"No. Mr. Silk was my dad."

"Was?" A frown flitted across her face.

"He died six years ago. A sudden heart attack. It was in the all the papers. I've been in charge of Silk Publications ever since." Now why had he said all that? Mia had been right on the mark about Julian being sick of his reputation preceding him—even before *Celebrity Gossip* had made his exploits famous.

Was he trying to impress her? If so, bad try. She'd made it obvious that she wasn't the kind of girl who'd be impressed by an inherited position and wealth, even if the family company had been teetering on the brink of bankruptcy when he'd taken over and he'd saved his mother and sisters from having to downgrade to coach class.

"I don't follow the society and financial sections," Mia said. "But I am sorry for your loss."

Her voice had softened. There was only sincerity behind it. Not a hint of the inner calculation over how much he was worth and whether she could snag him—reactions he'd come to recognize at fifty paces.

Julian gave his rolled-up sleeves a brisk shove. "Thanks."

Mia's eyes met his, and for a moment a warm current flowed between them, sweet and pure, unadulterated by her flip remarks and the surface charm of his initial attempts at seduction, which suddenly seemed rather puerile.

Petra clacked toward them. "Julian, you must join us. The shoot's breaking up, and Victor and I are taking the Sugar High team out for drinks."

"Not this time, Petra." He didn't want to take his eyes off Mia. Certainly not to schmooze a bunch of ad guys.

"Julian…" Petra's dark red lips pooched out. She moved herself into his line of sight, cutting off Mia. "I know it's a bore. But they *have* bought a six-page spread in the December issue, and Victor's minions are working on a long-term contract for future ad campaigns…"

Yammer, yammer, yammer. Julian let Petra rattle on, but he wasn't listening. He was watching Mia, who'd moved onto the set to lean over the model's dais and begin removing the hard candies. The overalls pulled snugly across her derriere. Even in baggy denim, Mia Kerrigan was all T&A, as ready for plucking as a ripe plum. But she was no easy fruit who'd fall into his open arms after one shake. She was a lofty reward he'd really have to work for, tantalizingly out of reach until a final, supreme effort delivered her to his arms….

Making the first taste of her juicy flesh all the sweeter.

The model rose off her perch, full breasts swinging as she shimmied into the robe Cress held out for her. Julian barely registered the outstanding multicolored body that made the other spectators gape. There was a smattering of appreciative applause as she stepped off the set like a queen, Cress holding her hand aloft.

The pair disappeared behind a door in the darkened part of the vast studio. A murmur of satisfaction came from the suits, while the photographer and production team carried on without comment. For them, a gorgeous nude woman, even one tricked out like a gingerbread house, was business as usual.

For Mia Kerrigan, too.

Another good reason for Julian to explore her world. Thoroughly.

"Julian?" Petra faked a light laugh. "You're not usually so distracted. I suppose I don't have to ask why."

He nodded. Let her think that. "This cover should fly off the stands."

"It's not exactly a new concept." Petra's sniping tone betrayed tendrils of jealousy, even though she was usually good at giving off the modern woman's anything-goes, live-for-the-moment, no-commitment vibe. "Demi Moore did it on the cover of *Vanity Fair* ages ago."

"We're doing it better." He paused. "Thanks to Mia Kerrigan. Where did you find her?"

"The artist? Oh, I don't know. She was in someone's Rolodex, I suppose. I think she'd done body painting for the ad campaign of a makeup company. Living Color." Petra shrugged. "Her fee was outrageous."

"She's worth it."

Petra's eyes narrowed as she followed Julian's gaze and realized that perhaps it wasn't the model he was slavering over. "Oh really?"

"As art director, I'm surprised you don't agree."

"But I do. The cover will be…spectacular. I was only saying it's not a new idea."

"*Hard Candy* should do a body-painting feature. A fashion spread, all in paint. I can speak to the managing editor about it, if you're not keen on the idea."

Petra smiled. "No, no, I'd love to make the proposal. It's a spectacular idea."

"Spectacular," Julian echoed, watching Mia walk to the back of the studio with her arms wrapped around a half dozen containers of edible paint.

"The crowds grow restless." Petra touched his shoulder. "We really should go."

"*You* should. I don't have to." Once more, Julian

counted himself lucky to be the boss. Sometimes, the burden was worth it. "Though I will step over to make my apologies."

As they walked toward the ad group, he touched Petra lightly on the arm, accustomed as he was to escorting the women of his family. Her face took on a glow that he could no longer attribute to the strobe lights. Those were being shut down one by one.

Apparently, Petra still carried a torch for him. Damn. So that's why his father had always said not to dip his pen into company ink. Once again, the old man's advice proved to be true.

Julian grimaced. A couple of years ago, after the *Hard Candy* launch party, he'd found himself alone in a chauffeured company car with Petra after they'd dropped off other members of the staff. She'd come on to him as if he'd been catnip, finishing up with an invitation to her place. He'd gone.

An obligatory dinner date had followed, then another night of Catwoman sex, then comments at the office about the scratches on his neck. Julian had realized the affair was getting complicated. Petra had surprised him by ending it before he did, parading a new model— an impossibly handsome twentysomething print model, in fact—past his office door.

Julian had been relieved to be replaced. Much later, he'd learned that he was supposed to have been jealous. Behind her mask of cool, Petra hadn't forgiven him for that mistake.

"THE DOMINATRIX has her claws in him," Cress said over the sound of rushing water.

"Quit looking." Regretfully, Mia dumped liquid

chocolate into the deep sink instead of sticking her face into the bucket like a horse at a trough. She was trying Atkins for the sixth time in an effort to take off her stubborn excess poundage. The water thinned the rich concoction and swirled it down the drain. "I don't care what they're doing."

Cress ignored her. "Ouch. He tried to get away and she grabbed him by the buttons. Or maybe the nipples. Her hands are all over him—pretending she cares about his stained shirt. Aha. Now she's pressing up against him, 'helping' with his suit coat—"

"Cress. I do not *care*."

"She's buttoning him up. Smoothing the coat over his shoulders. Clinging to his arm, doing the boob-press thing. Ooh, that bitch."

"I'm not gonna look," Mia said.

"They're leaving."

Mia counted to ten, then spun around. The studio *had* emptied—except for Julian. He was coming toward her.

"See ya," Cress said. He scooped up his supply kit and stuffed a handful of the remaining candies into his jeans pocket. "I'm taking Angelika to lunch. She has a sweet tooth, and I have just the lollipop for her."

Mia gave a vague wave. "Later."

Doors opened and closed in other areas of the studio. The photographer and his black-clad assistants had retreated to the office area, somewhere behind the large, hanging screens of backdrop material. Mia heard them arguing over whose turn it was to order in Chinese. She got busy, packing up the remainder of her gear in the big industrial toolbox she used as an art caddy.

Julian stole a candy and unwrapped it with a crinkling sound. He popped it into his mouth. "Got plans for lunch?"

"I'm meeting Cress in ten minutes."

"The bald guy?"

"He's a photo stylist."

"Whatever you say. He just left with the model."

"Yes, that's why we're meeting up," Mia insisted, even though he'd caught her in a lie. "In ten minutes." She snatched up a small plastic cup of purple paint that had been overlooked. The crew at the photographer's next shoot could graze on the remaining boxes of Sugar High candy.

She felt Julian's eyes on her. It was hard to ignore the magnetic pull they seemed to generate.

He cleared his throat. "Would you cancel if I asked you to come with me instead?"

"No. I don't do that to my friends."

"You don't like me," he said with the supreme confidence of the adored.

"Oh gosh. What gave you that idea?" Mia angled her head to look up at him, intending to be skeptical.

Not easy. He stood at least a head—maybe a head and a neck—above her five-two. Health and vigor radiated off him. The conservative business suit couldn't hide that his body was as lean and toned as an Olympic swimmer's. She'd know that even if she hadn't touched him through his shirt, or seen the shift of muscles when he'd tossed his jacket over his shoulder. She'd know even if she was locked in a sensory deprivation tank. His masculine aura was that strong.

Worse, he had the chiseled face of a Greek god…if Greek gods had been given hot-towel shaves and herbal facial wraps. Then there was the wealth, privilege and charm, not to mention the caustic humor that cut his arrogance to an acceptable level of confidence.

As far as she could see, the man didn't have a flaw. Not one single flaw.

Very irritating.

Mia was both repelled and fascinated by the perfection. Julian was at the other end of the spectrum from her usual boho crowd of artists, writers and other creative types, most of whom struggled to make rent as they stayed true to their muses.

However, she despised superficial judgments. It seemed only fair that she give Julian a chance to prove that he was more than the sum of his glossy parts and lady-killer reputation.

Oh sure. That's what Miss Hood had said before the Big Bad Wolf got his jaws around her.

Mia knew what she had to do. *Put him back in his place and then keep away.*

Julian shrugged. "What gave me that idea? Oh, I don't know. Read any gossip columns lately?"

"Nope. I tear Page Six into strips for papier-mâché."

"What a relief. It's all true, but now we can skip the usual explanations and apologies."

"All true?" Mia blurted.

Julian grinned. "I thought you weren't familiar with my exploits. Most of them greatly exaggerated, if I may add."

Ha! She could just imagine what *didn't* make it into the papers. "I overhear things. You're a player."

"Assume what you will, little girl."

Little girl? Was that a shot at her height? Maybe the cutesy features that she'd given up agonizing over? She might have been ticked if she wasn't positive his eyes had twinkled when he'd said it. He was deliberately provoking her!

Into doing what?

Mia glanced down into the cup of grape paint. Her grip tightened when Julian leaned even closer. If he tried to kiss her, she'd throw the congealing contents in his face.

He dipped a finger into the cup. Tasted it. "Very sweet."

"We thickened grape juice." Or, actually, added dollops of juice and food coloring to a concoction of sugar and cornstarch. It probably didn't taste very good at all.

Julian dipped again. "Have you tried it?"

He didn't wait for an answer. His glistening finger touched her lips, drawing slowly across them. First the bottom, then the upper, leaving them coated with the sugary paint. A hundred sensations rushed through Mia's body, surging upward to gather at her mouth. Her tingling lips swelled with anticipation.

Instinctively, her tongue darted out to lick away the thick grape coating. She made herself stop, her tongue curled against her upper lip before she reluctantly drew it back in. Sugar melted into her taste buds, but she hardly noticed. Her mind was on other flavors to come: the taste of hot, hard lips, warm male skin, pungent, salty, sweet…deliciously sexy.

"I want to taste," Julian said.

Her voice whispered, barely audible. "You—you already did."

His face was so close to hers she could have counted his nonexistent pores. His breath was warm and sweetened with the tang of peppermint. She knew that he would taste good, but not because of the candy.

Their noses bumped. "I want to taste *you*."

She swallowed. "What makes you think I'll taste any different than your thousand other conquests?"

"Every woman is unique."

"But this one doesn't want to be just another note in the Julian Silk hit parade." And yet she didn't pull away when his cheek grazed hers. His fingertips touched under her chin, tilting it up; instead of shaking him off, she felt her lips pout and her lids drift shut.

"No worry. You, Mia Kerrigan, are an entire song."

Big whoop, she thought in some dim, lazy part of her brain, where there was still a sliver of rationality that wasn't dying for his kiss. It was as if he were a spider who'd wrapped her in silken, sticky strands. She could not move. She was at his mercy. But lucky for her...

Julian kissed her.

Mercy.

The man really knew how to kiss. Of course he did. Practice makes perfect.

She couldn't rouse much disgust for that, not when his lips were covering hers with a sure, steady pressure that was somehow soft and hard at the same time, and easy, and deep, sending urgent signals to her fuzzy brain about wrapping her arms around him and pushing her breasts into his chest.

She held the cup of paint to the side and slid her free hand around to his back. He'd gripped her by the waist and was bending her under the force of his kiss. She arched—terribly, wonderfully conscious of the ache in her breasts as they rubbed against the rough denim of her overalls...the melting sensation between her thighs...

The prodding of a growing hard-on.

Whoa. The man was a quick draw. With a hefty six-shooter, by the feel of it.

"Umm," Mia said.

Julian took the opportunity to slip his velvet tongue into her mouth. Grape and peppermint. Sugar and spice. Seduction and delusion.

"That's enough."

He lifted his head and said, "You're wrong." His lips were stained purple from hers. "It's not enough." With a wicked quirk of one black eyebrow, he reached for her again.

She plastered a hand to his chest and pushed. "Listen to me. I said no."

He took his hands off her, straightening up. His eyes were dark and questioning, his hair ruffled, his tie a little askew. Impossibly attractive.

She quivered with frustration. Every inch of her skin was at war with her brain, the nerve endings screaming for appeasement. While she was attuned to her sexuality and usually listened to her body's needs when a walking advertisement for sex appeal strolled into her life, this was one time where she intended to lead with her head to protect her heart. Given his reputation, Julian Silk was a pleasure she'd have to deny herself.

And she needed to do so in a way that his overblown ego really understood, so that there'd be no teasing, chasing or seducing in their future.

None? A pang of longing ran through Mia like a strummed guitar.

"You didn't like the kiss?" Julian said, still cocky.

"The kiss was okay."

"Just okay?"

She shrugged. "If I had to rate it…" That gave her an idea. Oh, she was mean. But it was a perfect pinprick of an idea, sure to let the air out of his balloon.

She thrust a couple of fingers into the cup of paint

and swirled them through the purple goo. He smiled when she reached toward his face, as if he expected a reenactment of his smooth move and silken lines. He didn't even seem to notice when purple drips splattered his tie.

She bypassed his mouth and started finger painting his forehead.

"Hey!" He pulled back. Her fingertips skidded.

"Hold still."

He gripped her wrist. "What are you doing?"

She continued to stroke the paint over his skin, finishing quickly. "Settling your score."

"What does that mean?" He let go of her and put a hand up to his brow.

"No, don't smear it. Go and look in the mirror."

Frowning quizzically, Julian brushed aside the backdrop screens and went to stand before a wall-hung mirror. He put his hands at his belt and stared at the numbers she'd painted on his brow. "Seventeen?" His eyes glinted. "That's on a scale of one to ten, I take it?"

"Not exactly." She pursed her lips, trying to keep from laughing. "You don't recognize your own number?"

"I wore number twenty when I played soccer in school."

"Your *bachelor* number," she said.

He grew more quiet and less cocky. "Ah."

She pulled a tissue out of her pocket and wiped off her fingers, the stickiness shredding the fine paper. "See, it's like this. Maybe if you were number one, or at least in the top five…but *seventeen?* A girl's got to set her standards higher than Bachelor Seventeen. I'm sure you understand."

When he didn't respond, she wadded the tissue in a tight fist. Maybe she'd been a little hard on him.

Julian turned to look at her with a bemused expression. "What did you do, memorize *CG's* entire list of bachelors?"

Mia hesitated. Great. Now he'd think she was a gold digger. "I told you, I hear things."

That was true, sort of. One of the art models she often hired for body-painting experiments had come in a while back with the bachelor issue of *Celebrity Gossip*, joking that her accounts were overdrawn and she needed to snare a rich husband. While Mia had painted the model's skin, they'd flipped through the pages and laughed at the poses of the self-consciously sexy bachelors. There had been several pro athletes displaying their rippling muscles, an indistinguishable clump of Wall Street millionaires, one blue-collar guy for show, a couple of artists and a slew of actors—one of whom the model swore was as fruity as his Hanes briefs.

And then there was Julian. Number Seventeen. CEO of Silk Publications Ltd. and the brilliant mind behind the swift rise of *Hard Candy*, the glossy lifestyle magazine with a guy-power attitude. Since its inception, *Hard Candy* had stormed both the newsstands and pop culture trends with its cheeky articles about sex, sports, careers and entertainment, and even cheekier layouts of barely dressed pretty young Miss Thangs.

Mia had lingered over Julian's page for a minute or two, telling herself that she was only interested because she'd been booked for the *Hard Candy* cover shoot.

There had been a paparazzi shot of Julian doing the exiting-limo-with-hot-babe thing. One formal portrait of him wearing a serious expression and a suit and tie—probably lifted from his company's annual report. But the photo that had captured her attention was a candid, taken at the seashore with dunes and a weather-beaten beach house in the distance. Julian was building a sand castle, looking all brown and sun-bleached, wearing nothing but deck shoes and cutoff jeans, one arm wrapped around a little girl with a sun hat pulled down to her jet-black button eyes. The display of his sand-sprinkled muscles had been impressive, but what was most attractive was the sweetness of his kinship with the child—a niece, according to the caption.

"Number Seventeen tries harder," he said.

Mia laughed and shook her head. "Tempting, but no. I always go for the best." Oh, her parents would choke if they could hear her! While both of them had always preached modesty, they'd also wanted her to make something of herself—or at least marry very well. She'd disappointed them on all counts.

"Hmm. I'll keep that in mind for next year, when the new list is released." Julian sighed and rubbed his chin. "It's a tough task, but I'll take it on. Wining, dining, kissing and seducing my way up the list…"

If he was trying to make her jealous, he was succeeding.

Nonsense. She tossed her head. "Whatever. As long as it's not with *me*."

"Certainly not. I may never make it to the Number One slot you require. But a man's got to try."

She picked up the heavy toolbox, lugged it toward the door, then thought better and set it down. "Here," she said, digging into her pocket for another tissue. She handed it to Julian. The crooked purple numbers had dried on his forehead. He didn't seem to mind, and he carried them off with a certain slapdash style, but she was feeling petty.

"Reconsidering my offer?" Julian said, smirking at her like a cocky bastard as he scrubbed away the brand.

She snapped to. "Absolutely not."

"Till next year, then," he called after her as she wrapped her arms around the toolbox and hauled ass for the door. Show a guy like that one inch of vulnerability and he'd have her naked between the sheets before she could wrap her lips around a No, Thanks.

"Have fun," Mia muttered as the heavy metal door clanged shut. She stopped, shuddered as if a train had just whizzed past, then hefted her materials and headed for the street, making a mental note to invest her spare change in a condom factory now that Julian Silk was on a mission to seduce. If his reputation was correct, he'd already cut a swath through Manhattan. She'd better put out a warning bulletin to the boroughs.

3

A WEEK LATER, with many schemes regarding his seduction of Mia Kerrigan conjured and abandoned, Julian was still trying to figure out his next move when his kid sister, Nikki, came into the office looking for a job. Serendipity, he thought. She might be useful, for a change.

Nikki was twenty-three, a recent college graduate, just returned from a grand tour of Europe—two months sunning in Ibiza, partying in London and wining and dining in Venice. When he'd asked about museums and landmarks, Nikki talked about power-boating with Guiseppe and lashing Simon at the Dungeon. Julian shuddered to think.

"Jules, luv, you've got to give me a job!" In full drama princess mode, Nikki threw herself horizontally onto the new leather sofa that had replaced his dad's old leather one. She swung her feet onto the armrest, kicking away a pillow needlepointed by their mother, beloved by their father and sneered at by the designer who'd "done" the office when Julian moved in.

"Why?" he said, even though he already had an idea of how to combine their objectives. But Nikki had to think she'd persuaded him into giving her a real and valuable position in the company. She would treat a make-work job like the rest of her gifts—from the first edition *Little Women* left out in the rain to the Aston Martin she'd crumpled on the gatepost of their country house when she was applying lipstick in the rearview mirror while practicing her British accent.

"I can't be a decorative but useless heiress forever. Maybe for another few years, but what happens then?" Nikki waved her arms, happily chattering away while Julian listened with one ear while paging through his stack of messages. "Nobody cared about Stella McCartney until she started designing for Chloé. Gloria Vanderbilt had her jeans, Paloma Picasso did perfume...." She paused, reflecting on her ancient predecessors. And he'd thought she knew nothing about history.

"Look at Sofia Coppola." Nikki sighed. "I want to be my own person. I want respect. I mean, I didn't go to all the trouble of hiring a look-alike ringer to take my college finals only to hang the degree on a wall and never use it. But does anyone—"

Julian interrupted more forcefully. "Nikki, tell me you didn't."

She grinned at him from her supine position, her long dark hair spread across the cushions. "You're so easy to tease."

He rolled his eyes upward to ask his dad for forbearance, much as he had when Nikki had first informed him that she was getting a journalism degree so they could work side by side. If Jim Silk was watching, he was getting one helluva kick out of Nikki's latest idea. Nothing would have made him happier than to see his girls kept safe and close under Julian's protection. He'd said so, in fact, over the beep of heart monitors and the sobs of his wife. How could Julian decline the chore?

But there were limits. "Nik, do you really think you can just march in here and be handed a plum job?"

"Why not?" Nikki wrinkled her nose. "That's the point of being the boss's sister. And a shareholder. Anyway, who died and made you king?" She giggled at her wit. "Besides Dad."

"I worked my way up." At his sister's age, Julian had also hoped to choose his own career. Race-car driving, he remembered with some embarrassment. But he'd been the good son and had done as his father wished, starting as an intern at one of the Silk publications and moving from position to position until he knew all aspects of the business. When his father had died unexpectedly with the company in disarray, Julian had been well prepared to take over the reins.

Nikki sat up and flung back her hair. Uh-oh. She must be serious.

"I'm willing to do that," she said. Quite earnestly. "I'm not asking to be the next Anna Wintour by tomorrow. I can start as a columnist."

Julian humored her. "What kind of columnist?"

His sister scowled, distorting her pretty face. "I don't want to tell you because I know you'll say no."

"Oh god. Not *Leather & Chrome*," he said, citing the motorcycle magazine that was one of their smaller, more obscure publications. Nikki had gone through a rebellious biker-chick phase when she was seventeen. Their father's death had curtailed it before she could crack her head open or fall in with a truly dangerous crowd.

"Julian! You know I'm a vegan now. Leather is cruel. Plus, it really stinks and it made me sweat like a pig."

"Of course. I forgot." If something was a trend, Nikki would follow something.

Aha. *Trendy.* Which of their magazines was hottest right now? That was where his sister would want to go.

The answer came instantly: *Hard Candy.* Home of bikini-clad bimbos and tips on oral sex.

Nikki would be employed there over his dead body.

"How about a fashion magazine?" he suggested. That way, she'd only do damage to her credit cards.

She shook her head. "High fashion is for rich old white women."

He wanted to ask her how much she'd paid for her spike-heeled boots, distressed jeans and the skimpy snipped-silk top that showed off her navel ring, but he resisted. The last time he'd questioned Nikki's look, she'd come home with a tattoo that had sent their mother into a week-long dither. If he let her loose at *Hard Candy,* she'd be researching sex toys in a week. Or worse—posing for a spread wearing edible undergarments.

"Watch out. I may start you at *Puppy Monthly.*" Julian turned over a page in the ad sales projections for next spring. "What ever happened to Frodo, anyway?" Frodo was the teacup Chihuahua Nikki had carried in a designer bag everywhere she went…for about a month.

"He's Mom's now. She took him with her to the Vineyard while I was vacationing and got attached."

"So that's who was yipping in the kitchen last time I visited. I thought the cook had gone off her Zoloft again."

"Are you trying to distract me?"

"Usually that's easy to do."

"I know." Nikki sighed. "But I'm serious this time. I want to do something with my life."

"You could get married, like Lis." At twenty-nine, Elisabeth Silk Reingold was the oldest sister. She and her husband, Sam, lived in the Nashua countryside and had two little kids who called him Uncle Julie and gave him kisses that smelled like peanut butter.

"I'm way too young to get married," Nikki said, appalled at the thought. She studied her brother for a moment and apparently decided that he couldn't be serious. Her lips twitched. "I'd rather be like Very. She knows how to have fun."

Julian groaned. Very, short for Veronica, was the middle sister and his worst nightmare. She'd been in college and on track for a responsible life when their father's passing had hit her like a locomotive. Soon after, Very had dropped out with a vow to live every moment to the fullest. Ever since, she'd been racing with a jet-set crowd of club kids. When in residence, she stayed out till dawn, partied like a maniac and slept till noon, only getting clean and sober to pay sporadic visits to their mother. Next to Very, Nikki was almost responsible.

Maybe giving her a job wasn't a bad idea. She probably wouldn't stick it out, but at least for the short term it'd be easier for him to keep an eye on her.

Nikki's lashes flickered. "I was thinking I could write for…"

Not *Hard Candy*. Anything but. Julian seized on the idea he'd been toying with at the back of his mind ever since she'd barged into the office.

He held up a hand. "Wait. I have an assignment for you."

"An assignment? One measly assignment?"

"You don't start off as a columnist, Nik. That's a prestigious position you have to work up to. Most of our writers broke into the field doing freelance assignments."

"Oh." Nikki brightened. She got up and approached his desk, exuding genuine interest. "What's the assignment?"

Julian wondered if he was being smart. It could be disaster, bringing Nikki and Mia together. But setting his sister free to find her own story could lead to worse.

Plus, this way he'd have reason to see Mia again.

Not that his throbbing dick needed an excuse.

He shifted at the thought. "It's a simple project, to start you off. If you do well, I'll think about giving you a permanent position." At the magazine of *his* choice. "I want you to do background research on an artist. We're thinking of featuring her in a, uh, fashion layout, so I need you to—"

Nikki clapped her hands. "A feature article! Yippee!"

"Hold on. I didn't say you'd be writing the article. The first step is gathering background information."

"But why can't I write the article?" Nikki climbed onto a desk chair on her knees. "No way am I doing the drudge work so some other writer can sashay in and slap their name on my story."

"That's how it's done." Sometimes, but not for a relatively minor piece like this one. Mia Kerrigan might get a three-paragraph blurb. The focus of the layout would be on her luscious works of art.

Nikki leaned forward and put her elbows on his desk. Her boots stuck up in the air behind her. "Please let me write the article." She reached a hand across his desk. Batted her lashes. "Pretty please."

He gave her hand a pat, feeling very fatherly except for his motivations. Those were, well, sort of sleazy. But Nikki was an easygoing kid. She'd laugh if she found out his motive was dating and mating Mia. So…why not get two birds with one stone?

"We'll see," he said, "*if* you're responsible and thorough about gathering the preliminary research."

Nikki popped up. "Fab!" She went and grabbed her bag—a slim leather clutch now that Frodo was ensconced at the beach house with their mom—and pulled out a wafer-thin PDA. She stood with poised stylus. "What's the deal? Got a name and number?"

Julian turned on the phone and buzzed his executive assistant, Dustin Sheppard. "Shep, will you call Petra Lombardi over at...her office and get Mia Kerrigan's number for Nikki?"

"For *Nikki?*" came the disembodied voice.

She made a face at the intercom, temporarily holstering the stylus.

"I'm sending her on assignment. She'll be out in a minute." Julian checked his schedule. "Send my next appointment in as soon as she leaves."

"Yessir. Whatevah you say, sir."

Julian disconnected. "Wiseass."

"Who, me?" Nikki laughed. "Is there anything you can tell me about this artist? Like, what does she do, since it's a fashion layout—paint fabric? What's her name again?"

"Mia Kerrigan." Instantly, Mia's baby-doll face and full lips sprang to mind. They'd shared sweet candy kisses, but Julian figured Mia for being a tigress in bed. She had spark, verve, an electric energy. She had bite.

Nikki watched him through slitted eyes. "She must be a dog."

"Not at all. What makes you say that?"

"Because you'd already have her number if she wasn't."

"You make me sound very superficial."

"Oh, yes. I forgot. Females of any shape, form or species are fair game to the man who would be the World's Greatest Lover. Is she married?"

"Not as far as I know." Julian frowned. "And watch your mouth."

Nikki strutted to the door. "Julian, luv, regardless of deathbed promises, you're not my father."

"But I am your older brother and I do hold the purse strings." Their father had put Julian in control of the estate, though he had no authority over the trust funds that were released as each sibling reached age twenty-five. Very was going through hers like water.

"Give me some credit," Nikki said. "For once, I'm trying to earn money instead of spend it."

"And I'm proud of you." Julian joined her at the door. He kissed her cheek, relieved that she hadn't noticed how he'd avoided the question about Mia's career. Nikki would find out about the body painting soon enough, but he wanted her to think the potential layout and article were for a fashion magazine, not *Hard Candy*. "I expect you'll do a fine job."

"Thanks." Nikki hugged him. She'd always been an affectionate girl. Even when she'd sent a strippergram to a board meeting on his birthday, Julian couldn't help forgiving her. He felt the same way about the rest of the aggravating Silk women. If he hadn't cared so much for them, the burden of his father's expectations might be too heavy to contemplate. As it was, Julian managed by telling himself that at least he never doubted that they loved him back, even if they were doing their best to turn him gray before his time.

THE NEXT DAY, Mia was sitting on the top rung of scaffolding in a Riverside Drive ballroom when Nikki Silk arrived. The Gormans' butler—an honest-to-goodness butler even though he was dressed casually since the owners weren't in residence—announced the visitor with a twinge of annoyance before bowing out, firmly shutting the double doors behind him. Mia made a mental note to thank the old guy for looking after her on his downtime, even if he was only guarding her from stealing the silver.

"Hello?" the visitor called.

Mia switched off the hip-hop music blasting from her portable disk player. "Give me a sec," she bellowed, misjudging her volume. She nudged away the earphones. "I have to finish the gold-leafing while the sizing is tacky."

"That's all right. I can watch."

Mia glanced down at the rookie journalist whose face was turned up toward the ceiling arches. Nikki Silk was young, pretty and dressed like a crackpot Daisy Mae in a flared denim miniskirt, short white leather jacket and ankle boots with teeter-totter heels.

"I guess you're related to Julian?" Mia pounced her horsehair brush on the gold leaf she'd just applied. Small flakes drifted down onto Nikki's hair and face.

"Cool," she said, puffing at one of the snippets of gold. "I'm his sister."

Aha. Interesting. "He sent you here?"

"Well, he gave me the assignment."

"Is he serious?" When Nikki had called yesterday, Mia had felt suspicious enough of Julian's motives to consider denying the interview request. But if the proposed article was legit, the opportunity was too good to pass up.

Nikki put her hands on narrow hips. "Is there something wrong with me?"

"Not you. I meant the article. Is he serious about the article?"

"He'd better be." Nikki cocked a leg and crossed her arms. Her boot tapped the marble floor. "I'll shave his eyebrows while he's sleeping if he's setting me up."

Mia wasn't reassured. "Setting you up? Is that something he does frequently?"

"Not really, but he doesn't take me very seriously."

Mia thought of the women who reportedly dropped in and out of his love life like ducks at a shooting gallery. "What *does* he take seriously?"

Nikki picked a shred of gold leaf off her lip. "Lots of stuff," she admitted. "If you want to know the truth, he's kind of a bore, working all the time and giving orders. He thinks he's the boss of me, but he's not." She reconsidered. "Except I guess he would be if I get on to the *Hard Candy* staff."

"Then you're not already?" Definitely a setup, Mia decided as she peeled off another sheet of leafing, carefully laid it on the last bit of ungilded arch and pounced the brush to fill the crevices of the carving. She just couldn't figure out what game Julian was up to.

Nikki's voice rose to the twenty-four-foot domed ceiling. "I might as well confess. This is my first story."

Mia peered through the scaffolding. "We all have to start somewhere."

"Yes, but now that I've met you…" Nikki grew silent as she looked around the ballroom. Even littered with painting tarps, ladders and assorted supplies, it was an amazing room. Tall dove-gray walls were adorned with gilded French-style molding. The stone floor was flecked in gray, black and pink. Sconces and elaborate wall candelabra dripped crystals that matched the immense chandelier, presently shrouded in a protective linen covering.

"What's the problem?" Mia prodded.

"I'm confused. I thought you were involved in fashion, somehow. Julian tried to steer me toward working for a Silk fashion mag…" Nikki shook her head, gesturing at the room. "But you're a—a—"

"Decorative painter. I do a little of everything— trompe l'oeil, gilding, faux effects, murals."

"That's great, but I can't imagine what kind of a fashion layout he's thinking of." Nikki looked up at Mia, her eyes growing wide. One side of her mouth lifted. "Or maybe I can imagine. That dog."

"Really." Mia set aside her brush and the packet of leafing and started to climb down. "You mentioned *Hard Candy*, so I thought you knew about me."

Nikki stepped away from the rattling scaffolding. "Julian didn't say much at all. He might even have been secretive, now that I think about it."

Mia swung her body down the last few rungs and dropped to the floor. "Why is that?" she asked.

At the same moment Nikki said, "What does *Hard Candy* have to do with decorative painting?" She frowned. "Or fashion."

Mia studied Julian's sister, who was six or seven inches taller and at least fifteen pounds lighter than herself, reed thin in the way of young girls and anorexic ballerinas. She liked Nikki anyway. The girl had marched in here for an interview despite her lack of experience. There was moxie in those willowy genes. Maybe resilience.

"There's been a mix-up of some sort," Mia said, taking a flier that she could trust Nikki not to run back to her brother and tell all. "We need to share our information."

Nikki nodded. "And get the better of Julian."

"Is he putting one over on me?"

"One of us. Maybe."

"Then let's put our minds together. You start."

"I think…" Nikki looked Mia up and down, taking in the corkscrew curls and splattered canvas apron. "Even though you're not his usual, and he was playing it ultracool with me, he fancies you."

The odd stirring in the pit of her stomach disturbed Mia. Arousal she could identify and take care of. This was more than arousal. "Oh," she said, scoffing at her own reaction, "*fancy* is way too polite a word for what he feels for me."

"Yes." Nikki laughed. "He wants to frank you."

"Frank me?"

"That's what my girlfriends call it when we're being silly. You know, serve you the foot-long, the pork sausage, the—"

"I get it." Foot-long? If the rumors about Julian Silk's equipment and prowess were true…

Mia corralled her thoughts before they made her dizzy. As attractive and exciting as Julian was, she didn't need the distraction right now. And she really didn't need to be another of his throwaway "dates."

But *he* could be hers. Fun all the way around.

Mia blinked. *Forget about playtime. Consider your career.* "So you think he sent you here to gather information on me for his own use, not an article?"

"That's possible," Nikki said. "And it wouldn't be the first do-nothing task he's set for me—all with good intentions, according to him. When I interned at the family company one summer, Julian actually assigned another intern to shadow me and keep me out of trouble." The girl smirked. "Didn't work, of course."

"I'll bet." Mia almost pitied Julian the responsibility of looking after Nikki. Not that he deserved any lenience, since it appeared he gave as good as he got.

"I suppose you're right— he's playing us both." She flapped gold flecks off her apron. "Damn. My career could have used the boost of publicity."

Nikki swung from side to side as she gestured at the glorious ballroom. To have such a space in Manhattan was the epitome of luxury. "You seem to be doing fine without the publicity."

"Ah, but that's where my explanation comes in." Mia lifted the apron off and laid it over a rung of the scaffolding. "I'm not only a decorative painter, though that's been my bread and butter. My true calling is body painting."

"*Body* painting?" Nikki's penciled brows made twin Arcs de Triomphe. "Is that a career?"

"Not for many. But I'm getting there. I've painted for parties, for galleries, and the past year I've gotten several advertising jobs that have drawn attention in the media and in the trade."

"Like what? Oh, wait a mo." Nikki dug through a denim shoulder pack until she withdrew a micro-recorder. She fiddled around, rewinding the tape and testing one-two-three before she was satisfied. She held it out and clicked a button. "What advertising work have you done?"

Mia opened her mouth, but Nikki made a quick dive at the recorder. "I'm talking to Mia Kerrigan, body painter." She held it out again. "Go."

"There were a few small print ads, but my most well-known work so far was for the Living Color cosmetics campaign."

"I know that one!" Nikki squealed. "Finally my clandestine subscription to *Elle* pays off. You're talking about the ads where the models were painted in makeup colors…?"

"Yes, to reflect the product names. For the River of Color line, I painted several models like a rushing river and we photographed them lying head to toe among rocks and rushes."

"The peach!" Nikki spoke into the recorder. "Tell about the peach."

Mia grinned. "The peach caused a minor sensation. That was for their Peachy Keen blush and lipstick. A few magazines banned the ads and the company was delighted. The brouhaha over censorship gained them tons of free publicity."

"All because the peach was really an ass, right?"

"Well, yes." She'd painted Angelika's derriere so skillfully it had looked absolutely authentic when photographed close up with extraneous body parts cropped out. The resulting ad had been beautiful and luscious, but fairly unremarkable. The kicker had been when the reader turned the page to a similar photo of Angelika's outthrust bottom with a male model poised to take a bite, one hand squeezing the sensuous curves of the "peach."

Mia brought Nikki over to one of the window seats that overlooked the street and told her about doing the Living Color ads and how that had led to a certain notoriety. She spoke about the art pieces she painted and photographed on her own time, for her own pleasure, but also how she was building a body-painting portfolio. Her ultimate goal was to win the gold medal at the upcoming International Expo and have a gallery show.

Nikki proved to be less scatterbrained than she first

appeared. She paid attention to the details and asked smart questions. The only area that Mia glossed over was her family background. Her parents had requested anonymity long ago, but it still hurt a bit to be reminded that they were ashamed of her ventures.

After a while, the butler came back and looked inside. "Still here? I suppose you'll be wanting refreshments."

"Oh, no, that's not necessary, thanks." The butler flustered Mia. He was too posh for her blood, even when he was practically off duty. While her parents' wealth was fairly impressive, it was never ostentatious. She came from good Puritan stock, where parsimony and modesty had ruled for generations.

Nikki, however, had no problem giving the butler orders. "Actually, I'm parched. Fetch me a Perrier and lime, will you, luv?"

"I should be getting back to work," Mia said.

Nikki checked the recorder. "You haven't explained about the *Hard Candy* connection yet."

"I recently completed a body-painting assignment for the magazine's cover." She described the edible woman theme and how she'd achieved the look. "Julian was there, and that's when he mentioned a 'fashion' layout, with the models wearing only my paint. It's odd that he didn't tell you."

"Not that odd. He didn't come right out and say so, but I know my brother. He doesn't want me to work at *Hard Candy*."

"Why not? Is he like W.C. Fields?"

"Huh?"

"Thinking you're too good to work for your own— Oh, never mind."

"It's simple, really, but devious of him. He said you'd

be featured in a fashion layout, but not what kind. Obviously because he didn't want me getting in at *Hard Candy*. The magazine is pure sex. Even the offices are pretty well testosterone saturated, and my brother is so overprotective," explained Nikki. "Or he tries to be. I usually don't let him, except when he gets this weary expression and I start to feel sorry for him, because he *does* have to deal with the three of us and even I can imagine what a headache that is."

"Three sisters," Mia said, remembering the bachelor bio.

"There's me, Very and Lis. Since our dad died, Julian feels responsible for us. He's really very patient and loving. We all know we can count on him, no matter what kind of trouble we're in."

Mia's respect for Julian increased. She didn't need actual feelings complicating the matter, but there they were.

Nikki made a choking sound. "Ick, how sappy! I'm forgetting that Jules tried to mislead us about the article. But I'll show him." She clicked off the recorder. "I believe you'd make a fabulous feature article, Mia. My brother might interfere, but somehow, someway, I'm going to get us both into *Hard Candy*."

She shoved the recorder into her pack and stood, throwing out her chin. "Julian can go suck a lemon drop."

The image made Mia smile, especially since she already knew what Julian tasted like when flavored with candy.

She rose, shaking her head. "I'm not so sure that's smart, Nikki."

"You said you could use the publicity."

"Sure. But I don't want to cause trouble—"

"You don't?" Nikki looked astonished, as if the

thought of keeping peace had never occurred to her. "Oh, come on! Julian is just begging for trouble."

"He's powerful," Mia said. *Could hire me and fire me a hundred times over.*

"But kind."

"Arrogant." *And deserves to be hoisted on his own petard.*

"Not cruel, though."

"He's also dangerously attractive." *You can say that again.*

"Pah." Nikki's eyes narrowed. "You can resist."

Someone has to, Mia thought. *But why me?*

"You won't have to do anything but keep your mouth closed," Nikki said. "I'll turn in the background info to Julian like an obedient little airhead, and he'll think I'm none the wiser that the fashion spread—if there really is one—was meant for *Hard Candy.* Meanwhile, I'll get started on an article. I can pitch it to the magazine even if Julian doesn't follow through. If you hear from him, play dumb. Remember, it's possible that he's only interested in getting into your—" Nikki's lashes dropped to Mia's lower half "—painter's pants."

"So it's true that he's had a lot of…relationships?" Mia said, even though she was slightly uncomfortable talking about Julian's love life with his sister. Nikki didn't seem bothered at all—she was as open as a book of the Kama Sutra.

"I don't get to actually see him in operation because he's discreet, but the way I hear it, he's so smooth, most girls slide into bed without a struggle. Then they slide right out just as fast."

"He doesn't ever get serious?"

"Not as far as I know." Nikki shrugged. "He *never*

brings them home to meet family. I'm not sure why, except that he's a stickler for doing things the right way, especially since he got put in charge of the family business. Maybe none of the women are good enough to make the cut?"

Mia was intrigued. And somewhat intimidated. She wanted to know more, but the butler returned, carrying a tray with tall glasses of Perrier on the rocks.

Nikki met him halfway into the room. "A tall cool one," she said, sassily eyeing the reserved butler.

He nodded. "As requested, miss."

The young woman picked up the glass, tilted her head back and drank down the entire contents, her long, elegant neck showing each big swallow. She plunked the glass back on the tray with a click of ice cubes.

"See ya, Mia." Nikki let out a girlish giggle, snatched the lime slice off the edge of the glass and sashayed out the door with her lips puckered into a moue around it.

For a moment, Mia sympathized with Julian for being stuck trying to control such a handful. Even the stony butler looked dazed by the spectacle that was Nikki Silk.

4

JULIAN HAD THOUGHT that getting into Mia's apartment building would be difficult—*if* she was serious about rejecting him and not just playing coy. As with many of the challenges in his life, the task turned out to be easy.

He simply followed the argyle sock.

The argyle sock was standing on the stoop smoking a cigarette. Certain that a bald man painted plaid from neck to toe had to be one of Mia's models, Julian approached. The guy tossed the butt, making a motion to stub it out before realizing he was wearing only paper booties.

Julian ground the butt under the leather sole of his wingtips. "Going in?"

"I am," Argyle said, shuddering inside a flimsy unbelted kimono. "I'm catching a chill, and so is my snookums." He chirped and patted his thigh. For a moment Julian was worried that he was about to be introduced to a body part he didn't care to meet, but then an ugly pinkish cat peeped out from a pot of shrubbery in the corner.

"Come along, Mrs. Snookums." The cat crawled across the stoop, her belly low to the ground. It was hairless and shivering, and looked remarkably like Argyle except that it wasn't plaid.

The weather was cool for early September—sixty degrees. The cement steps of the row house were not particularly hospitable, even to one wearing real woolens instead of a faux-painted version. Either way, Julian thought Argyle and his cat were taking a chance lounging out here in almost no clothes. Mia's neighborhood in the West Thirties wasn't the safest.

Argyle pressed the buzzer. The intercom crackled, breaking up as a male voice answered. "Let me in, honey," Argyle said.

Julian caught the door at the answering buzz. "After you."

"Going up to Mia's?"

He nodded.

"You're not a model." Argyle tucked Mrs. Snookums under his arm and gave Julian's suit a look. His eyes were a watery blue rimmed in pink. "You must be from the ad agency. She said someone might drop by for a look-see." Argyle started up the steps, entirely too trusting. "Well, come on, then."

Julian climbed four flights, each becoming progressively narrower, steeper and more twisty. Argyle was a wiry fellow who jogged upward with his robe billowing. By the time Julian got to the top, he was angling his shoulders sideways. The last time an ascent had been as tight, he'd been in a deathtrap rock chimney in the Himalayas.

He'd gone climbing three years ago, Julian remembered. His last lengthy, stress-free, solo vacation. He'd come back to disaster—Very had been arrested for DUI and his mother had become friendly with a dignified older couple who'd claimed to be cousins of the Vanderbilts and had persuaded her to invest fifty thousand in their emerald mine in Brazil. Julian had vowed never to be out of touch again.

The door to Mia's place was open. Music blasted from it, preparing him for the explosion of light and jumble of color inside. The decor was surrealistic—giant poppies affixed to the ceiling, mad abstract paintings, peacock feathers, papier-mâché fruit as big as bowling balls on the floor, Roman columns, piles of pillows in every color and pattern. One area was filled with enough broken-down furniture to stock a rummage sale. Thankfully, the walls and ceilings were a blinding snowcap white. But there seemed to be too many of them for one small studio apartment—they jutted here and there and slanted in every direction. Julian had to duck beneath an overhanging lintel to enter.

His next impression was movement—bodies swaying to the music. Some of them were stripped half-naked, their exposed skin painted in various plaids. Julian counted six of the plaid people, equally divided between men and women when he included Argyle. They danced, they strolled, they sprawled on a low double bed stacked with pillows and tucked into a gable end hung with sheer curtains.

At the center of the mad plaid circus was Mia, dressed in only a loose smock that reached midthigh. Her bare legs were splotched with random streaks of paint. She was bent over a nude model reclining on a hard wooden chair set upon a dais, shaking her bootie to the music as she drew crisscrossing lines over the model's legs with an artist's brush, turning them into navy blue and yellow plaid.

Julian's gaze went from the model's bare breasts to Mia's round butt. Every time she rocked to the beat, the hem of her smock flipped up, flashing an expanse of smooth thigh. When she bent way over, still bobbing, the tail of the loose shirt was pulled even higher. An especially vigorous wiggle momentarily revealed the twin globes of a perfect round ass. She straightened, one hand reaching behind to tug the smock back down over the provocative red thong that peeped out from the apex of her thighs.

The flash had been involuntary and brief, but heat surged through Julian's veins. He tried to look away to take in the rest of the scene, but his eyes couldn't stay away from Mia's bouncing bottom. The second most amazing thing was that no one else seemed aroused. Or even to notice.

"Brought you a visitor, Mia," Argyle announced, more concerned with pulling the cat's claws away from his kimono. He went to the CD player and turned it down a few notches. "From the ad agency."

Mia whirled. "But you're too ear—" the pink drained from her cheeks "—ly."

Julian gave a casual wave despite a body that had grown as stiff as a cigar store Indian.

"Julian." She shifted the artist's palette to one hand and frowned down at her skimpy shirt and bare legs. One stocking-clad foot moved on top of the other. He saw that the paint splotches that decorated her skin weren't entirely random, but patches of plaid test patterns.

"I'm sorry if I've come at a bad time." He regretted that his presence had made her uncomfortable. She'd seemed so free and natural. So happy.

She shrugged. "It's always a madhouse around here."

He raised his brows.

She waited a questioning beat but he wasn't sure

what to say to explain his arrival. After Nikki had turned in the background info on Mia, including her address and phone number, curiosity had gotten the better of him. He'd come with an excuse—an offer, perhaps even genuine. But the scene in Mia's studio had knocked him out of his nonargyle socks. The glib words that usually flowed without conscious thought were lodged somewhere in his throat.

"Well," she said, setting her palette on the crowded table. "Let me introduce you. This is the garret where I live and work, and these are my friends."

She pointed. "Stefan, on the bed with Leslie." A reclining bearded man, fully clothed, chatted to a slim blonde perched on the edge wearing a bikini top and a schoolgirl-plaid skirt. Every inch of exposed skin was painted to match the skirt, even her face. The white of her eyes and pink of her lips grew when she glanced at Julian and mouthed hello.

He returned the smile. The bearded man frowned.

Mia continued. "This is Fred—" Argyle man "—and Maurizio." Maurizio was a ponytailed dude noshing in a minuscule open kitchen area. He waved a cheese slicer and a packet of crackers. Although he was stripped down to his boxers, only his chest was plaid, airbrushed a pale jaundice yellow and sketched in with a herringbone pattern that turned his bulging pecs into a piece of Escher artwork.

"This is Sue," Mia said, indicating an older woman with buzz-cut silver hair and tartan skin from the neck down. Julian thought she wore a thong, but he didn't want to stare.

"And Cherie." The brunette in the chair, unabashedly nude even though she only wore paint on her legs. Her breasts were small and rather unobtrusive, considering that the nipples stood out like pencil erasers. When Julian nodded at her, she flicked her tongue across her lips and winked.

"Everyone," Mia said, "this is Julian Silk."

"Oh!" Fred, aka Argyle, put his hands on his hips. "Naughty boy. I thought he was from the ad agency."

"Do we know him?" Stefan asked, rising up to one elbow.

Julian couldn't remember many of the names. His head was ready to explode. He'd been to wild photo shoots before, including the *Hard Candy* bikini calendar shoot with naked, oiled babes, tropical heat, rum punch on demand and a much more sultry air than could be found in a fifth-floor walk-up attic. Maybe that was the difference. Mia's friends seemed quite casual about it all, as if the body-painting extravaganza was an everyday occurrence.

"Ooh, the big boss from *Hard Candy*," Cherie said. She moved in the chair, hooking an arm over the backrest and tilting one breast higher. She studied Julian with a tight little smile. "Mia was just telling us about you, Mr. Silk."

"Julian," he said.

"Julian," she purred.

Another Petra. Lovely, but potentially lethal. He crossed her off his list, despite the honed body and the champagne-glass tits. After a moment's thought, he realized that his recent reluctance wasn't only from caution. Mia made other women seem calculating and almost bland. Juiceless.

She'd seen him looking. With an irritated nose twitch, she tossed Cherie a scarf. "We have a visitor, Lady Godiva. Keep the naughty bits under wraps."

Cherie shook out the scarf, seductively lowered it across her front like a veil and then tied it around her hips. "There, I'm decent."

Mia rolled her eyes. "No modesty. This is what I get for hiring a nudist."

She retrieved the palette and approached Cherie again, squinting at the pattern of the plaid. "Don't know if I'm happy with these colors…"

"I can only stay another half hour," Cherie said. "I booked a job downtown. What a trek!"

"Someone grab the Polaroid for me," Mia said. "We'll try some test shots. Maurizio? Want to bring your chest over here? I need to see the contrast."

Julian found the camera on the table and put it into her extended hand. She glanced up with a distracted thank-you. "Oh, Julian. I forgot. Was there something I can do for you?"

Either she was very good at playing it cool, or his renowned charisma truly had no effect on her. He was tending to go with the latter until he remembered their kiss. A woman didn't kiss a man she could take or leave like *that*.

"I'd hoped to speak to you in private."

"Should have called for an appointment then." Mia framed a shot of Cherie's extended legs and snapped a photo. She bent at the waist to get a close-up, her own legs straight, knees glued together. The tail of the smock lifted across the back of her thighs, dangerously close to revealing her thong again.

The view was so enticing Julian felt as though he'd been granted a ringside seat at a strip club. But instead of tucking a bill into a convenient crevice, he battled the urge to tug the shirt down to keep her rear end decently covered. Maurizio, crossing to the dais, had finally noticed.

"No modesty," the muscle man said, reaching out to pat Mia's behind as he slid into place between Cherie's legs.

"Whoops." Mia felt for the back of her shirt. Julian caught her eye. She colored slightly. "Maybe you should come back another time? This is only a test shoot, but it's going to take a while yet. We tend to get a little goofy. Even, uh, wild."

"I can wait. And I'm an expert at getting wild."

A sexy laugh came from the dais as Cherie folded her legs around the male model in a suggestive pose. Mia glanced from them to Julian, in his suit and tie. "In the middle of the workday? Be honest, now. This isn't really your scene."

"No, but I'm always up for new experiences. If you don't mind an observer, that is."

"All right." Mia waved him to a chair. "As long as you keep out of my way. I'll forget you're here, so if you get thirsty or hungry, go to the kitchen and help yourself." Her ripe little mouth puckered. "Enjoy yourself."

"Oh, I will."

He settled down to watch, seated in the one space of sanity in the kooky studio—a lime-green easy chair positioned against the wall with a reading lamp and a side table stacked with worn paperbacks. Romance novels. He picked one up, found the used bookstore stamp on the inside cover. The well-thumbed book sprang open to a love scene.

He skimmed a few paragraphs. Mia had a telling taste in literature. But, of course, he already knew how sensually alive she was. The proof was in the flush of her skin, the brightness of her eyes, the shape of her mouth opening to his.

He returned his attention to the work in progress. Mia

shot dozens of Polaroids, rearranging the poses and pairings, then took even more test shots. Eventually, she released Cherie to make her appointment. The other models scattered, taking a break while Mia worked on Maurizio's herringbone chest, managing to laugh and talk with him while never losing her focus. Her hand was skilled; the paintbrush was always in motion.

No one approached Julian, though they sneaked frequent looks at him. All except Mia. She spared no glance at all. In fact, she seemed to have forgotten his presence.

Julian realized that he was as out of place here as Mia would be in a Park Avenue drawing room. He sank deeper into the cushions, trying to get comfortable. To prove to himself that he still could. He wasn't, as his sisters accused, a stick-in-the-mud whose only interest was work.

Mia continued to ignore him. Which only succeeded in keeping his interest aroused.

After a while, he let his mind drift into fantasy. Mia was naked on the curtained bed, rounded in all the right places. She was looking at him, seeing all of him. And licking her lips. He beckoned her with a curled finger, and she crawled forward on hands and knees, her breasts swaying. Oh, yeah, she wanted him. She really did. Eagerly, she pounced and stripped him. Within seconds, he was in her hands, her deft artist's fingers teasing him as she opened those decadent lips of hers and slid them over the head of his penis.

A couple of the models broke out into loud laughter. Julian blinked, coming out of the fantasy. Not the right time to continue the imaginary scenario, but there was no doubt in his mind. With Mia's skills at handiwork, she'd be an attentive and inventive lover.

Cherie emerged from a glass door that led to what must be the bath. No longer plaid, she was dressed in jeans and a tight top, with wet hair. She grabbed a portfolio, blew air kisses all around and then flicked a card at Julian on her way to the door. He let it fall. His hands were loosely linked over a fully engorged boner.

Mia's lashes flickered in his direction.

The door shut behind Cherie. He gulped. Plucked the card off his shirt front and made a show of examining the content before tucking it into his pocket. "On my way to the sixteenth spot," he said, under his breath but loud enough for Mia to hear.

She flounced off to another area of the studio and with a whoosh pulled down a sheet of heavy paper from a roller hung near the ceiling. "Let's move, gang. I need some real photos before we lose the natural light."

The door buzzed in the middle of the setup. Mia was involved with arranging a tangled knot of plaid limbs. Twister gone Celtic.

"I'll get it," Julian said, even though she wasn't paying attention. He went over to the intercom and pressed the button. "Who is it?"

"Cress. I've got the stash."

"The stash?" Julian wondered if the photo shoot concluded with a good old-fashioned bong party. These people seemed the type.

"Let me up." Cress sounded cranky. "I'm being chased by a clan of dekilted Scotsmen."

Julian buzzed him in, left the door open and returned to his chair. In seconds, the young black man from the cover shoot appeared, his arms filled with plaid fabrics, dangling shopping bags and a bulging tote. He zipped straight through the studio and tossed the "stash" on the bed, beside Stefan, who hadn't moved except to take off his shoes and prop his dirty feet on the pillows. Something of a fantasy-killer, that was.

Cress dusted off his hands. "Mia, my pet. This stuff is god-awful tacky. It's *Braveheart* regurgitated."

On the makeshift set, Mia's head poked out from behind a plaid thigh. "Yeah, but it's also a paying job."

"A mere pittance compared to the *Hard Candy* shoot. Why be this painstaking with a measly little print ad that'll soon be lining bird cages?"

"I can use it in my portfolio," she murmured. "I'm creating art, remember?"

"She's creating art," Cress said to the air, pushing his sunglasses up to his head. He blinked at the variety of the models' intertwined plaids. "Ugh. Clash art." But he got to work positioning the lights.

"We need a stand-in for Cherie," said Mia, once she'd finished arranging the first pose and was standing off to the side, considering the composition.

"Stefan?" Cress called.

A loud snore came from the bed. Clearly fake. Julian snorted.

Mia and Cress looked at him. Air whistled between the photo stylist's teeth. "So…we meet again. Or don't meet." He walked up to Julian with an open hand. "Cressley Godwin."

"Julian Silk." They shook hands.

"Mine's worse than yours."

"Pardon?"

"The moniker."

"Oh, I don't know. It's no fun being called Silk Shorts all through school."

"Unless you wear them," Mia said. "And I bet you do."

Julian let his gaze slide slowly across her, putting a little heat into it—just enough to get her warmed up and aware of him. "A tempting proposition, but I'll have to decline that wager." He did a James Dean one-corner lip quirk. Gave her a flick of his chin. "You just want to get my clothes off."

Mia's mouth dropped open.

"Yes, but only so she can slap paint on you," Cress said.

"No thanks. I'm here as an observer."

"So you're one of those." Cress nodded sadly, turning to Mia with a glum expression. "He likes to watch."

Self-consciously, she put both hands over her bottom, tugging down on the shirt hem in back, which only made it rise in front, tenting over her breasts and flirting with her upper thighs. Julian wondered why she didn't put on pants.

Maybe she *liked* to be watched...?

"Come on, Julian, be a sport," she said, bright and jittery. "Pose for me. This is only a test shot for my own use. You'll never be seen outside this room, I promise."

"Why can't Cress do it?"

"I need his eye. Plus, he'll be arranging the fabrics and the other crap we have to sell in this ad."

"For God's sake, will you take the picture already?" said the blonde positioned on the paper scroll. She was twined around Maurizio, the Latino hunk. "My thigh is cramping."

The others nodded, adding their complaints. "I need to get to yoga class."

"I'm cold."

"Someone's been eating cheese."

"Please," Mia said, half pleading, half pushing Julian toward the set. "Just take off your pants and get down on the floor and stick your legs up there, near Leslie's—" She waved at the contorted couples.

"Hold on," he said. "I'm not taking off my pants."

"It'll be difficult to paint you with them on."

"Paint me? I don't remember agreeing to that either."

"But that's the point! I'm doing a color test. Don't argue with me." She grabbed his belt and started unbuckling. For a moment, Julian was too stunned to react—particularly when she ducked a little to slide down his pants, briefly aligning her mouth with his groin and making the previous fantasy pop into his head. He closed his eyes and summoned up thoughts of board meetings, computer manuals, anything to keep body parts from popping, too.

Something wet tickled his thighs. He squinted at Mia, on her hands and knees, all right, but not even remotely interested in giving him a hummer. She was hurriedly slapping green paint onto his legs. *Thwap, thwap.*

His trousers were puddled around his ankles, the lining getting splattered with green dots. He cupped his hands down low, hoping his shirttail covered vital areas. The irony didn't escape him. "I didn't agree to this."

Mia glanced up. "Nice boxer briefs. But not silk. I am *sooo* disappointed."

Just deserts for leering at her. "Can I get out of my shoes and socks?"

"Yeah, strip for me, sugar," one of the models said. Unfortunately, it was Argyle.

"Let's be professionals, shall we?" Mia helped Julian step out of his pants, which, under other circumstances, might have pleased him. But the sexy mood was killed. "Mr. Silk is doing me a favor."

She smiled at him as he bent and peeled off his socks.

Definitely killed. No man looked good in bare legs and dark socks. He slipped off his jacket, wondering what he'd gotten himself into and if it would help him get into Mia.

But he was already into Mia. Just not in the one way he expected.

The group continued to mutter complaints. "Hold still a little while longer," Mia soothed. "The sooner Julian is positioned, the sooner I can let you guys go."

Ah, what the hell. He gave himself up, arms outflung. "Go ahead. Position me."

"We're not shooting *The Joy of Sex*," she whispered as she guided him onto the set. The paper backdrop crinkled beneath his bare toes. He felt absurd, but liberated. His normal business day didn't include posing with a troupe of half-naked artsy types. This was the kind of thing he'd growl at Very for doing.

Mia told him to get down on the floor. "Don't worry about your shirt and tie. They won't be in the picture. Nor your face. All I need's a handy pair of legs so I can test out the composition and this new green color. The navy blue I did on Cherie wasn't working."

Seemed like a lot of bother to Julian, but he'd never paid all that much attention to the ins and outs of production. He did as told, feeling utterly foolish, like a helpless turtle. If his board of directors could see him now, they'd be apoplectic with shock.

Cress circled the group, draping them with fabric. Mia snapped photos, the shutter whirring. They rearranged body parts and took more shots. Julian was dismissed early on, thankfully, but instead of hurrying off to wash and dress he stayed close, fascinated. Not with the process, so much. With Mia. She drew his gaze and held it. He was enchanted, like a child at a candy-store window.

After a while, it occurred to him that he was no longer the seducer.

He was seduced.

5

"THANKS FOR being a trooper."

Julian seemed to wince at Mia's cheery words. Was he still embarrassed?

She finished washing out her brushes at the work sink and absently ran over the bristles with the pad of her thumb, thinking that she probably shouldn't have pushed him into posing for her.

Then again, why not? Loosening up was good for him. He'd seemed so out of place, decked out in full business attire while the rest of them hung loose. At the back of her mind had been the notion of proving to him that their worlds could never coincide—they could only collide. Scare him off, so to speak.

He'd surprised her.

Usually, she liked surprises. And she had enjoyed the incredible sight of the great and mighty magazine magnate, de-trousered and on his back with his hairy, naked legs up in the air. She hadn't *really* needed him for the shoot. That had been a ploy.

But he'd met the challenge, with his sense of humor—and even dignity, of a sort—intact. Once again, she'd learned that there was more to the man than surface charm and a mind for business.

"I have one regret," he said.

She looked up. He was watching her with his eyes all black and shiny. Goose bumps prickled her skin. A draft seemed to fly up her loose shirt, except it wasn't cold. It was warm and moist. She pressed her thighs together.

The butt end of the brushes rattled as she dropped them into a big glass jar. "What's your regret?"

They were interrupted by laughter. Sue, Maurizio and Fred were in the shower room—the only semienclosed space in the studio apartment. Steam curled from the foot of open space above the three-quarter walls made of sandblasted glass framed in black metal.

Julian stared at their silhouettes, wavering in and out against the opaque glass. One of the men snapped a towel at Sue's butt. The cat came skittering out from the half-open door, wearing a wet washcloth.

"Go ahead," Mia said, amused by his goggling. Despite the glass walls—or because of them—the shower room was as much a part of the open studio as the other work/sleep/eat areas. Her models loved the luxury of the new bathroom, which she'd recently installed. Especially the oversize shower stall. "Join them."

A smile teased her lips. She knew Julian wouldn't, even though he remained pantless with his legs painted green. "That's your regret, isn't it? You've never had a ménage à quatre?"

He shook his head, eyes still gleaming. The man had mischief on his mind and if she didn't want to find out the details of his naughty thoughts, she'd better quit teasing him. And keep Cress around as a buffer.

"Is that what they're doing? It looks more like horseplay to me."

She acted unaffected. "I wouldn't know. I've never engaged in a ménage of any sort."

"I can introduce you to one of my girlfriends…"

"Hah!" She tossed her curls out of her eyes. "Tell me, why is it that men, and even a lot of women, only go for the woman-man-woman combo? If I did decide to try a ménage à trois, I'd want two men at my beck and call."

Julian's brows inched upward. "Then I'll introduce you to one of my male friends…"

"Would you, really?"

He didn't hesitate. "No. I want you all to myself."

Pleasure unfurled inside her. "There's that ego again."

"Yes. When it comes to certain things…" his gaze coasted down and then up her body on a lazy return trip "…I'm greedy."

She felt the look in a visceral way. A fine tension tugged inside her, tightening in sync with his leisurely examination, producing an arousal that sent hot shards prickling through her veins.

"Greedy," she said, "but still wanting." And she turned away from him, helplessly brushing a hand over the back of her shirt. More than almost anything, she wanted to put on a pair of shorts, but she couldn't do it while he was watching. He'd know that he'd gotten to her. She didn't want him to realize that she was annoyed because he'd made her aware of her body in a way that she never was while working.

The trio emerged from the bath, taking over the studio with their energetic antics. Stefan had already departed with his girlfriend, Leslie, a low-level model who did a lot of catalog work and filled in her schedule with arty experimental jobs like Mia's. Stefan was an underemployed artist who'd rather guard Leslie than hustle for his own jobs.

Mia passed out goodbye hugs and pay envelopes containing hard cash, then shooed the group out the door. Often posing sessions became lazy all-day affairs with cheap wine and lots of fun talk. Today, she needed to be businesslike. There were plans to finalize with Cress regarding the actual shoot next week. And, well, Julian's presence was a damper, even for her most off-beat friends.

"They're not typical models," he said after she'd closed the door. "Are they professionals?"

Mia glanced at Cress. He was working on her computer, loading shots from a digital camera so they could play with the images. She had to handle Julian on her own. Both of them bare-legged and daubed with paint. How surreal.

"Leslie and Cherie are, and Sue was one when she was young, but now she's a writer. Maurizio is an actor."

"A personal trainer," Cress said without turning away from the computer.

"Actor hyphen personal trainer," Mia amended. "Fred is…"

"A hairless freak of nature," said Cress, nodding his own bald head. "Like owner, like Mrs. Snookums."

Mia pooh-poohed him. "Fred is just a guy I know. He sort of latched on to me, so I decided it was easier to keep him than get rid of him. He grew on me."

"Like mold on Cheddar," Cress said automatically.

She shook her head, accustomed to the sarcasm between Cress and Fred. "They're all my friends. They work for free when I need them, but I pay if I can."

"Strange lot," Julian said.

"Maybe to you. Not to me."

He smiled. "Makes sense. You're strange, too."

"Said the man without pants." Her face was warm. Consciously, she dialed back her emotions so Julian wouldn't start thinking that he'd caused them. She was an emotional person, that was all. She tried to be sarcastic and tough, but anyone who knew her for long realized that she wore her heart on her sleeve. Which was why she ended up keeping people like Fred, delivering dinners to Miss Delaney downstairs and bringing blankets and 800 numbers to the teenage runaways who roamed the streets around the Port Authority.

"My participation was all *your* doing," Julian said. He seemed intent on getting her riled up.

"What about Cress?" she asked. "Do you approve of him?"

"What's not to?" Cress murmured. "I'm a model citizen."

Julian straightened his tie. "Sure, I approve. He's almost normal."

"Normal." Mia shuddered. "Did you hear that, Cress? You're normal."

"Almost."

"Is there something wrong with normal?" asked Julian.

"It's not my goal in life." She started tidying up the photo set. "You'd better get back into your pants before someone mistakes you for being one of us."

"I have to clean up first."

She waved at the shower room. "It's all yours."

"I need a buddy, like the other models. What if I accidentally wander into the deep end?"

She suppressed a smile. "Cress will go with you."

"But it's you who needs washing." Julian blinked at her legs. "I'll do you, if you do me."

A lump as big as a fist formed in her throat, blocking her air. She inhaled, almost wheezing. *He'd do her? Oh, yeah. He'd do her up right!*

Cress swiveled in the desk chair. His sunglasses fell off his head and clattered on the wood floor. He didn't even pick them up.

"I can do myself," she managed to say.

"Plug-in or battery-operated?" Julian replied, and Cress laughed so hard it was possible he'd choke before she did it for him.

Her face had gone from warm to red-hot. "Just shut up, both of you," she mumbled, her clamped lips twitching. A snort of laughter flew out her nose.

"I'll be in here, if you need me." Julian disappeared into the bathing area. She watched his shadow through the glass before he moved farther into the room, wondering if he would only wash the paint off his legs or if he planned to strip and shower....

Cress got up and handed her the digital camera. "You know what they say. Take a picture, it'll last longer."

She held a finger over her lips. "Shh."

He put his mouth near her ear. "You know you want to join him. Should I leave?"

"God, no!" She gripped her friend's arm.

Behind the frosted glass, Julian's wavery silhouette had reappeared, frozen in a listening posture.

"Stay," Mia said under her breath. "I need a buffer."

"You mean a cock block." Cress pried her fingers off his arm. "Sorry. Can't do it. That's sorority sister territory. There's a law among men that we don't run interference for the other side."

Her voice rose. "Be a friend."

"This is me," Cress said as he grabbed his jacket off

the back of the desk chair, "being a friend. You just don't realize it yet."

Part of her wanted to hang off his legs to keep him with her. The other part was listening to the sound of rushing water, watching as the shadow Julian took off his shirt, and wondering if his chest was as hairy as his legs. She liked smooth skin for her work, but there was something cuddly about a furry man.

She licked her lips. *Once more, with meaning.* "Please, Cress. I beg of you. Don't put me at his mercy."

Cress rolled his eyes. "Spare me the dramatics, sugar."

She caved and started to laugh at herself. "Okay, okay. You're right. No big deal. I'll tell him no, thank you, and then he can leave."

"Or you can go the other way. How long has it been since you've had sex?"

She counted back as she followed Cress to the door. "Not that long. About three months."

"That's not long? I couldn't last three weeks."

"You're a man. A walking hormone kind of man. You couldn't last three days."

"I had a long weekend once at a family reunion in Vermont that was hell on earth. Every woman there was related to me. And most of them were packing butt cheeks the size of canned hams."

"Nearly four months," Mia said, remembering. "After Matthew, my libido went into hibernation." It had been a long, hot summer with her friendly BOB— battery-operated boyfriend. Energizer was her brand of choice, but she'd never tell Julian that.

"Matthew was the one with the body fluid phobia," Cress remembered.

She nodded. Matthew had been a nice guy, but too neurotic. By the end of the affair, having sex with him had been like going to the dentist, what with all the sterilizing mouthwashes and dental dams. Even early on, there hadn't been even one moment where she'd felt as alive and aroused as she did with Julian.

"Then you've got to take advantage of this situation." Cress moved into the hall. "There's a man you really like in your shower, Mia. Go on. You deserve a little fun."

"I already told him no."

"Change your mind. Woman's prerogative."

"I called him Bachelor Seventeen!"

"So what? He liked that." Cress started down the stairs.

"It could get complicated," Mia threw out and then regretted it. She was practically whining. Ugh. The lesson to always put others' needs before her own had been pounded into her as a child. She'd tried to overcome that training and become a hedonist instead, but sometimes she slipped. Poor needy Matthew was a case in point.

Julian would be a total indulgence. All for herself. No redeeming virtues, just pure pleasure.

Cress kept going. She leaned on the jamb, listened to the creaking treads and decided that she needed a female best friend, not a male who didn't even try to understand the complicated feelings that sex aroused in a woman. Even so-bad-for-you-it-was-too-good-to-pass-up Bachelor Seventeen sex.

She could go to Julian and pretend that she was content with a fling, but it'd never work. Maybe for him, but not for her.

Nope. The only way to get rid of him for good was to convince him that she was not interested. Definitely not interested.

JULIAN HAD NEVER washed as slowly as he did while waiting for Mia's desire to overcome her reservations. He hadn't expected that to take so long.

Mia appeared to be fairly unaware of her effect on men. And yet she was one of the most sensuous women he'd ever met. She was sexier with bare feet, paint-splotched legs and tousled hair than other women were in a thousand dollars' worth of designer underwear.

She had doubts about his sincerity. *And who could blame her,* a nagging internal voice said. Even so, if he bided his time, her innate sexuality would take over. She'd succumb to their mutual attraction.

He was almost sure of it.

He'd started washing down his second leg before a shadow moved outside the door. Mia peeped inside. "So you found the washcloths?"

"I went into the cupboard. Your friends left a pile of wet cloths on the bottom of the shower stall."

"They're slobs." She sounded distracted. And she wasn't looking at him.

He watched her in the steamy mirror as she bounced glances off the white walls and stainless-steel free-standing sinks when they both knew what—who—she really wanted to look at. She was a funny mix of bold and bashful.

"Where are you from?"

"From?" she said, surprised into looking directly at him. "Right here. City born and bred. Why?"

"You're different than other women. I can't get a handle on you."

"You mean you can't put me into a box."

"That might be it." Julian propped his leg on the wall of the spacious mosaic-tiled shower stall. It was almost a room. Considering the modest size of the apartment, a bathroom of such capaciousness seemed like a needless extravagance.

Not that he'd object. It was too easy to imagine a naked Mia looking over her shoulder as she stood poised with her hands braced on the tiled wall and her squeezeable, outthrust ass rising from the clouds of steam. He would take hold and sink himself between those voluptuous cheeks....

Inside the cotton boxer briefs Mia had commented on, his groin felt heavy and full. Damn. He had to stop these erotic visions.

Or fulfill them.

"I hate boxes," she said.

Boxes, not boxers. Use the big head.

All right—focus. He had hated boxes, too. At one time. Now he lived his life in them. Apartments, offices, elevators, in-and-out boxes, magazine pages where space was measured in precise centimeters.

Julian squeezed a sponge to sluice water over his leg, diluting the paint. There wasn't a straight angle in Mia's place—except for the shower stall.

He looked up, catching her staring at him, the hard sparkle in her blue-green eyes a contrast to the curl of her lashes, her soft rounded cheeks and ripe red lips. He swallowed, looked away—suddenly almost as unsure as she. Strange.

"Why such a large shower?" he asked.

"You saw why. Body painting requires lots of soap and water, and it usually seems that everyone's washing off at once."

"Then *you* built this?"

She nodded. "My landlord okayed the renovations and gave me a long lease for my trouble."

There were four showerheads, including a rain pan overhead. To keep the spray at a minimum, he'd turned on only one of them. Even so, the longer he stood posing in the shower the wetter his shorts were getting.

Mia cleared her throat. "Um, if you don't hurry, the hot water will cut out."

"Then you'd better get over here, hmm?"

"No. I can wait."

"Come on. You're safe. Nothing will happen." *That you don't want.* "I'm only Bachelor Seventeen, after all. My powers aren't that strong."

"Yes, that's true," Mia said thoughtfully, irritating him until he realized that's what she was trying to do. She wasn't that good an actress.

She edged closer, eyeing the spray, then his clinging briefs. "You'll get me wet."

A tight chuckle rasped in his throat. "Ohhh, sweetheart, that's what I'm hoping."

She flushed. "I didn't mean—"

"Come on." He grabbed her arm and pulled her into the shower, not even trying to keep her out of the water. She yelped, but didn't pull away, so he wrapped an arm around her waist, tucking her beneath his chin. The sweet fruit scent of her hair tickled in his nostrils.

She gave a little sigh and melted into him. Her palm

slid across his bare stomach, fingers plucking at his waistband. "You're not wearing wet underwear home. You might as well strip."

Whoa! So much for the bashful Mia.

He waited a few seconds before he spoke into her hair. "Is that a good idea—freeing the monster? He has his own agenda."

"The monster?" She snickered. "Guess what? I've never been afraid of monsters." She pulled back, dropping a skeptical glance at the fullness in his shorts. "Especially ones with agendas."

He hooked his thumbs in the waistband and slid it past his navel, then paused. "I thought you weren't interested."

Mia forced her eyes back up to his. "I'm not. It's just that nudity is nothing out of the ordinary around here. I deal with it all the time. You're only another body to me." She shrugged. "I doubt if even the monster can make me—" her hand waved through the rising steam "—make me, um, blink."

"Oh yeah? Is that a dare?"

She looked at her fluttery fingers, then frowned and crossed her arms. "Nope. It's a fact."

Julian spread his feet and rested his hands on his hip bones. His erection swelled, pushing against the wet cotton. *Good boy.* The bigger, the better.

Mia's confidence wavered. She reversed one step, putting her backside into the shower spray without noticing. He grinned to himself. Any way you looked at it, she'd backed herself into a tight situation.

Her chin jutted, daring him. "What's wrong? Are you shy?"

"Not that I've noticed."

"Then…" She twirled a finger, pointing from his

shorts to his ankles. "I want you washed, dressed and out of here. So take 'em off."

"Soon enough," he said. "I thought I'd do this first."

He was on her before she could process his intent. He slipped his hands under the hem of her shirt and held her by the hips, bringing his mouth down to capture hers in a deep, abrupt kiss.

She made a sound in her throat, halfway between a protest and approval. He used his tongue to open her mouth wider, seeking the hot, slick interior. The first intimate surrender of many.

She wrenched away, panting. "Hey! I told you to get naked, not to kiss me."

"I don't follow orders well." He spread his fingers, squeezing the flesh of her tempting bottom. "Besides, I didn't want to leave here with any regrets. Not kissing you would have qualified."

Her eyes narrowed, but again she didn't retreat. She pushed even closer. Defiant. He felt a tug as she gripped the front of his shorts. "You don't follow orders at all."

Suddenly she jerked the clinging fabric downward so his hard cock popped out. Her face remained tilted upward, eyes locked on his as she bent a little at the waist to reach farther, shoving the wet shorts down his thighs until they'd puddled around his ankles.

"Don't look," he said. Taunting.

Contrary as she was, she looked. Her pupils shrunk to pinpoints.

Every nerve in his body seemed to be sending messages straight to his swaying erection. Commands to get harder, to seep moisture, to seek relief. And damn if he didn't have to stand still as she stared, feeling himself pulsing, throbbing, the sensitive foreskin stretched taut to the point of pain.

His fingers itched to touch Mia and find the sweet succor hidden beneath her scarlet thong. Instead he clenched his fists and spoke through gritted teeth. "Don't blink. You said you wouldn't blink."

She clamped her lower lip between her teeth. Not blinking. After a few moments, she let go and pouted, her lip dented like a bruised fruit. "Nothing I haven't seen before. Just an ordinary monster."

Her breathlessness nullified the flip intent.

"You blinked," he accused.

"No, I didn't."

"Yes, you did." He kicked the sodden briefs away. The shower spray beat past Mia's body, spattering across their legs. Rivulets of multicolored paint stained the water washing toward the drain.

"I *had* to blink," she said. "It's a natural physiological response."

"So's this." He touched his thumb to her lip.

She winced.

"Did that kiss hurt you?" He brought his face next to hers, dropping his voice down low. "You're all swollen. And soft."

"You're all swollen, too."

"But not soft."

"No-o-o-o," she groaned as he pushed against her, his erection a rigid bar against her belly. "You're not soft."

"I can be." He held her face in his hands and kissed her, flicking a soft tongue between her lips. Their wet mouths made small smacking sounds as they kissed, once, twice, ten times—quick suckling kisses as sweet and juicy as an orange split into sections.

One more, he thought. And then one more. He couldn't stop tasting her.

Her hair hung in damp ringlets against her cheeks. Her eyelids quivered. "What are you doing to me, Julian?" She pressed her hands over his. "We have to stop. This isn't—isn't—"

"Don't be that way," he said, as she forced his hands down. He put them back on her hips. Her skin was so wet that when she squirmed his hands slipped over the flexing muscle to the tempting cheeks, cushy as pillows. He traced the line of her thong between them, then slid a finger under the wet satin strap, brushing a darkly exciting caress over her intimate parts, parting the plump folds—

She gasped and pushed him away. "This is not professional."

He had to shake his head to break up the sexual haze dulling it, blinking away the flying water drops. "I'm never professional when I'm naked."

"But *I* am."

Mia whipped her shirt down to cover her ass, then made a swooping leap to grab his underwear and escape the shower. "I'll run down to the laundry room and get these dry. Back in ten minutes."

Julian let out a groan and slapped his hands on the mosaic tiles, bracing himself under the spray. He'd almost had her.

He lowered his head and gritted his teeth. The ache in his balls was so fierce it was nearly debilitating, but what really consumed him was the soft kisses they'd shared and, for a few moments, the promise in Mia's eyes.

She'd wanted him. Even more, she'd *liked* him.

Something to build on.

He'd looked up into the spray and was reaching for

his erection when the hot water abruptly turned cold, sending him to the far corner of the shower stall, leaping and swearing.

"Mia," he growled. She'd probably turned on the kitchen faucet, for spite.

Icy droplets ricocheted around the enclosure, making him tingle. He was still hot. And ready. No cold shower could cure that.

NIKKI REFUSED the executive assistant's offer of a seat. Her feet were killing her, but everyone knew that you had to suffer for fashion. Her skintight pencil skirt was already a mass of wrinkles after a crosstown cab ride; sitting would make it worse.

She tugged the skirt down, smoothing it over her hip bones. Determined to look like a professional, she'd dressed conservatively for the meeting with the managing editor of *Hard Candy*. Four-inch stiletto heels qualified, didn't they? They *were* black.

A frosty blonde with a perfectly made-up face walked into the editor's reception area with a manila folder, aiming to drop it onto the desk. Her gaze flew over the guest with disinterest, until she reached Nikki's face.

Then she smiled. "Nikki Silk?"

"Yesss…"

"What are you doing here?" The blonde veered in for a double-cheek air kiss, bringing back memories of stilted family holidays with female relatives who never took off their head-to-toe Chanel and pearls. Up close, Nikki saw that threads of lipstick had seeped into the nearly invisible lines around the woman's lips.

"Is Julian with you?" the blonde asked. There was a shift in the depths of her crystalline eyes.

Nikki made a face. "Hell no. Absolutely not. And please don't mention this to him either, Ms....?"

The smile became a light laugh. "Petra Lombardi. We met at one of those benefits your family is always hosting, for some disease I can't remember. It was at the St. Regis, and you were in a beaded red gown that was too old for you. I was Julian's date."

"I'm sorry, I don't remember."

"Ancient news." Petra shrugged prettily. "So many parties, so many introductions." She arched her brows at Nikki. "So very many men. Who can keep track?"

"I know Julian can't."

Petra's smile dropped away. "Mmm...*Julian*." Her lips puckered as she threw a hard glance at the editor's assistant, who was watching them from behind the desk while murmuring into her headset.

Petra regathered herself, nostrils flaring. "So, Nikki, what brings you to *Hard Candy*?" She gave a just-us-girlfriends chuckle. "And why is it a secret?"

"Only a secret from Julian—for now. He doesn't want me employed here."

Petra's eyes narrowed. "You're coming to work at *Hard Candy*?"

"Not yet. But we'll see." Butterflies danced in Nikki's hollow stomach as she fingered the strap of her purse. "I'm going in to pitch an article to the editor."

"Oh, how sweet. But I can't imagine Julian objecting to that. Writing should be a pleasant, harmless sideline for you."

Sideline? Nikki winced at the accurate barb. Why shouldn't the entire world assume she was a dilettante? She'd given them plenty of reason. Only Mia Kerrigan had treated her like a halfway competent person, and that was probably because she didn't give a flying fig about how many times Nikki's name was mentioned in the gossip columns. Or Julian's, for that matter.

"I want to surprise him," she said. "Surprise all of my family, in fact." She held a finger over her lips, not trusting Petra, but guessing that the woman would suck up to anyone named Silk. "So *shhh.*"

"As you wish."

"Ms. Silk?" the assistant said. "Mr. Morrisey will see you now."

"Thanks," Nikki said, flipping her hair to make herself believe that she wouldn't crumple if she was laughed out of the office. If she was really lucky, she'd find a way to charm the editor into keeping quiet around Julian, at least until the article was accepted for publication. "See you around, Petra."

Petra's smile was cool and careful. "Looking forward to it, Nikki."

6

"SPEAK OF the devil," Mia said into her cell phone as she trod along the sidewalk to her home sweet tenement. She'd put in a full day finishing the Gormans' ballroom, then lugged her toolbox with her on the subway and another three blocks from her stop. Her muscles were like rubber, her hair was limp and falling out of its clip, her deodorant had given out hours ago and her clothes were crusty with paint spatters.

And waiting on her stoop was Julian Silk, looking as handsome as the devil. In this case, the devil had dressed down from Prada to jeans, sneakers and layered T-shirts, with attractive beard stubble and a big bag of Chinese takeout. But he was still the devil.

There to tempt her with his goodies.

And the food, too.

"Not Julian," Nikki shrieked into Mia's ear. The girl was so dramatic she could star on Broadway. "He never leaves work before six."

Mia lurked behind a beefy man delivering cartons of tomatoes to the Tibetan restaurant down the block. Did they have tomatoes in Tibet? She thought they only had yak milk. "He did today. He's sitting out front of my building."

"Sitting out front," Nikki repeated like a psychiatrist on cruise control.

"My building. With Chinese food. I recognize the Garden of the Floating Lotus Blossom logo. I'm going to have to invite him up, aren't I? I mean, there's no way out of it. Unless I double back and go to Cress's place instead." Mia's ankles wobbled at the thought.

"This is strange," Nikki mused. "Julian usually takes his new girlfriends out to a fine restaurant, the sort of place where you hand over a credit card without looking at the bill. He gives them the full show—wine, lobster, compliments, paparazzi...."

The delivery guy wheeled away, and Mia darted behind a mound of garbage bags. The stench was horrible. She put down her toolbox and squeezed her nose shut. "Whad does id mean?"

There was silence on Nikki's end. Julian's sister had secured interest in a potential article from the editor of *Hard Candy* and had called Mia to set up another interview, this time intending to concentrate on the sexier angle of her body-painting sideline. They'd lapsed into harmless girl talk before going on to the ever-fascinating subject of how they should proceed with Julian. Though they'd shared a giggle over Mia's telling of his fish-out-of-water episode at the plaid test shoot, she hadn't mentioned how she'd just about had a meltdown when she'd stripped him in the shower. Some things a sister didn't need to know, and the effect the sight of her naked brother had on a supposedly with-it woman was one of them.

When Mia had returned from the laundry room with his dry shorts and a semblance of control, he'd already been dressed and ready to go. She'd melted again at the thought of him free-balling beneath the proper business suit. Julian had departed with a wink and no promise, not the only one left dangling.

She'd had a few regrets of her own. But now here he was, unannounced. Planning what?

"Maybe he thinks of you as a buddy?" Nikki suggested, but then they both said, "Naaah."

There was movement in one of the ripped garbage bags. "I gotta go," Mia said, and snapped shut her phone. A whiskery nose appeared from behind the shredded plastic. She grabbed her kit and bolted onto the sidewalk. She had love and compassion for all of God's living creatures, but rats were one neighborhood denizen she avoided under any circumstance.

Even when that meant putting her in temptation's path. She squared her sore shoulders and called, "Hello, Julian."

He waved. "Why were you hiding behind the trash?"

Cripes. "Thought I saw an interesting cast-off, but it was only a broken picture frame. Street salvage is one of my hobbies." *That* should put him off.

He met her at the bottom of the cement stairs and took the heavy toolbox. "Can I go with you sometime?"

"Why would you want to? Don't Silks buy everything they need on Madison Avenue?"

"Not friends."

"I'm sure Barneys was having a special sale on them, too."

"That was girlfriends." Julian laughed, but there was a trace of sarcastic truth in his words.

Mia climbed the steps, digging her keys out from the bottom of her shoulder bag. "So now you want to be friends, huh?"

"For a start."

She hesitated. Why not? After she showed him the day-to-day truth of her lifestyle—which did not include facials, tailors, limos and gilded invitations—he'd be too dumbstruck to even think of having sex with her.

"Great. We can begin right away." Except that her thigh muscles were whimpering and her head felt too heavy for her neck. All the way home, she'd been looking forward to climbing into bed with her other BOB— the TV clicker. "After I have a shower. I smell like a monkey."

Julian sniffed. "I don't mind, especially if we both end up reeking of hot jungle love."

"Friends don't let friends have meaningless sex. Besides, I had onions for lunch and my breath must stink." She was sounding like quite the prize. Why wasn't he giving up?

"The garlic shrimp will take care of that."

"I'm allergic to shellfish." Especially lobster masquerading as a seduction.

"I meant for me."

"Don't get your hopes up. I kiss friends only on the cheek." She pushed the door open to the lobby with a dingy linoleum tile floor.

Immediately a security chain jingled and an elderly lady in a terry cloth turban and a floral housecoat poked her head out into the hallway from apartment 1A. "Mia, is that you?

"Yes, Miss Delaney."

"Did you finish the ballroom like you'd hoped?"

"I sure did. It looks incredible. I'm going back next week to take photos for my portfolio."

"You must remember to show me."

"Sure. I'm going up now, Miss Delaney."

"Do I smell Chinese food?"

"Oh, yes. I almost forgot." Mia took the takeout bag from Julian. "We ordered too much. You know how my eyes are always bigger than my stomach. I was hoping you wouldn't mind taking a few of the dishes off my hands—"

She approached Miss Delaney's door, rummaging inside the bag. "We have soup and pea pods with water chestnuts and Mongolian beef. This one appears to be some kind of lo mein—"

"I don't care for the pea pods—it's like chewing on a leaf. What kind of soup?"

"Shark fin," Julian said.

Miss Delaney peered at him through the upper half of her bifocals. "A new young man?" she stage-whispered to Mia.

"Just a friend," Mia stage-whispered back. "Like Edmund Flax."

Miss Delaney cackled. "I'll take the soup and the lo mein. If you have spring rolls, that would be a meal and I could invite Edmund down for dinner…"

"How about garlic shrimp?"

"That will do. You're a dear. Stop by on your way up and extend my invitation to Edmund, will you?"

Mia repacked the cartons. "Sure thing."

"I must go take my curlers out. Have a nice evening." Miss Delaney's door clunked shut.

"I meant to introduce you," Mia said, rolling down the top of the paper bag. "That was Miss Delaney. Alberta. She taught school on the East Side for fifty-two years. Then a gang-banger cracked her in the skull with a lead pipe and the school board forced her to retire."

"Addled?"

"Not a bit. But she uses a walker now, so I do a lot of her grocery shopping. I hope you don't mind about the food…"

"I'm happy to share."

Mia gave him a quick smile. She reached for her shoulder bag, but he said, "Let me," and her sore muscles were so grateful they wanted to grab and cling and kiss him.

She didn't let them, settling for a "Thanks."

At the third-floor landing she stopped and went to knock at the door of Edmund Flax, a small elderly black man who lived in genteel poverty in a room furnished with secondhand books and a hot plate. He had no phone, but much dignity. He spent several evenings a week at Miss Delaney's, who insisted they were "just friends" when Mia teased her about being courted.

Mia and Julian continued the climb to her studio. On the next flight of twisting steps, they ran into Lance Wheatley, a thirty-year-old doctoral candidate at Columbia who lived directly under Mia's attic apartment and was frequently disgruntled, mostly because he believed she was having orgies without him.

"Hi, Lance."

"Mia."

They maneuvered around each other. Lance stared at Julian and seemed to be on the verge of recognizing him. Mia couldn't imagine Lance reading the gossip rags, but he said nothing more. Perhaps he was only jealous again.

"Finally," Julian said, after the other man had disappeared around the twisting staircase.

"One more flight," Mia said.

"You misunderstand. I was saying that finally there's a person who's not in love with you."

She scoffed. He probably lived in a building with a private elevator and anonymous neighbors. "No one's *in love* with me. But Lance did ask me out."

"You didn't go?"

"Nope. Other than a missing sense of humor, he's too perfect. By my mother's standards." Lance was very presentable in a subdued, clean-cut, well-educated way, which was everything that her mother wanted for Mia in a husband, and exactly what she found to be boring.

"Too perfect..." Julian was oddly serious. "How do I stack up in that department?"

"You're perfect, too, but in a different way. An over-the-top way. Much too well-known, for one thing. Too rich, too handsome...*and* you have ten times the sex appeal any normal man needs." An indecent amount, she thought, becoming sharply aware of the warmth of his body as he stood close behind her while she unlocked the door. It wasn't that he crowded her, exactly; he just had a way of being there, so big and male and shockingly handsome that it was easier on her nerves not to look at him.

His voice dropped, becoming more intimate. He did that very well. Smooth as silk, one might say if one was smitten. "Is it possible to have too much sex appeal?"

"In my mother's opinion, absolutely. She doesn't think that sex is very seemly."

"It's not." Julian knocked his chin lightly against the back of her head. "Good thing I don't want to date your mother."

"You don't want to date me, either," Mia reminded him as they entered her apartment. She dropped the bag of takeout on the floor and collapsed into the armchair to remove her shoes and socks. She got halfway and then was too tired to lift her other foot. Maybe later.

She rested her head on the back of the chair and closed her eyes. "I guess you can make yourself at home, since we're going to be *friends*," she said. Friends. The platonic kind. Not tumble-buddies.

"To start," he reiterated, even though their start already included hot, naked bodies and even hotter kisses.

He knelt, picked up her foot and placed it on his thigh. He unlaced her shoe, slipped it off along with her sock and then held her heel in his hand. His thumb took a deep stroke across her instep.

"What are you doing?" she asked in such a lazy voice it was clear she didn't want him to stop.

"I can see that you're beat."

"It was a hard day's work. Michelangelo must have been a hobbled crone by the time he finished the Sistine Chapel." Julian's big warm hands covered her foot. Both thumbs pressed into her sole. She let out a moan that was almost orgasmic.

"Painting bodies?"

"Mmm. Ballroom."

"Is that a body-painting euphemism for something I don't want to picture?"

She chuckled. "No, really, I was painting a ballroom. Didn't Nikki report to you about that?"

His fingers stilled. She twiddled her toes and he resumed the sensuous massage. Now and then his hand strayed upward to give her calf a squeeze. Cold tingles broke out on her warm skin.

"What do you know about my sister?" he asked.

"You mean your spy?"

"I don't need a spy. I'm perfectly capable of getting anything I want out of you."

She might have protested, but she didn't want the delicious kneading to stop. "That's probably true, now that I know you have magic fingers. I'm *so* weak. Do you know shiatsu?"

"I'll get a how-to book." He sat back on the carpet and pulled her other foot into his lap. "Nikki was doing preliminary work for the article I mentioned earlier. A painted-fashion layout in *Hard Candy*."

Mia cracked an eye. His head was bowed. She couldn't see his expression, but she believed him. Nikki's mission hadn't been only a personal reconnaissance for his own benefit. "There's really going to be an article?" Mia relaxed another degree. "I suspected that you were playing me with promises of fame and fortune."

"You're not the kind of girl to be lured by that…are you?"

She jabbed him with her foot. "I don't know. I might be. No one's ever tried to buy me before." Except her parents, in a way, who'd withdrawn their support for her college education when she wouldn't give up her creative ambitions for an approved major at an approved school. She'd been what most people would call a starving artist ever since, but at least she was free.

"I don't want to buy you, Mia."

"Good."

"Nikki came to me, looking for a job."

"And you, being a loving big brother, threw her a bone with a fairly harmless assignment?"

"That's about it, but I won't deny that I also had an interest in acquiring personal information about you. However, there would have been easier ways than sending Nikki."

"She's…ah…"

"Very young and very spoiled."

"But she's trying, and she really wants to please you." *And torment you,* Mia silently added with a smile.

"She turned in an excellent background brief on you. No drama at all. I was pleasantly surprised."

Mia had been watching him from beneath her lashes. His face changed when he talked about Nikki, reminding her of the easy joy he'd showed in the beach photo from the bachelor article. One of his most attractive qualities. She could almost believe that the coolly urbane man, who'd flustered her at the cover shoot, and the gossip pages' smooth bachelor with his string of glossy girlfriends, were the facade.

Part of her did believe that. But there was another part that knew how important facades were, whether they were genuine or faux. A man could be a serial lover and a loving brother at the same time. She probably wasn't the first woman to fool herself into believing that *this time* was special for Julian. Maybe he'd even tried the let's-be-friends ploy before, to get a woman's guard down.

Mia reluctantly pulled her feet off his lap. "I want you to tell me all about your sisters," she said, "but first I need to take that shower."

"I'll come, too." He gave her an innocent smile. "I have to wash my hands."

"You can use the kitchen sink." She waved at the minimal kitchen that had been fitted into one of the attic nooks. "There's a microwave, if you want to warm up the food. I'll be out in ten minutes."

"I'll be waiting."

No doubt. He *was* the devil her father had always told her to look out for.

"I KNEW I'D get you into bed," Julian said, more than ten minutes later. She'd lingered in the shower, thinking of him waiting for her, thinking of him getting impatient and joining her in the shower, touching herself as she considered how that would be, naked against the shower wall with his hands all over her, and his mouth on her breasts, his tongue licking her, tasting her—

She'd heard of men whipping off a quick one to take off the edge. So far, that didn't seem to work the same way for a woman. She'd only heightened her responses.

It didn't help that Julian was using his eyes like a paintbrush loaded with liquid chocolate, even while they talked about prosaic things like the vital stats of his three younger sisters and the Mets' chances of getting into the playoffs. Forget the Chinese food. She wanted to eat *him* up.

"I really need to get a couch," she announced, when their hands had brushed for the umpteenth time over the carton of pot stickers. Her diet wasn't the only resolution that might end up broken this day.

They'd taken a tray to her bed, which wasn't the first time she'd hosted a meal there. The studio apartment wasn't conventionally furnished. For sitting, she had the secondhand armchair and heaps of floor pillows. The only table of any size was used as a work surface, forever cluttered with paints, chalk, brushes and tins of cleaning solvents. The kitchen had a couple square feet of counter space and a stool, so that left her bed to serve as the communal lounging and dining area, which worked fine except for latte spills and guests who rubbed off on her pillows.

But then she'd never had *Julian* in her bed. He was reclining across the foot of it, his long legs stretched toward her, casually crossed at the ankles, framing the fullness at his crotch, which she was *not* looking at—

Yep. The floor pillows might have been a wiser option, but her body had refused, even though the hot shower and equally hot fantasy had loosened her up considerably.

"A couch would be too normal for you," he said.

"True." She stabbed her chopsticks into the carton of pea pods. "Want some?"

"Sure." He leaned forward on his elbow with his mouth open.

She fed him one. He chewed, his cheeks hollowing and his shadowed jaw moving up and down in a way that seemed erotic. *Everything* seemed erotic with Julian.

"Like chewing on a leaf," he said.

She smiled. "Did you go to work today?"

"I did. Left early for a dental appointment."

Then it wasn't visiting her that had had drawn him out of his usual patterns. Damn.

"Whitening?" she guessed. Had to be. His teeth were perfect enough to be featured in a toothpaste ad.

"Just a cleaning."

"How come you didn't shave?"

He rubbed a hand across the stubble. "Didn't feel like it. What's with this interest in my hygiene?"

She shoveled in a mouthful of the slimy green pods.

His gaze moved along her bare legs, crossed Indian style. She flipped shut the front of her robe. She'd put on loose men's boxers and a sleeveless tee, but that hadn't seemed like enough coverage. Not with Mr. Hot Black Brooding Eyes around. A radiation suit might do it.

"Maybe you wanted me to join you in the shower for a hygiene check," he guessed.

"Don't flatter yourself."

"You didn't seem to mind last time."

"I told you. Nudity is standard operating procedure to me."

"Right. What's a little skin between friends?" He reached across and skated his palm along her leg beneath the robe. "So soft. Did you shave your legs in the shower? Is that what took you so long?"

"No." She rearranged herself so that she could close her thighs. Her inner muscles squeezed tight, almost spasmodically, as if his hand had gone higher and he'd slipped a ticklish finger inside her.

Ohmigod. Stop thinking that way.

"You lotioned up," he guessed.

"No." She thrust the pea pods back on the tray and tried the next carton without paying attention. Curry sauce. *Yeow.* The spices burned on her tongue, making her eyes water. "Beer," she croaked. "Water."

Julian jumped up to go to the minifridge. She panted with her tongue out. Thank god. Anything to break up the tension. Turned out *she* was the dawg.

In heat. She flapped a hand at her flushed face.

"I brought both." He handed her a bottle of water and set a couple of beers on the tray.

"Thanks." She drank, making glugging sounds.

He settled back into place. "You don't like spicy foods?"

"I love to try them, but I have supersensitive taste buds, so I usually regret it."

"Supersensitive taste buds. I like the sound of that. What's your favorite taste?"

"Sweets," she said quickly, before she could blurt out something embarrassing about their candy-flavored kisses lingering on her tongue long after the taste had passed. "I'm a chocoholic, but I like other candies, too."

Julian's lips curved. "Ever lick chocolate off bare skin?"

"For me, that would be mixing business with pleasure."

"Only if you did it with a paid model." He tapped himself. "I'm free."

Her mouth went dry; she drained the remaining water. "But we have a professional connection…sort of."

"I'll call Nikki right now and tell her the article is canceled."

"You can't do that to her! She's all excited about—" Mia stopped.

"About what?" Julian frowned with suspicion. "What have you two been talking about? Sharing secrets?"

"Not so much. But I know she's eager to be involved in Silk Publishing. Why don't you give her a staff job on one of your magazines?"

"I'm considering it, as soon as I decide which publication can withstand a massive dose of Nikki's nonsense."

"That's very controlling."

He shrugged his head. "Yeah, I know. But that's my job."

"To boss your sister? I don't think so."

"Call it duty, then. I'm the man of the family."

Mia thumped her chest. "I am man, hear me roar. Do you really think your sisters aren't capable of making their own decisions?"

"You haven't met Very—Veronica. She's hell-bent on self-destruction. Hasn't made a wise decision since our dad died." Julian moved the tray to the floor, keeping only the beers. He twisted off the tops and handed one to Mia. "You're a girl. You wouldn't understand."

"I understand what it's like to be on my own and making my own choices. It's hard. Especially without the Silk bank accounts to fall back on. But there's an empowerment in it, too. The struggle makes success so much sweeter." She tipped her beer at him. "*You* wouldn't understand that."

His eyes darkened, but he took the blow without getting all huffy and having to bluster about his many successes to bolster his ego. "You have a point. But I still say that our situations differ."

"Yes, maybe so. But I don't see why you can't encourage Nikki, since she wants to do something more with her life than shopping and manicures."

"I *am* encouraging her. I'm also being cautious."

"Oh…" Mia waved her hand, feeling frustrated and impotent, the way she used to when she was seventeen. She'd chosen to grab hold of the independence she craved, but the lingering wish to make her parents proud remained. It still ate at her, knowing that from their viewpoint, none of her triumphs had been the right sort.

"Why don't you just set Nikki free and wish for the best?" Mia said. "That's what I'd do."

Julian sat across from her, knees bent, denim-clad thighs spread and his feet tucked under his butt. He threw his head back and she watched his Adam's apple move in his throat as he took a large swallow of the beer.

He lowered the bottle. "It's not that simple. I made a promise to look after her—all of them."

"I get it. Still, that doesn't mean you pull their puppet strings. You'd hate for your father to do be doing that to you, I bet."

"How'd you guess?" Julian's smile was nostalgic.

"But, you know, he did it anyway, and I'd give anything to have him still doing it."

"Of course you would." It was different, having your father gone for good versus having him tucked safely away in another world, giving stuffy church sermons and running a vast charity network on the Upper East Side. "I'm sorry—I'm just blowing my mouth off."

"No, it's good to have a real conversation with a woman."

She made a face as if she believed he was spouting a line to flatter her, when she tended to believe him. "What kind do you usually have? Superficial?"

He angled toward her, studying her face very intently. "You don't think very much of me, do you?"

She tilted back. "I'm starting to."

"Starting to…?"

Her breath came short. "If we're going to be friends, I have to like you, at least. And, well, it's turning out that's not very hard to do. You're a nice man, Julian. Somewhat domineering and arrogant, but nice."

"Thanks. And you're nice, too. Somewhat goofy and intentionally obtuse, but nice."

"Obtuse? Gee, thanks."

"Don't worry. I plan on opening your eyes."

He'd gotten closer, leaning forward on his arms with his splayed hands bracketing her legs. The heat that was always there between them became thicker, almost humid. Her head sang with warnings, but her only recourse to stay out of range was to drop back onto her elbows, which proved inadvisable. The position put her breasts practically in his face and even though she squirmed, the only place for her legs was on either side of his body. She felt so…open.

"Have I dominated you?" he asked with a wolfish grin.

"You are right now, and you know it."

"Mmm-hmm. And you like it."

He brushed his face across her stomach, just barely touching. His teeth caught the loose tie of her belt and tugged it free. She clenched inside, wanting him but knowing she should say no, like a dieter being offered a cupcake. Fortunately, she'd already broken her diet.

The bristles of his light beard scraped between her breasts as he nudged the lapels of her robe open with his nose. "You smell so good," he said with a low growl, rubbing his cheek against her breast.

Her back arched. Her nipple peaked beneath the thin cotton T-shirt, begging for his attention. An involuntary offer, but one she was no longer capable of taking back. She knew they couldn't be friends—that had been a reach from the beginning, a last straw to grasp so she could justify having him here.

But why? She'd never felt it necessary to justify sex. Not before Julian. Was it because he was so obviously bad for her? Or…

Oh hell. The reasons didn't matter. She was already a lost cause.

Mia reached for the scoop neck of her ribbed tee and pulled it down with one hard yank, baring her left breast. Her heart hammered wildly. This wasn't an offer; it was a blatant inducement.

Julian's eyes went once to her face before the thick black lashes dropped. He made a reverent humming sound as his lips closed over her nipple. The initial contact was riveting, but then the vibrations went through her as if she were a cello being played by a master. Lovely. She started to melt. To swoon.

At first, he held her nipple delicately between his teeth and twanged it with his tongue. But soon his mouth had opened and he'd sucked her flesh into the hot interior, taking in as much as he could manage, pulling on her nipple with a sensation so strong she felt it through her entire body.

Mia's eyes rolled back in her head.

This was heaven on earth.

Forgive me, Mom and Dad. I'm about to sin.

7

JULIAN LOWERED himself from all fours, resisting the urge to cover Mia completely. He kept most of his weight off her. He didn't want to overwhelm her. Not yet.

She trembled, even so. Especially when he slid a hand beneath her shirt, across her satin skin and cupped her other breast. The plump weight, the natural shape so soft and pliant to his touch, worked on his libido in a way no silicone-enhanced starlet ever had.

He started to lift his head, then stopped and played with her nipple a while longer, averse to letting go. When he finally did, the little pink button was glistening with wetness and as hard as a bullet. "You have beautiful breasts."

Mia blew out a long breath. "I've never had complaints. But, you know, they came with a pair of hips most women would trade in. Kind of a matched set."

"Your ass is fantastic." He thought of her swaying and bobbing to the beat, flashing her thong at him. "Especially when it bounces." Smiling at her, he jiggled her breast in his hand, making his passions skyrocket.

Her lips twitched. "Oh yeah. My body is a playground."

"A wonderland."

"And I like to invite my friends over to play."

A short sharp burst of jealousy stung him. "You mean I have to share?"

She blinked. "Is that a problem with you rich-boy types?"

"I hadn't thought it through."

She pushed at him, trying to turn over onto her side. "Then maybe this isn't a good idea. We should go back to being platonic friends, not friends with benefits." She muttered into a pillow. "Even though that's never gonna work either."

"Hey, wait." He folded his arms around her, nuzzling his face into her hair. She tried to bat him away, but he found her ear and licked and nipped and tickled until she relaxed with a shudder and a sigh. "Don't make me stop," he coaxed. "This is so nice." He stroked the length of her body, reaching her smooth thigh inside the baggy leg of her shorts. Damn, she was hot, like a steam machine.

"It should be special, not just nice. *Nice.* Bleh."

Where had that come from? He'd been taking it easy, going along thinking that she'd balk at the full-on seduction with all the romantic trimmings. She was a blunt girl, a bold, free, sexy one.

But still a girl.

He kissed her lobe, behind her ear, the cord at the side of her neck. "What do you want? Tell me and I'll give it to you."

"I don't want *stuff.*"

"That's not what I meant—"

She slipped from his arms and climbed out of bed. He caught at her robe to keep her, but she let it slide off her arms and left it behind, stalking across the studio apartment without a backward glance.

He sat up gingerly and threw away the armful of

empty terry cloth. Okay, so how the hell had that happened? He was usually a Ferrari when it came to his moves. This time, it was she who'd taken over and gone in reverse—from sixty to zero with one wicked screech of the brakes. She'd just laid the wrong kind of rubber across his flattened corpse.

Mia adjusted her top with her back to him. She ran her hands through her damp ringlets, then took a deep noisy breath as she turned. "Listen." She strolled toward the bed. "We both know you're a hot guy. When I'm with you, when you touch me, I want to have sex with you—"

He interrupted. "That's not one-sided."

She waved with dismissal, as if that was a given. He admired her confidence. In his experiences with other women, he'd discovered that even the most stunning of them could be needy and insecure.

"The point is—" Her face twisted. "Ack. What *is* the point? I'm not sure how we came to this. It's like…you're another of the people who appeared in my life and somehow end up sticking around. Almost like…"

"I'm a friend?"

She dropped her hands. "Yeah."

"I wouldn't mind that. In fact, I'd like it a lot." He scooted to the edge of the bed, giving his fly a tug over his semideflated boner. There was that. "But what about the sex thing?"

Silence.

"We should go ahead and do it," she blurted.

"Oh?" He wasn't jumping too fast this time.

"Just to get it out of the way."

"That never works," he said.

"You've tried?"

"No-o-o-o." He hadn't run across too many women who wanted to be just friends. "But common sense says…"

She sighed and plopped beside him. "You're right. Dammit. Sex is complicated with emotion, no matter what. I don't want to end up broken-hearted and resentful."

He'd just talked himself out of a quickie. A first, but not regrettable. Mia was worth exploring, even if they never came together again.

Yeah, like there was any chance of *that* happening. He knew they'd wind up in bed. But for once, getting there was going to be as good as the act. His only qualm was her mention of broken hearts. He'd thought they could avoid that complication, but there he was again, forgetting that Mia was a girl.

Luckily, he had his own emotions under control and didn't get caught up in the drama of these things. These flings.

"So what should we do?" He took her hand, threading their fingers into a knot. "How do we handle *this*?" He gave her hand a squeeze, ignoring the pleasure that touching her gave him. A friendship first? Amazing.

After a moment's thought, Mia bumped his shoulder. Her eyes slid sideways, peeking at him from the mop of her tangled curls. "If you really want to be my friend, come back at 2 a.m. tomorrow morning. And be prepared to go to places beyond your wildest imagination."

"That sounds rather sexy."

She laughed, her eyes snapping, her effervescence returned. "Aw, Julian. You would think that! But you'll see. You'll see a lot more than you think."

"WHAT ON earth?" Mia said when Julian emerged from the limousine outside her building at the arranged time. The vehicle was black; not an ostentatious stretch, but it was still a limo.

He'd thought of ditching it down the block and then decided that she might get a kick out of a ride. "I was at a benefit dinner all evening. The speeches ran long. It seemed easiest to come straight here."

"In a limo!"

He noticed that she wore jeans, a heavy sweatshirt and boots. A red bandanna covered her hair, and she carried work gloves. Not a limo-riding outfit, unlike his tux.

"This is impossible." She fingered his lapel, then dusted off his shoulder with a slap of the gloves. "Gorgeous suit. Far too fancy for what I'd planned. You might as well go home."

"I brought clothes to change into. We can send the limo away, if you'd prefer." He wanted to shake himself for not thinking. Showing up in a limo was not the way to enter Mia's world.

She reconsidered, dragging her teeth across her lower lip. "What kind of clothes?"

"Your kind." Truth was, he had a bag in the trunk with several choices, from blue collar to boating wear. Having no idea what Mia intended, he'd wanted to be prepared. But he couldn't admit that. Dressing down for Chinese food hadn't fooled her, and explaining that a tux was work wear for him would only cement their positions as polar opposites.

"All right," she said with a heavy sigh, though he could see that her humor was intact. She seemed to be suppressing a smile that he didn't fully understand. "I guess we can go back upstairs for you to change, but you can't take too long or all the best junk will be gone before we get there."

Junk? Was that street slang, or did she actually mean *junk?*

A guy on the other side of the street put his hands up to his mouth and shouted, "Nice ride!"

Mia waved. "Hey, Goldman. I'm going to the prom!"

"Where's the corsage?" The man's laughter faded as he continued along the street toward the neon invitation of a few seedy porn shops and strip clubs.

The chauffeur had opened the trunk. Instead of removing the entire bag, Julian dug to the bottom and pulled out a jacket and a pair of jeans. Damn. He'd forgotten appropriate footwear. His Cole Haan wingtips would have to do.

"Where are we going?" He peeled off the tux jacket and slung it into the trunk. "Why not use my, um, *ride?*"

Mia's eyes widened. "Oh wow, that would be something. At least we'd be in the right neighborhood for a limo instead of…" She gestured at the corner, where a couple of wiseguy wannabes had staggered out of Mambo Italiano and were lighting cigarettes while they watched the limo through slitted eyes.

Julian had been keeping his eye on them, as well. He hated that Mia had been waiting outside for him in a disreputable area, even if she did seem to be on friendly terms with the after-hours crowd. And the morning crowd, and the afternoon crowd. Meanwhile, he still hadn't met his "new" neighbor who'd moved into his condo building a year ago.

"I don't get the joke," he said.

"You'll find out. We're heading toward the Upper East Side, where the pickings are good."

Pickings? *Aha.*

If she thought that he'd be put off, his little sex kitten was toying with the wrong ball of yarn. "Then let's take the limo," he suggested. "It's here. It's paid for. All night long."

"Huh. All night long, is it?" Mia winked. "You know what? That's not a bad idea." Her eyes danced; her sweet face glowed. The kitten liked mischief. Julian knew that she was trying to put one over on him. He didn't care.

They climbed into the car. Mia scooted across the padded leather seat. "Fancy," she said admiringly, but she didn't appear to be overwhelmed by the opulence. Instead, she picked up the phone and matter-of-factly gave the driver directions. "Onward and upward to the East Side, driver. Put the pedal to the metal and lay some rubber."

The limo pulled smoothly away from the curb. Julian had to admit he was disappointed. He'd collected a speeding ticket or ten in the days when he'd zipped around Manhattan in a sports car. He was more practical lately. With constant phone calls and paperwork to deal with, using a chauffeured car was a more efficient use of time. And if that meant that he was becoming his father, who'd scheduled his life by the minute in degrees of importance, starting at the top with business concerns and family to the bottom tier of taking care of himself...

An uneasy tremor went through Julian. He wasn't his father. Not yet.

Especially with cuddly, outrageous Mia onboard.

"Have you guessed?" She tossed him a pair of work gloves. "It's garbage night. We're going salvaging."

"I guessed." He pulled on the gloves and reached out his hands like claws, making monster noises. She let out an obligatory shriek. He grabbed her and nuzzled her into the corner, hugging her curves. "You and me in a garbage bin, baby," he teased, taking gentle, growling bites of her neck. "Grrr. Sounds like fun."

She shoved him away. "You can't do street salvage in a designer tuxedo."

"I can do anything in a tuxedo. I'm the James Bond of Dumpster diving."

She sat up straight, breathing kind of funny. "We'll see about that." She tucked stray curls beneath her bandanna. "Strong men have quailed when faced with a rival gang of garbage pickers."

"Will this be dangerous?" He removed the gloves and then his pants, working them past his shoes. Why not? She'd already seen him naked.

"Not really. We'll have to look out for other scavengers. They can get proprietary about who spotted which broken chair first. I operate under the hands-on rule." She was busily watching the streets change from the rundown tenements of her neighborhood to the gray canyons of midtown. When she turned to look at him, her eyes dropped to his unclad legs. The lip-licking smile and wink she did made him fumble with the zipper of his jeans.

He lifted his butt off the car seat and jerked up the pants. "Tell me about the rule."

She was breathing funny again. "First one to lay a hand on the item owns it."

"I like that." He zipped the jeans and reached across the roomy limo to press his palm to her cheek. "Mine."

Pink mottled the skin beneath his hand. "That's

sweet, but also possessive and bossy. Anyway, you can't lay claim. I haven't been tossed out." Her lids dropped and then blinked open, revealing eyes filled with a sudden sadness. He felt the tension in her jaw. "At least…not that way. It was my decision."

"What was?"

"Leaving home."

"Were you a runaway?"

"Of a sort, but it's not the sad case you imagine. More just me declaring my independence and my parents washing their hands of me. We've been distant ever since."

He nodded to himself. That explained her lack of money and the assortment of strange friends who substituted as family. "Estranged?"

"Not completely. I call them now and then, to let them know I'm still alive. We see each other at holidays, but it's strained." She wrinkled her nose. "They're good, conservative people. My father's a Methodist minister and my mother is…a lady. Forever and always, a lady. They just don't understand my lifestyle. Too outlandish."

Julian pictured them, a God-fearing couple living in a small parsonage, where they cut coupons and prayed for their daughter's soul. They'd be the kind to share their meager income with the less fortunate. That would be where Mia got her generosity and belief in the goodness of humankind. But she was also a city child, blessed with curiosity and imagination, attracted to the color and variety and even tawdriness all around her.

"You should try harder to get along," he said. "They must miss you being a part of their life."

She shook her head. "They miss the *me* they wanted me to be, not the *me* I am."

His fingers moved across her ear, tracing the swirl of the cartilage. "The *me* you are is pretty damn fine." He tweaked her lobe, unable to keep his hands off her.

"Thanks." She shivered and rubbed her head against her hunched shoulder, nudging his hand away. Twice now she'd done that, but not because she didn't like him touching her. He could feel the response in her even without physical contact. She pulsed and swelled and shimmered with it, filling the air between them with expectation.

He'd never known such a deep and abiding desire. The kind that was so good he almost didn't want it to be over. As if he were a kid waiting for Christmas morning. Or waiting through the last few seconds of a big sporting victory, before the raucous celebration commenced.

"We're here." Quickly, Mia lowered her window and pressed a button on the control panel to drop the partition between them and the driver. "Please continue north along Park. Drive very slowly."

"What are you looking for?" Julian asked when she hung halfway out the window.

"Good salvage. The garbage trucks only pick up big pieces a couple of nights a week, so that's when the hunt is on."

They were cruising by the side streets off Park. Sixty-sixth, Sixty-seventh. Julian paused to admire Mia's rump before joining her at the window, his hand on the small of her back as he poked his head out beside hers. "No luck yet?"

"An old mattress and a lamp with a tattered shade. Nice booty for someone, but I'm looking for wooden pieces."

Nice booty. His hand strayed lower. "What for?"

"I fix them up, paint or tile them and sell the pieces at a ritzy little shop in the Village run by a friend of mine. We like to joke that some of the same people who threw out the stuff buy them back in their new transformations, never the wiser. Now take your hand off my ass and keep your eyes peeled, 'kay? I'm not used to trolling from a limo."

"Well, neither am I."

She laughed. "Good to know…although I'm not sure I believe you." Suddenly she let out a yip. "Stop the car! Look—what's that?"

Halfway down the block, beneath a royal-blue awning, a doorman in epaulets was trundling a large object covered in a tarp out of his building. Julian squinted. "Might be a desk. Hold on."

He reached for the control panel. The sun roof opened with a *whir.* He stood on the seat, looked out at the dazzling lights along Park Avenue, then peered back inside the car, gesturing for Mia to join him. "Bird's-eye view."

Taking his hand, she climbed up beside him. "You're brilliant. I don't know why I've never thought of salvaging from a limo before." She cocked her head, looking at him with stars in her eyes. "This is the way to go, all right."

The doorman had set the object on the curb. He removed the covering with a snap. "It's a bureau," Julian said. "Looks off-kilter."

"Who cares?" Mia bounced. "I want it. Let's go!"

"Wait. There's a car…" A dinged-up sedan with a popped trunk had turned onto Seventy-first from Third.

"Then we have to hurry." Mia disappeared and shot out the limo door two seconds later. "Haul ass, Julian. The race is on."

He followed, stopping only to grab the gloves she'd left scattered on the street. She was running pell-mell past the limestone townhouses and the graceful glass-and-stone facades of the apartment buildings, shouting over her shoulder for him to catch up. From the opposite direction, the car bore down, headlights washing the street like a movie set. Mia ran into the glare, her red high-tops slapping the asphalt, arms pumping.

Julian sprinted, slipping a little in his dress shoes. He and Mia arrived beneath the awning together, mere seconds before the car. She flung herself at the tilted bureau. *"Mine."*

The car screeched to a halt. Secured in the trunk by cords was a tatty sofa with stained cushions and a pair of ladderback chairs. A sour face looked out from the driver's window. "Hey, lady. I saw it first!"

"No, you didn't." Mia hugged the bureau. "And anyway, I called it."

Julian slapped his hand on a half-open drawer. "Me, too."

She beamed up at him before waving the car off. "Take the rummage sale to the suburbs, buddy."

With a final four-letter-word insult and a gun of his engine, the driver gave up.

"You're nuts." Julian stepped back and studied the bureau. A knob was missing along with the leg, and the top was scratched. "This is a piece of junk."

Mia jiggled the drawer until it slid into place. "Solid construction, great lines. Look at that carved detailing! I probably won't even paint this one—it needs only fixing and refinishing." She ran a hand along an ogee edge. "I might even keep it for my place. I need a place to store my collection of vintage silk flowers. Mrs. Snookums has been shredding them."

The limo driver had swung around the block and parked at the curb. The bemused doorman watched as Julian removed his cuff links and rolled up the sleeves of his formal white shirt. He and Mia put on the gloves and helped the driver hoist the bureau into the trunk.

Mia saluted the doorman. "Thanks, sir. She'll have a good home."

After that, she decreed the limousine the perfect undercover vehicle for her salvage operation. It belonged in the neighborhood, so the roving street pickers overlooked them as the limo purred by, swooping in upon choice lots. They had a minor tussle over a headboard with a hotheaded trio of gay men wheeling a dolly, then another race to the wire for an armchair and matching footstool that Mia gave up when their rivals—dancers from American Ballet Theater—convinced her they needed to furnish a barren apartment. "I always support the arts," Mia said, and received a backstage invitation to their next performance.

When the limo returned to her building hours later, the capacious trunk and extra seat were both full. Julian had torn his shirt on a jagged piece of trim molding and jammed his thumb dropping a chipped marble bust of a laurel-wreath-wearing philosopher into the trunk, whereas Mia had thrived. She was now fast friends with their driver, Joe Damone from the Bronx; over a broken coffee table, she'd taken the number of a girl who stood a skinny six feet tall and wanted to be a model; she'd even left business cards at the doors of several houses undergoing renovation.

"I hope that wasn't too horrible for you," she said

when they parked near her building and started unloading the loot. It was nearly 4:00 a.m. and the street was as quiet as a city street ever could be. Meaning that even the insane people were home in bed.

"It was a fascinating evening," Julian said. He looked up and saw that the skies had lightened to a charcoal-gray tinged with rose. "Morning, I should say. Sort of a distaff *Lady and the Tramp*."

"If you're the gentleman, that makes *me* the tramp." Mia shrugged and skipped down the steps from unlocking the front door for Joe, who had volunteered to cart the furnishings to the fifth floor. Julian had already decided that the bedazzled chauffeur had earned a very large tip.

"You know what I mean," he said.

"Sure." She patted his cheek with a gloved hand. "But what *I* meant was that I hoped you weren't embarrassed about running into that couple—the Stuckuppers?" Her blink was altogether too guileless.

"The Stukenvilles." Longtime friends of his parents'. They'd arrived at their Lexington town house after a late evening at the opera, only to find Julian and Mia evaluating the merits of their neighbor's cast-off dining table. The double take the older couple had given them after belatedly recognizing Julian as a scruffy street scavenger had been classic.

"Didn't bother me a bit," he said, although he imagined that his mother would be informed via the Upper East Side grapevine. As long as the Silk Publishing board of directors didn't get wind of the adventure, he was okay.

Mia adjusted her bandanna, maintaining the pleasantly false expression. "They were awfully nice, inviting us in for a nightcap."

"Agreed."

"Poor Joe didn't mean to knock over the Lladró shepherdess. There was just so much clutter. Not much room for a big man like him to move around in."

"No harm done," Julian said easily. He ignored a twinge at the thought that Mia preferred Joe's bulging muscles and simple, straightforward personality. It was difficult to tell, with the way she openly embraced everyone she met.

She'd assumed that the Stukenvilles' dutiful invitation had been sincere and had included all of them, so she'd prodded Joe inside even though he was reluctant. Julian had relished the surprise on Esther Stukenville's face when the three of them had sat side by side by side on her Louis XIV love seat.

"The museum benefit that Mr. Stukenville mentioned does sound like a lovely event. I certainly hope that you attend—for the sake of the endowment fund."

"Another boring affair." Julian shrugged. "I'll write a check instead."

Mia's features puckered. "That's nice, but meaningless. I adore museums and galleries. When's the last time you went to one?"

"To view the exhibits? It's been a while." Was she angling for an invitation? He could just imagine the buzz Mia would create with the staid museum crowd. She'd probably show up in a garish dress with tassels or sequins, drink too much champagne and lead the party guests in a samba line.

Julian smiled at the image. No affair with Mia would be boring, which was the understatement of the decade.

"Saturday afternoon," she said. "I'll take you to a gallery I know and open your eyes."

"Are you asking me for a date?"

"Oh no. I'm welcoming you into my world, as a friend."

He'd take that, as often as he could, even though her secretive little smile was impossible to read. He felt as if she was stringing him along, but for what reason? Maybe only for fun.

Joe lumbered out of the building to collect another piece of furniture. Julian flexed his muscles, shifted Plato to one side and helped the driver unload the bureau. "Can we get spaghetti afterward?" he asked, looking over his shoulder at Mia as they carried the heavy piece up her stoop.

"Why spaghetti?" She closed the trunk and followed close behind.

"Don't you remember your Disney movies?"

It took her a moment to think of the noodle kiss between the cartoon dogs in *Lady and the Tramp*. She shook her head at his nonsense, smiling up at him from beneath the bandanna that had slipped down her forehead. "If that's your way of asking for a kiss, I can see why you're only Bachelor Seventeen."

"Hey, man," Joe Damone said under his breath as they maneuvered inside. "Next time, don't ask. Ya just gotta grab the girl and kiss her."

FOR THE FOLLOWING week, Mia woke with an unfamiliar feeling in her stomach. An excitement. She'd always been an optimistic person who greeted every new day with enthusiasm, but this was different. This was unprecedented, stimulating and alarming all at once.

She'd enjoyed herself immensely.

Over the weekend, Julian had taken her to the Frick

and they'd wandered around the quiet shining rooms with their hands in their pockets and an unspoken electricity crackling in the air between them. When the drawing-room elegance became too tasteful to bear, she grabbed his arm and brought him to the gallery where Stefan, Leslie's guy, was showing two of his ink drawings.

The shoestring operation wasn't like any gallery she could imagine Julian attending, such as the swank spaces in Soho with paintings as expensive as houses on the walls. Stefan's gallery was two dark, dank rooms on the third floor of a nondescript building, with bad lighting and experimental artists who sneered at success. Julian studied the weird, complicated drawings, so dense with pen strokes they were almost black, moved on to another work that featured mangled doll parts and broken egg-shells, then looked at Mia with an admirably straight face to ask her if he could get his spaghetti now, as a reward.

They returned to her street to eat at Mambo Italiano, an inexpensive but cozy bistro, where they discussed the meaning of art and beauty, moved on to a debate about whether or not talent was corrupted by money and finally finished with a long, lovely chat about their favorite places in the world. Their choices ran the gamut from Yankee Stadium in September to eating chocolate sundaes at Rumpelmayer's to the view of the Saturday night action from Mia's fire escape. But if she had to pin it down, her ultimate favorite place was sitting in an empty pew in her father's church, on a quiet afternoon with the sun flooding through the stained-glass windows and the organist in the choir loft practicing a hymn, sustaining each note until the music grew so grand it hummed in a person's bones.

"Why?" Julian asked, and she explained that it

wasn't about religion or solitude, exactly. There was simply no better definition for any word at anytime than her favorite moment and *exalted*.

Julian was reluctant to choose his favorite, but finally she dragged it out of him. If he closed his eyes and concentrated, he said the place he returned to in his mind was the knee cubbyhole in his father's enormous walnut-burl desk. He remembered hiding there as a child, waiting for his dad to come in after dinner to smoke a cigar and finish the newspaper. They'd played a game where his dad pretended not to see him and announced that the squeaks and movements under his desk must be mice and he would have to lure them out with bits of biscuits and cheese.

When Julian finished, his voice was hushed and his face somber despite a fond smile; tears welled in Mia's eyes.

But she'd blinked them away and leaned in for the promised kiss. No noodle, just garlic and tomato, Italian spices and the deeply satisfying but frightening pleasure of knowing that she was beginning to fall in love.

8

"PLEASE, PLEASE, PLEASE, can I get prints of some of these shots?" Nikki asked. Even though her article was focusing on body painting, she'd come to observe Mia and Cress at work, as they lit and styled the Gorman ballroom for shots to go into their portfolios. Mia's next clients would be impressed by the work she'd done, just as the Gormans had oohed over the Hudson River Valley mural she'd restored for the Keenes, et cetera, et cetera.

Mia straightened from peering through the camera viewfinder. *Et cetera, et cetera?* Apparently she was feeling very *Anna and the King of Siam.* Must be the ballroom. Buffed and glowing, it made her think of hoop skirts and waltzes and men in tuxedos....

She smiled to herself. Julian would do very well.

"Then I can submit photos with the article," Nikki prodded. "Especially if you'll give me reprints from your body-painting portfolio. I've *got* to have the infamous peach."

Mia gave a start. "Oh. Sure. No problem. I'll print extras."

"Head still in the clouds?" Cress said slyly, sidling up to her with a fistful of clipped stems. He'd arranged several extravagant bouquets in the gold-leafed niches. Flowers were his favorite finishing touch.

Even though he'd crawled out of bed at 4 a.m. to search for bargain blooms at the flower market, the extra cost had made Mia wince. After paying her models in advance for the plaid shoot, recently completed, she was pinched for ready cash until the fees for her past few jobs arrived in the mail. Despite doing fairly well, self-employment was a constant struggle in an expensive city like New York. Luckily, she'd received a number of feelers lately for the more lucrative body-painting jobs. Perhaps word had leaked out about the *Hard Candy* cover.

"You've been walking around with that dumb look on your face ever since the other weekend," Cress continued. "Which you just happened to spend with Bachelor Seventeen."

"Shhh." Mia's glance touched on Nikki, jotting into a new spiral-bound notebook, seated on a window seat out of the way. "I don't want my love life detailed in *Hard Candy*."

"Don't worry. That magazine is all about sex. You and Julian belong in the pages of *Chaste Confessions*."

She snorted. "Just because we haven't done it yet, doesn't mean we won't."

"It's taking you long enough. Even Stefan has stopped taking swipes at Julian's intentions. Fred's halfway in love with the guy himself. What are you waiting for, girl?"

"We're still pretending we're friends." Although she'd never made out with a "friend" in the back of a movie theater at a weekday matinee the way she had the past week with Julian, unless she counted the awkward forays of an art school classmate who hadn't realized he was gay. Mia had known as soon as he squeezed her breasts as if they were mangoes ready to burst. She'd introduced the guy to the glories of gay bars, and he'd been much happier with his fruit shopping ever since.

"Are you holding out on him to prove you're different from the rest of his women?"

Out of the corner of her eye, Mia saw Nikki's head lift. She was listening. *Shit.*

"Absolutely not. You know I don't play games like that."

"You're playing some kind of game." Cress lowered his Gucci shades. "I just haven't figured it out yet."

"Clue me in when you do." Mia sighed. She truly didn't know where she was going with Julian. A friendship? A fling? A full-blown affair?

Were those her only choices?

Something inside her clicked into place and she reflexively squeezed the shutter button. The camera whirred. Both she and Cress jumped. "Hold on! I didn't set the music stands yet," he said, darting off.

Mia stood stock-still. *Oh damn.*

Not only was she falling in love with Julian, she was hoping for a real relationship. A long-term love affair. A commitment. Maybe even—

Oh double damn!

The man was a notorious bachelor. And even if he wasn't, even if he actually *wanted* a—a—

A W *word,* Mia said inside her head, not willing to voice the term to herself. Julian might want one of those apron-clad creatures, but *she* was an unconventional artist. A bad fit. She'd seen the life her parents had pushed her toward—always, like the road to hell, with the best of intentions—and she'd rejected it.

Rejecting the same from Julian was another thing.

Not that he'd ask. The *M* word was not on his mind. He was having fun with her, stepping out of his box for brief interludes, pretending that they could play Skittle-flavored tonsil hockey at 3 p.m. and still be pals.

"All set," Cress called.

Mia got busy snapping photos of the gleaming ballroom. Nikki came over to watch and ask questions about upcoming body-painting jobs, looking for a sexy angle. Mia told her about an advertising concept she'd recently been hired to create for a new chocolate-scented perfume. Someone at the *Hard Candy* cover shoot had recommended her, according to a rep from the perfume company. Probably the photographer. Mia had made a mental note to send him a thank-you.

Cress set up from another angle, and then they did close-ups of the detail work. They were packing up and Nikki was standing around picking at her nails when the butler opened the doors and announced, with an aggrieved air, that yet another visitor had arrived, insisting he be let in. "A Mr. Julian Silk."

He appeared beside the butler. "Is this a party, or what?"

"Julian!" Delight flooded Mia at the sight of him in a navy-blue pinstriped business suit with a silk tie in gleaming pewter and a precisely folded pocket square. He looked rich, but not in a way that was only about his wealth. Julian was rich with character and heart, and basic male sex appeal.

In that area, he was a gazillionaire.

"What are you doing here, Jules?" Nikki tossed her head, making her long dark hair fly. "Are you spying on me?"

"I had no idea you were here." He stopped and looked

from her to Mia and back again. A frown drew his brows together. "Why *are* you here?"

"Why are *you* here?" came the sassy retort.

"Mia mentioned that she'd be doing the final shoot of the ballroom today, so I wanted to see it." He lifted a hand to wave at her, holding the other behind his back. "Surprise."

Mia returned the gesture, feeling a little unsure, the way she often did around Julian. He upset her balance, yet she wanted nothing more than to let go and fall into his arms.

"What do you have behind your back?" Nikki clipped across the marble floor. Julian tried to back away and she rushed him, playfully attacking until she'd forced his arm out. He held a bottle of champagne and a florist's tissue-paper cone out of her reach—barely, as Nikki was only a few inches shorter than him in her steep sandals.

Nikki read the label. "Veuve Cliquot. My, my. What are we celebrating?"

Julian held his sister's hands away as he brought the bottle down. "This is for Mia. A congratulations for her new job. And finishing the old one."

"What?" Mia was flustered, especially when she took the bouquet and saw that he'd also brought her a dozen red roses. "That is, thank you, Julian. But I don't understand. I only got the perfume job this morning. How did you—"

"He's romancing you," Nikki said, standing beside her brother, one arm wrapped around his shoulders. She laid her head on his chest and made kissing noises. "Jules and Mia, sittin' in a tree…"

He elbowed her. "How old are you again?"

"Just having a little fun." Nikki smacked his cheek. "I'm out of here. I'll see you around, Jules baby." She whipped up her red leather attaché and slung the long strap across her chest, making an unusually hasty exit.

"Hold on," Cress said, grabbing the aluminum photographer's case he'd finished packing. "I'll come with you."

Ditto, Mia thought. Could they be any more obvious?

She peeled the paper away from the roses. Red velvet petals, long-stemmed, bountiful. Talk about obvious. There could be no question about *this* gesture being romantic. Extremely corny, too, she tried to tell herself.

Her brows arched at Julian. "Champagne and roses in the middle of the day? Is this how the upper crust lives?"

"Too ostentatious?" He stepped closer, looking sheepish. "You've been working hard. I wanted you to have a little luxury." His hands slid into the pockets of his trousers, a brushed chrome watch glinting at his wrist where his sleeve rucked up. Except when he dressed down to be with her, he always seemed to gleam with prosperity. "I didn't intend to run Nikki and Cress off like that."

"'S'okay. We were finished anyway."

"Please tell me that you haven't hired my sister to be your assistant."

"No."

"She ran out without answering my question. Why was she here?"

Mia chewed her lip. Blatantly deceiving him was not her style. "Mmm, well…Nikki's been interviewing me. She wants to do that article—the way you suggested." Sort of. "I'm not sure how far she's taken the idea…"

Not a lie, but not full disclosure, either. It was up to Nikki to give him the news about her attempts to break into print with *Hard Candy*.

Julian gave a short laugh. "Figures. That's what I get for sending her to you."

"Of course she was going to seize the opportunity. I've only known Nikki a short while, but within five seconds I saw that she's no shrinking violet."

"I'll discuss it with her."

Mia tugged his tie. "You're cute when you get all stern and fatherly."

He angled toward her. "You think?"

She pulled the tie taut, reeling him in finger by finger. "I must have one of those Greek complexes because I find myself *very* attracted to you."

"Considering your father really is a Father…"

"Methodists are ministers, but I get the reference. Too Freudian for me." She touched her lips to his. "I'm a simple girl. I like meat and potatoes, honest answers and uncomplicated sex." How often she got them was another matter.

Julian's nose bumped into hers; her hand was gripping the knot of his tie. "Then ask me a question."

Her heart seemed to be beating in her throat. Given her earlier revelation, she had to know. "Why did you bring me champagne and roses?"

His head tilted sideways and his mouth found hers. One searing stroke of his tongue over her lips and she was moving into his arms, kissing him with a sweet rush of need. "For this," he whispered, and licked his tongue across the roof of her mouth. "For you." Deeper now, a sucking kiss. "All of you." He slipped a hand under her baby-doll tee and thumbed her nipple, tweaking it into hardness. "And the *us* that's just beginning."

She was breathless. "Oh—ohhh my goodness…" A stark-naked hunger burned inside her. "That's what I hoped you'd say."

"Then why didn't you tell me earlier so we didn't waste so much time?"

She blinked. "It wasn't a waste, being friends first."

"No—of course not. Just…" He cupped her breast and squeezed, holding the bottle of champagne at the small of her back. "We could have become friends afterward instead."

But then it wouldn't have happened at all, she wanted to say, but stopped herself. How was she to know? While she'd gone into this assuming he was a love-them-and-leave-them type, she now believed there was more to Julian than a relentless male desire to score. What she still couldn't grasp was that they were meant to be together forever.

Fine. There is no reason to pretend that this is a lasting love. Take your pleasure in him—and let that be all.

"Put down the champagne," she directed. "We don't need it. I'm already high as a kite."

He did, ducking beneath her hands. She let them run through his hair, raven-black and silky short, across his expensive suit, the fabric so fine and smooth she caressed it as if it were his skin.

"Dance with me," she said when he'd straightened.

Except for the camera on its tripod, the untouched ballroom waited for them, gilded and polished, sparkling like a jewel, a Cinderella fantasy to make any woman melt.

"We have no music," he said, but then he started to hum. "Cheek to Cheek."

Heaven, she thought. *Oh yes. I'm in heaven.* Delight bubbled in her laughter as Julian took her with a gentle, firm touch, guiding her in the first sweeping swing across the glossy marble floor. She'd been right; this was an intoxication beyond champagne.

They danced, moving in swaying circles that slowed as their lips met and the humming became an incoherent murmur of pleasure. Too heavenly, too perfect. Mia closed her eyes tight enough to make them water. If she didn't bring her feet back down to touch the ground, she was going to lose her practicality and wind up like the rest of Julian's conquests—too dazzled to protect themselves.

The only way to hold her own was to show him that she wasn't a prize to be won or a body to be seduced. She was the mistress of her own love affairs.

It was time to get serious about not being serious.

She gripped him tightly and leaned in to whisper seductively, "Julian? Can you come to my studio tonight? I'll be experimenting with flavored paints for my new ad campaign and I could use a fresh set of taste buds."

He groaned. "Ah, Mia, what you do to me."

She laughed with a crazy, rising, leaping, soaring joy that was not at all what she'd intended. "Lover, you ain't seen nothin' yet."

"THIS IS ONE of the rare occasions when I cook," Mia called to Julian from the kitchen area when he walked in her open door eight hours later.

He'd hoped for some kind of glowing candle, lace and satin scene keyed for seduction, but of course, that wasn't Mia. Her place was the same as always—bright lights, background music, colorful atmosphere. The photo set was ready for action, with the camera on its tripod.

But there was one glaring exception that gave him hope. Her friends were not included. Unless Fred was hiding in the shower stall, they were alone at last.

Julian was hugely relieved, even without the romantic scenario. However, he realized, approaching the kitchen area where she was stirring one of her edible paint concoctions, she *did* intend to work.

He looked into the double boiler set atop her miniature range. Melting chocolate, dark and silky. "What are you making?"

"Bittersweet ganache," she said. "I think. There are several varieties here, ready for testing." Dishes, spoons and measuring cups littered the counter. "Don't get me wrong. I'm no culinary genius. A friend came by to help me with the blends."

Julian glanced around the studio. Who'd he miss?

"Don't worry, she's gone," Mia said.

He put his arms around her. "Thank God."

"You don't like my friends?"

"Sure. But I like them better when they're not always here." He reached a finger toward the chocolate mixture.

She tapped him with a wooden spoon. "I don't do orgies, despite what Lance, my downstairs neighbor, thinks."

"I was only worried about observers."

"Critiquing your technique?"

He chuckled. "My technique is beyond reproach."

"I'm sure. But we'll see how you do, covered head to toe in chocolate like an Easter bunny." Her bottom moved against him, acting like a magnet and pulling his blood south to thicken in his groin. She laughed softly at his purring response, and suddenly the close confines of the kitchen nook seemed all the seduction setup he needed.

His fingers spread over the soft curve of her stomach. "Ah, sweetheart. Double dip me and find out."

She gave another of the flirtatious little booty wiggles. "Why do I get the feeling you're not taking my experiment seriously?"

Maybe because he was already so hot for her that he'd bust a thermometer. "I'm serious," he vowed. "Say the word and I'll get straight down to business."

Taking him seriously, she moved the double boiler off the burner and shut it off. "Pour this chocolate into a bowl." She ducked under his arm. "I'll get the set ready."

"You're planning to take photos then. This is for real."

She was kicking the scattered floor pillows into a pile, but stopped and dusted curls off her forehead, sending him a slanted glance beneath her palm. "I told you it was. I have that job with the cosmetics company. I need to test my edible paints."

"I was hoping that was only an excuse to get me naked."

"Nope. My intentions are pure."

"Mine aren't," he muttered, scraping chocolate out of the pan. "But I'll do whatever you like, as long as it's just between you and me. And you burn the negatives."

"Then it's the test shots that bother you." She wrinkled her nose. "Sorry. Of course they're private. But, really, I'm surprised you care, after being featured in that magazine and showing up in so many gossip columns…"

"I didn't ask to be in *Celebrity Gossip*."

"They had a personal photo, didn't they?"

"Not one I gave them." He carried the dish of melted chocolate out of the kitchen to her photo set. "They bought a snapshot from someone who I thought was a friend. Except for the business portrait that's in the public domain, the others were paparazzi shots."

"A friend sold you out?" Mia took the dish, set it aside and then turned back to twine her arms around his waist. "That's a terrible invasion of privacy. All along, I've been believing that you enjoy the notoriety of being Bachelor Seventeen. Doesn't everyone want to be a celebrity?"

"Not me." He concentrated on her face, trying to keep serious even with her breasts pressed to his chest and distracting him badly. "There are a few younger people involved with Silk Publishing who think it's an advantage, but just as many from the old school who say my current reputation hurts our image. I haven't aligned with either side, although I have to respect my board of directors. And they've asked me to keep out of the limelight."

Julian stroked Mia's back, contemplating the predicament. His father would have frowned on the excessive publicity. On the other hand, the launch of *Hard Candy* would not have been as successful without the extra attention Julian had garnered as a playboy. His board was touchy about possible scandal, but very, very happy with the bottom line.

Mia was looking up at him with her forehead creased by an adorable concern, as if she'd forgotten about their plans for the evening. He turned the conversation back to the here and now. "I can't believe we're really alone. Are you sure there'll be no interruptions? Where's Cress?"

"Cress is out buttering up Angelika, the model from the cover shoot."

"Literally buttering her up?" Julian was bemused by the possibilities. "With your crowd, I can't be sure when you're serious."

"No foodstuffs involved, I assure you. Angelika's a macrobiotic model who weighs about sixty pounds." Mia gave his chest a pat and resumed straightening up the studio area. "Cress is coaxing her. She wasn't crazy about the head-to-toe mess of the *Hard Candy* shoot, but I want her for the perfume ads, exorbitant fee and all. She has the best skin for chocolate. Smooth as satin, no flaws, no unsightly lumps or bumps."

Julian was watching Mia bend over. "I like a few lumps and bumps. In the appropriate places."

She straightened, holding a full ashtray. Her eyes were bright. "Good to know you're not one of those guys who's forgotten what a normal female body looks like. I don't come airbrushed."

He raised his brows. "But you will come."

Laughing, she went to dump the cigarette butts and briskly wash her hands. "Couldn't resist, huh?"

"I'm a sucker for a bad double entendre."

She gave a hand clap. "Well, if we're going to do this, let's get the show on the road. Strip down."

Taken aback by the matter-of-fact command, he watched her disappear into the bathroom. This might be business, but it was also still an evening of seduction, right? He hadn't expected her openness to translate into such a straightforward approach. What was wrong with a few soft words and slow kisses?

Oh well. He was down to his boxer shorts when Mia walked out of the bathroom carrying an armful of clean towels.

She scanned him. "You can leave those on." Her tongue darted across her lips. Her lashes lowered. "At least for now."

That was more like it. His trousers dropped to the floor with a clunk of the belt buckle.

"I don't think I've explained about my new client," she said, reverting to briskness as she shook out a few of the towels and draping them close at hand. She straightened the edge of a tarp that bore traces of recent experiments with chocolate paint.

The new client with the big-bucks ad campaign, the one she'd been so excited about that morning in the ballroom. He knew more of the details than she was aware, but he was certainly interested to hear what she intended to do with him. And *to* him.

"A major cosmetics company is launching a new scent called Sweet. It's supposed to smell like chocolate, though I haven't received a sample yet. Their advertising agency heard about the work I did for *Hard Candy*, and they want me to create the images for the Sweet campaign. I was working on those with Leslie earlier today. I want you for taste experiments."

"Taste experiments," he repeated. "Sounds intriguing."

"I'm being serious, Julian."

"Then why did I strip?" He gestured as if he were going to retrieve his pants.

"No, no, keep your clothes off. I need your skin."

He shook his head. "You said you wanted my taste buds. You *said*—"

"Oh, I need those, too. See…" Mia stood over her table of supplies, stirring and arranging paintbrushes. "There's going to be a launch party—a media event. You've been to that kind of thing, so you know how lavish and often outrageous they can be. The wilder, the better. My employers want a rotating display of models wearing edible designs, in chocolate and other sweet flavors. So I need to come up with paints that will taste good, not melt, and stand up to—" finally, she looked at him, her eyes revealing that she was feeling less businesslike than he'd thought "—wear and tear."

"Exactly what kind of wear and tear?"

"The models will be striking many different poses throughout the evening. The client is even considering whether the guests should be encouraged to sample the paints. So I have to be prepared for anything—moving and touching and tasting and rubbing and—" She ran out of breath and when she took another one, her breasts swelled, round and full inside her skimpy tank top with spaghetti straps. "You get the picture."

"You're saying you want to paint me."

"Sort of…" With a bashful grimace, she took him by one arm and led him to the tarp. Her gaze rose to meet his, her face glowing with an arousing mixture of shy anticipation and outright seduction. The tip of her tongue touched her lip. "I also want to taste you."

"Taste me?"

"To see if I've gotten the flavors of the body paints right."

He imagined her working on him, dabbing the candy paints across his bare skin, serious with concentration as she stuck out her tongue and licked a clean path straight to his—

Raise the Big Top! His shorts were tenting.

"Uh, I hate to be a party pooper, but can't you just use a spoon?"

She shook her head, looking like an overgrown poodle with her curls bouncing every which way. "The paints taste different on skin. Plus, there's the wearability factor. They must hold up to a lot of action. The models may even be expected to dance."

"And how will we…" He ran a finger along the neckline of her top, following the curvaceous contours into the warm hollow between her breasts and then out again. Her nipples peaked gratifyingly. "How will we test that?"

Her mouth tipped up into a wry grin. "I could put on some Madonna and make you vogue for me, but I can think of more enjoyable activities that would do as a demonstration."

"So can I." He moved in to kiss her, but she stuck a paintbrush between them, making a broad swipe of glistening red paint across his chest. He flinched. "That's cold."

"Here, let's try the chocolate." She picked up another brush and layered a stripe of the warm midnight-dark liquid next to the red. "Bittersweet chocolate and strawberry. Always a good combination."

He glanced down. "I'm dripping."

She shot an amused glance at the obvious erection straining against his shorts. "Already?"

"Not me, the chocolate," he said with a moan, although she was probably right. He was ready for action. If she insisted on drawing out her experiment, he would soon be in desperate need of the towels she'd so thoughtfully supplied. There'd be much less mess if he could lose himself in her.

Mia, of course, was not averse to a mess. She plopped another full load of the bittersweet paint onto his chest, layering it thickly and watching with an almost scientific interest as a rivulet ran across his stomach to pool at his navel just inside the waistband of his shorts.

"Maybe you should take them off," she said, gesturing. Her round cheeks pinkened. "In the name of science."

"Maybe you should take them off," he said. His voice dropped, grating in his tight throat. "In the name of *sex*."

9

MIA CLENCHED her fingers around the shaft of the paint-brush and swallowed. "Take it easy, cowboy. I have serious work to do before we reach that point."

She didn't know why she insisted on continuing the charade. While everything she'd said was true, experimenting with Julian could never be anything but personal. The sight of him stripped down to his skivvies was making her brain freeze. Add in an erotic painting session and all she wanted was to quit pretending and have her gluttonous way with him until they were both satisfied.

She'd never been good at keeping control of herself. Luckily, the life she led required a noticeable *lack* of restraint.

"We need the table," she blurted. "Would you...?" She pointed. "Put it there."

Julian retrieved the rolling table, muscles flexing as he pushed the wheels onto the tarp. "You want me..." He slapped the padded surface. It was a massage table, a handy height for her work, and comfortable for the models, especially when she was perfecting a design that required them to remain still for hours at a time.

She nodded. "Jump aboard."

He hopped on, sitting with his legs dangling. "Horizontal?"

"Not for now. I want to test the thickness of the paints when you're upright."

The globule of edible paint at his navel had coagulated, halting its downward path. Her mouth watered at the sight, especially when she lowered her gaze to take in the arousal that bobbed inside his boxers whenever he moved. With her previous male models, she'd never been anything but professional, but with Julian she wanted to dip the engorged head of his penis in candy-apple red or ripe-plum purple, paint stripes and swirls below that and then suck on him like a lollipop, no restraint, no concerns...

She shuddered, turning to focus on her paints. Her hand shook as she reached for the glossy lime color.

Julian was watching. "Do I get to taste?"

Oh boy, here we go.

"Sure." She dabbed the paint onto the back of her hand and held it up to him. "What do you think?"

He took her hand and licked. "Mmm. *Sweet*."

"It's lime. It's supposed to be sour."

He grinned, his eyes bright like high-intensity spotlights. "Then it must be your skin I'm tasting."

"Oh please. Stop with the cheesy compliments." She laughed anyway, glad to break the tension. "So...ahem. The lime paint was troublesome at the *Hard Candy* shoot. I should load the airbrush, because spraying it on will probably work better with this glossy texture—"

"But a thin layer isn't as lickable."

She pursed her lips. "True."

"Is this for real? The models will be edible?"

"That's what I'm told."

Julian hooted. "So the party guests will just grab hold of an arm, say, and—" He took hers and scooped a handful of chocolate straight out of the bucket. He smeared it along her, up to her shoulder. She shivered even though the paint was warm and really sort of erotic in a syrupy melt-my-bones way. "And swoop right in for a nibble?"

He lowered his open mouth to her biceps and took a deep sucking taste, sliding the flat of his tongue over her skin. His lips and tongue tickled there, opening and closing and flickering, stoking the fire inside her so it roared through her as if she were a chimney. Beads of perspiration popped out along her hairline and at the back of her neck.

"Um, yes, tha-that's the theory. But really, it's more for show—to be scandalous. I don't expect any of the guests will ac-actually be eating off the models, except for a gag, maybe—" She faltered. He was nipping at her collarbone, sending a shivering response over her nerve endings. "Julian…stop. There's no paint there."

His head raised. "No? Then how come you taste so good?"

"We're getting off track. I'm supposed to be paint-ing *you*."

"And tasting me."

She sighed. "Yesss."

He leaned back, propping his hands behind him on the table so his chest was on display.

She stared for a moment at the sculptural ripples and swells. His natural skin tone was a delicious pale golden brown, like butter melting on toast. "I should have waxed you first."

"No thanks." He squinted an eye and frowned at the patch of hair that thinned out over his pectorals. "Be-sides, I'm not very hairy."

"I like a really smooth canvas." She swirled a small brush in the lime paint. *Start at the neck. A neck isn't sexy.*

"Hmm." He shifted and brushed a hand inside the waistband of his boxers, sliding them a little lower, out of the spot where the slab of muscles in his abdomen creased across his navel. A narrow trail of black silken hair led her eyes downward—not that she needed directions when he was so aroused.

"There's always plucking," she said to loosen up her thickening tongue. *Keep it flexible. The better to wrap around his body parts...*

His brows shot up. "Now you're just trying to threaten me."

"Yup. Behave or I'll get my tweezers and do this job properly."

"I might consider shaving." He reached over and slid his fingers along the drawstring waistband of her velour sweat pants, riding low on her hips.

She jumped. "Get your hand out of there."

He smiled wickedly as his fingertips danced across her bare stomach. "Nice and smooth. And very warm..."

"Cold can be fun, too." She darted the paintbrush at his chest—one, two and done.

Julian sucked in a breath. "Not so cold, but it tingles a little."

I'll make him tingle a lot. Mia followed with her mouth, forming a tiny *O* with her lips and locking them around one of his lime-green nipples. She sucked the nubbin clean, then pursed her lips and blew a whistling breath to chill his warm, wet flesh.

His chest heaved. "Jeez," he groaned.

"You like that?" She gave the other nipple the same treatment, then weakened and rolled her cheek against his chest, never mind the previous stripes of paint. Blindly, she set the paintbrush on the table so her hands were free to creep along his torso. Each muscle was so firm, so warm, so satiny soft and yet hard as stone…

She pushed him down onto the table. He landed on his elbows, head still raised, watching as she took the bittersweet chocolate and tilted the dish over his abdomen. A thick, short stream of the chocolate poured onto him, and she reached in, swirling the head of a brush through the liquid. She painted a starburst pattern over his chest, ending a ray on each nipple with a tickling flick of the soft brush. He gritted his teeth. His stomach muscles twitched.

"Hmm." She stepped back, considering the design. "More of the red, I think."

"You forgot to taste," he said when she returned to the work table.

"I'll get to that. Wait until I've applied a few of the other flavors."

"I don't know how long I can wait."

She acted unconcerned. He didn't have to know that she was burning up inside. "When I'm doing an involved project, my models might pose for an hour at a time before I let them move."

He groaned.

"But you're only an amateur." She came back with a new flavor, stirring it with her finger. "I'll go easy on you."

"Don't worry. I can take it."

"Oh? You're awfully cocky for a man who's busting out of his shorts." She smiled. "Put your head back. Give me your throat."

He tilted obediently, closing his eyes. "What for? Planning a vampire theme?"

"Nope. I just thought I'd like to taste you—" she stroked a finger over the long line of his throat "—right here." She ducked toward him, her tongue eagerly stretching to slurp up the stripe of pale candied paint. Her mouth lingered at the hollow of his throat, where the sticky liquid had pooled, where his strong pulse beat against her tongue.

She popped up her head. A drop of the pearly paint had escaped from the corner of her mouth and she licked it up, reveling under his molten stare. She blinked. "Yum. Delicious."

"What flavor?" His voice was so dry it almost crackled.

"A new one. Passion fruit." She scooped up another dollop. "Want to try?"

"Sure."

"Open up."

"I'd rather taste it off your skin."

Her brow arched. "Who says you're not?"

His mouth opened. She leaned over him, letting the paint drip off her finger onto his tongue. He waited a moment, but when she made no other move, he caught her finger gently between his teeth. "There you go," she crooned, shocked by the erotic intimacy of having him suck on her index finger, pulling it deeper as his hot tongue stroked and curled, holding the helpless finger tight against the roof of his mouth. Her beaded nipples tingled in response, aching to feel his mouth. She rubbed her thighs together. The heat inside her was growing impossible to ignore.

He reached a hand around her waist, letting go of her finger as he pulled her closer, between his legs, locking them around her.

His chocolate-covered chest loomed. She pushed at it. "What are you—"

"Be still." He lifted the cup of passion fruit paint to his mouth, taking a big gulp before setting it aside. She had a quick glimpse of the paint coating his tongue, and then he was kissing her, one hand holding and tilting the back of her head.

Her mouth opened to receive his rapacious kiss. His tongue invaded, sweet and tart with the mouthful of passion fruit that oozed between them. Some of it leaked out, dripping off their chins, but neither cared. She gasped for breath and twisted her body in between his legs, wanting to squeeze in even closer as his tongue dove recklessly into her mouth, demanding, taking, driving her wild.

He slowed and suckled from her lips. She felt raw and swollen, sticky all over, but still needing more. A small protest flew from her when he pulled back. He started to slide off the table, but she clutched at his shoulders, holding him in place. "Hey!"

"I want you, Mia. In the bed."

"Later. I'm not finished here."

"What else is there?"

"I've barely even painted you. I made a new blood-orange-flavored paint, and melted all these chocolates. There's an almond ganache and a cherry chocolate to taste-test and I need to see how much skin shows through the white choc—"

"Later," he repeated. "We can do all that later."

"You won't! Not after you've had your way—"

His eyes pinned her. "Babe, promise me free access to your sweet body and I'll do anything you want."

She blinked. Okay, that sounded pretty damn good, but she didn't like the sense of being railroaded. "Wait a minute. I'm not bartering—"

"Me neither." He pushed off the table, put his hands around her waist and lifted her straight off her feet. Maybe if he'd carried her in his arms, she would have laughed and went with it, but instead she found herself slung ignominiously over his shoulder.

Her mouth dropped open in surprise. He was carrying her to bed like a caveman and—oooh, dammit—she liked it! Her stomach clenched, but so did her sex. Already she was running with moisture.

"Julian, please." She squirmed her belly against the rock of his shoulder, elevating herself by using his shoulder blades for leverage. "Put me down."

"As soon as I get you to the bed," he said easily, shifting the balance of her weight so she dipped farther over his shoulder. The floor tilted at her and she kicked, protesting with a screech garbled by laughter.

"I'm not kidding!" she howled.

He slapped her bottom. Hard.

She yelped, her body jerking to a shocked stop. *"Julian!"*

The bastard laughed. And spanked her again before throwing her down on the bed. He'd climbed on top of her before she could gather herself together. He pushed down with his arms, making the mattress rock, then pressed his face against her breasts. "This is more like it. Soft and bouncy."

She could not stop giggling. "But you hit me!"

"A couple of spanks. You're not hurt." He pushed her tank top up over her head, keeping it tangled around her wrists so that he could hold her down with only one hand. The other went to her breasts, taking a greedy hold and pushing her nipple higher toward his mouth.

She closed her eyes and moaned at the tantalizing

pull of his lips and tongue. *Oh yes.* That was what she'd been wanting. To feed him. To please him.

"I'm not hurt," she whispered. Only amazed by how easily he could put her outside of her very wide comfort zone.

Her butt stung a little, but most of the damage was to her pride. She was supposed to be running this show, but he'd taken control. And she really couldn't protest with any vehemence, not when laughter was rising out of her like champagne bubbles and he only had to touch between her legs to feel how wet he'd made her.

She rocked her hips, pushing against his erection. "But you're still a bossy male. I'm gonna get you back for that."

He lifted his head to smile with a flash of white teeth. "I look forward to it." She wanted him back at her breast, but he was busy sliding his hand between her thighs to urge them wider. "Come on, kitten. Open up. Let me stroke you."

"Now you ask." She strained against him, struggling with her own desires more than his demands. Was she really and truly ready to take this risk?

His hand reached into her pants; he nudged the waistband past her hips and discovered that she wore no underwear. "Ahh." His fingers threaded through the tidy patch of curly hair, stroking deliciously as he parted her swollen folds and delved inside. She was almost embarrassed by her copious moisture, but the look on his face belonged to a man who'd found paradise.

She took advantage of his preoccupation and heaved her body off the bed, gripping his shoulders and rolling him sideways. There was an instant when he resisted, but then he gave in and let her climb astride him.

"I like this." She propped her hands on either side of his arms and dragging her tight, aching nipples through the patch of chocolate on his chest. "War paint," she said, getting it on her face as she scraped the sweet stuff off his lean muscles. She nipped at him, teasing his nipples now that she knew he liked that. Her hips swayed, grinding her against his rigid shaft.

Reluctantly, she lifted herself a few inches to tug at his boxers. "Come on, tiger. Open up. Show me what you've got."

"All for you." He ground out the words between his teeth when she'd freed him. He was incredibly erect. His penis arched against his stomach, engorged and pulsing, the skin so taut it was almost shiny.

"The monster," she said, reaching for him. "Lucky me."

He twisted her off his body, rolling back on top of her. "I like to be on top."

She'd noticed, but there was not time to say so when she felt herself slipping off the edge of the mattress. She reached for him, gulping a plaintive "Help!"

Julian dragged her to safety, his long fingers digging into her buttocks. He stripped off her pants, looked at her open sex and smiled. She dropped a hand between her legs, blatantly stroking herself, hoping that he'd lose control and plunge inside her at last.

"Give me two seconds," he said, and then he was gone.

"Gah!" Restlessly, Mia threw a couple of the pillows off the bed. She wanted room to spread out and offer herself like a pagan goddess tempting the king.

Julian came back with a small tub of the edible paint—a deep, luscious bright orange. He used his fingers to apply it to her mound and then went deeper, gently probing inside her until she was thoroughly painted with the sweet goop. "Now," he said, lowering himself between her legs after he'd set the paint on the floor, "I will taste *you*."

His face disappeared between her thighs. But he didn't lick her yet—he put his big hand over her and held her firmly. Her head rolled against the flat of the bed, senseless with a surging desire. It was as if she really were an orange and he'd squeezed the juices from her succulent flesh, sending them coursing through the rest of her body in a sweet syrupy surge of pleasure.

His mouth covered her with a wet warmth. For minutes, he licked inside her, teasing, suckling, before finally running his tongue higher to flick the hard pearl of her most sensitive nerve endings. He lapped her there, using just the right pressure as she ground against his mouth. Such an intense sensation shot through that she let out a little scream and reflexively clamped her thighs around his head, coming fast and hard in a cataclysmic rush.

He pried her legs open, lifting himself up so she could see his panting face. His mouth was shiny with her liquid and his eyes were glossed over. Ridden with the unending climax, she bucked and twisted, trying to close her bent legs to contain the insane ecstasy. Agony. Ecstasy....

"Give me your hands." He took them and placed them around her ankles where her feet were tucked up near her quivering bottom. While she held herself open, he was free to cup her ass in both hands and lift her higher toward his mouth. She arched off the bed when he sucked her clit between his teeth, strumming it with his tongue until she was coming again in glorious waves that ran through her with more force than she'd believed possible.

When it was over, Mia went limp. Utterly exhausted, her limbs flopped every which way.

"You're incredible," Julian murmured, shimmying up beside her.

Lazily, she patted his back, lingering over the satin slickness of his perspiring skin. "How did I taste?"

"Like the sweetest sin."

She smiled. "I do feel sinful." One of her legs nudged between his. For a moment, his hot erection pressed against her thigh, until she shifted, raising her leg to let him slide along her swollen labia, burrowing into the warmth and moisture as she closed her thighs around him. "Where's that paint? I want to try."

"Believe me, I'd love it, but you can do that later. Right now I want to be inside you."

He made no move except to wince a little when she squeezed closer, keeping his erection trapped. "When you're ready," he added, languidly caressing her hip despite the tension in his voice.

A light, tingling shiver ran through Mia. He was thoughtful and kind and so sexy that she'd always be ready. Always.

They kissed, tangling their tongues. A warm, loving moment. She tasted her own pungency, mixed with the sharp sweetness of the blood-orange paint. Soon her hips began to rock in a slow sensuous rhythm.

"I think I'm ready." Understatement of the millennium. She was hollow and achy, hungering to have him filling her to the brim.

"Do you have a condom handy?"

"In the nightstand." A rickety wooden piece, salvaged off the street. The drawer stuck when he opened it. "You didn't bring any?"

He waved negligently at the other side of the room. "They're way over there."

She flipped from her side onto her back. He moved between her legs, holding the condom packet in his mouth as he steered his penis to her flowing center. The flared head rubbed in her juices, dipping just slightly inside her before he withdrew and quickly sheathed himself.

"Ready?" he asked.

"And willing," she said.

She drew her knees up and closed her eyes, dying a hundred deaths as she waited for the piercing pleasure to come. She wanted it so bad. So bad. Hard and fast, like her first climax. But he entered her slowly, deliberately. She murmured with surprised approval, coasting on a lovely current of sensation as their first joining grew into a moment she would never forget. She was able to focus on the heavy warmth of his body, the slippery slide of skin against skin, the feel of herself stretching to accept his girth. Her insides seemed to melt, molding to his length as he slowly pushed deeper and deeper until he was in her to the hilt.

She hugged him to her breasts. "Oh, Julian…"

He dropped a kiss on her forehead, then reared up, pulling out with an excruciating slowness so that she felt every inch of his ridged shaft. His hands wrapped around her hips, tilting her so when he pushed back inside there was a new friction, a delicious awareness of exactly how deep he was going.

"Oh. Wow. *Julian.*" Her arms moved across the rumpled bed, searching for something to hold on to. There was nothing. She ran her hands back and forth, back and forth, her body singing with sensation.

He plunged into her, going harder and faster and

deeper. She loved it, opening her eyes to see his face. He was almost ugly, straining toward a powerful climax, the cords on his neck standing out and sweat dripping off his forehead. And yet he was beautiful.

"Mia," he groaned, locking his gaze with hers.

"Julian."

She was riveted. This was more than sex—it was true intimacy. A connection of souls. Something she'd scoff at later when her head was on straight, but right now…ohhh…she loved him. She loved him from her head to her toes, with every breath in her lungs and beat of her heart.

He drove forward, impaling her as he went rigid as the first hot pulse passed through him, then began to move again with short hard strokes that sent her over the edge. She wrapped him in her arms and legs, tightening inside, milking every drop of pleasure from their spasming bodies.

They collapsed. Beneath her hands the knotted muscles in his back relaxed. She petted him, caressed him, trying to wet her lips with a tongue that had gone dry.

After a minute or two, she pressed an emphatic kiss on his shoulder. "That was something."

His face was buried in the lone remaining pillow, but he angled it to reveal one squinted eye and the corner of a slanted grin. "Can't you come up with a better word than that?"

"Sure." She thought about it, wondering if she should tell him that she'd turned from a swinging single into a lovestruck female who fancied herself in love with Bachelor Seventeen.

Not yet. Her pride wouldn't let her show her heart so

soon, especially when she wanted to offer it to him on a silver platter.

And yet…

Even if she couldn't tell him she was falling in love with him, she *could* let him know that he'd touched her soul.

She nuzzled his neck and whispered huskily, "You transported me, Julian. I believe—" her chest tightened, barely holding back the love that wanted to pour from her heart "—I believe you've given me a brand-new definition for *exalted*."

"Aw, my little sweetheart," he said, taking her into his arms. They nestled together in bed without speaking further, but for Mia that was enough. Right now, in this perfect moment, her satisfaction was complete.

SEVERAL DAYS LATER, Julian made a date with Nikki for lunch. She'd been suspiciously silent lately, and ever since he'd run into her hanging around Mia and Cress at the ballroom, he'd been nagged by curiosity. From what Mia had said—or not said—he knew only that Nikki was attempting to write an article.

Which wouldn't be so bad, as long as his sister stuck to an innocuous story about Mia's career in decorative painting. Nikki would be safe at a design magazine, if only he could manage to keep her there. She'd probably bolt the first time an editor asked her to write a scut-work article about roofing materials or mortgage applications.

He arrived right on time at the Columbus Avenue eatery and asked for an outdoor table so he could keep an eye out for Nikki, who was notoriously late. Fifteen minutes later, the September sun had grown warm on his navy pinstripe. He took off the jacket and rolled up his shirtsleeves, watching the crowd parading past. There was no end to tattoos and goatees. A queenly woman walked by in a dress that could have passed for rags but was probably worth hundreds, and he thought he saw a famous hound-faced Italian director whose booming laugh emerged from a wizened frame.

But still no Nikki. Julian opened a folder and began to sign various contracts that had been needing his signature for a week. When he was finished, he checked his watch, studiously avoiding eye contact with two women at an adjacent table who'd recognized him. Five more Nikki-less minutes had gone by. He hadn't brought enough paperwork.

His cell phone chirped. "Yes, Nikki," he said once he'd retrieved the phone from his breast pocket.

"I'm on Central Park West, a couple of blocks away. I'll be there in five minutes. I stopped off at this fabulous preseason sale and time got away from me. Well, so did my credit card! But it was totally worth it. I got a pair of knee-high boots marked down to three hundred."

"Only three?"

"They were originally *eight!* And they're pink goatskin. Like buttah."

"Aren't you a vegan?" Nikki could never be accused of consistency.

"They're boots. I'm not going to eat them." Sounds of a skirmish came from the phone. Julian heard Nikki say, "Whoopsie. Excuse me, sir. Yeah, well, same to you."

"Nikki, can you please concentrate on getting your butt over here without getting arrested?"

She laughed. "What do you want? I'm walking and talking, walking and talking."

"Try less talking and more walking. I'll get our order

in so I can get back to the office on time. You still like Caesar salad, right?"

"Not if they use anchovies. Let me—"

Julian beeped off before she could go off on another tangent. He waved over a waiter in a striped polo shirt who'd been hovering expectantly. "One chicken pita and a Caesar salad. Two Long Island iced teas." He thought of the alcohol. "Make one of them a virgin. My party will be here presently."

Minutes later, Nikki arrived loaded down with glossy orange shopping bags. Julian blinked at them, suddenly remembering Mia, candied in orange paint, her body writhing under his mouth.

"What's with you?" Nikki glanced at his face as she handed off her bags one by one to the waiter who piled them on a spare chair. "You're all sweaty. Are you sick?"

Julian dabbed his forehead with a napkin. "It's the sun."

Sort of. Mia did have the burning intensity of a thousand white-hot suns, especially when she was coming around his tongue.

The waiter brought their drinks, and Julian reached for his, hoping the alcohol would knock the happy hormones out of his brain. He had to be rational to deal with his sister's off-kilter kookiness.

Nikki smacked her lips. Her nose wrinkled and she took another sip. "What is this? Regular iced tea?" Not fooled by the look-alike servings, she grabbed his drink and swallowed a cube-rattling mouthful. "Ahh, that's better."

"You're too young to drink at lunchtime."

"No, you're too old. Aren't you thirty-four now? That's almost middle-aged." She jabbed him. "Ever since you took over for Daddy, you've turned into a Mr.

Serious Sourpuss. Soon you'll be having three-martini lunches at the St. Regis."

Another memory hit Julian: the first time his father had taken him to the King Cole Bar and Lounge at the fancy hotel. Just men, he'd said. Julian had been twelve, old enough to be thrilled about shedding his sisters, young enough to be impressed by his dad's largesse. He'd studied every move his father had made, from how he perused a menu to the casually authoritative two-finger signal to their waiter. Jim Silk had been *the* man.

Julian shrugged at Nikki. "Got to grow up sometime. You might take a cue."

"Remember the fun we used to have as kids, when you'd come home from school? The city was your oyster and you made us girls feel like pearls. Then you brought that weird girl home, the one who chanted three times a day, wore a driftwood necklace and convinced you to give up meat—"

"That didn't last. Neither did she." Fiona Schuyler, who called herself just Sky. A Barnard girl desperate to be artistic despite a noticeable lack of talent. His parents had been appalled, especially because he'd never liked a girl well enough to bring her for a visit. But Sky had been heavy into the *Kama Sutra* and, well, he'd been nineteen.

Julian scowled. "Nikki, it appears you're trying to distract me. You must know I want to talk about this article you're writing about Mia."

For a moment, Nikki was struck speechless. Then she fumed. "She told you about that?"

"Not in so many words—"

"I thought Mia was stand-up. She—" Nikki blinked. "What do you mean—not in so many words?"

"She didn't share any of the details, but that's not important. I saw you at the ballroom with my own eyes. It's fine with me if you want to take a stab at a feature article, but I'd like to be informed. Send it to me when you're finished and I'll see where I can place it."

"You just want to boss me."

"I'm offering *help*."

"Sometimes that's the same thing, especially with you."

"There's nothing wrong with that."

She reached across the bistro table and squeezed his hand, making a moue with her pink-glossed lips. "There is if I'm trying to achieve something on my own."

Sympathy gripped him, but only for a moment. "Then you'd better try another profession. Maybe…fashion design?"

"Please. Every other girl I know is claiming to have her own line of clothing in the works. That's so ten years ago."

"Magazine work is not as glamorous as you think."

"Petra says it is."

"Petra Lombardi, the art director?"

Nikki bit her lip. "Well…yes. She took me to lunch."

"Nikki, you are *not* working at *Hard Candy*."

"Why not?" she said with a fine whine.

"Just trust me. It's not the place for you." He had another suspicion. "This article about Mia, is it—"

"Here's our food," Nikki cried with ten times more enthusiasm than salad warranted. Her expression of delight drooped when the server set a plate in front of her. "Julian, you ordered me a Caesar. I told you! I'm not into anchovies anymore. I was talking to this guy who told me how fisherman have these nets that…"

Julian let her talk, thinking that she'd distracted him.

If she'd already been in contact with the staff at *Hard Candy*, he had all the information he needed. Fortunately, Petra Lombardi was easily bought. Nikki would have to be satisfied with a job at another magazine, preferably one where she wouldn't be tempted by a fast crowd that thrived on celebrities and sex. A safe magazine, such as *Knitting Pretty*. Yes, that would do just fine. Now he only had to convince his sassy sister. Fat chance.

10

AFTER FINISHING LUNCH with Nikki, Julian returned to the office, two phone calls on his immediate agenda. He made the pleasant one first since he wasn't especially eager to get involved with Petra again, for any reason.

Mia picked up after six rings. He'd been about to hang up.

"Hello. Speak fast, my glaze is drying."

"It's Julian." He paused, expecting…

"Oh, yeah?"

…more enthusiasm than *that*. "Sorry if I'm calling at a bad time."

"You've got fab timing. Three days after we boinked like bunnies. I'd say that's exactly what the Guy's Guide to Dating calls for. Not so soon that you look eager, but enough time to let the girl cool down on the warm gushy feelings."

"Why are you so sarcastic? Are you mad at me?" *Women*.

Mia made a *pffft* sound. "Men," she said, and he could almost hear her rolling her eyes.

"I sent flowers." The next morning, after leaving Mia's studio, he'd practically rolled on boneless legs to the closest florist and picked out every flower that reminded him of Mia. The huge bouquet had been bright, unconventional and crazy colorful, just like her.

"They're lovely. Thank you so much." Flat as a desktop.

"You don't like flowers?"

"I don't like them if you send them to all the women you have sex with."

"Not *all* of them…."

She let out a short laugh. "That's comforting."

"Mia, where are you? I don't like this. I'm coming over."

She blew out a breath. "You can't. I'm on a job. One I'm botching." He heard the clang of a paint can. "Listen, I'm sorry. I don't know what got into me." She chuckled drily. "Except you. And not just that way. You're under my skin and I—I guess that I started thinking—"

He wanted to speak, tell her that he felt the same way and maybe that's what had scared him from calling right away, but she hushed him. "No explanations, okay? For some reason, I was having an attack of morning-after remorse. But I'm better now. And the flowers were very sweet, even though I don't expect—" She drew in a breath. "What I mean is that I realize that I'm not the kind of girl you want to bring home to Mother."

Not since the disaster that had been Sky. He had learned his lessons the first time.

Or maybe not.

"I'd bring you home in a heartbeat," he said without thinking it through. The reality was, he'd been the responsible one looking after his sisters for the past six years. In that time, he'd lost the part of himself that used to be fun and spontaneous. Even his well-publicized— and exaggerated—love life was more predictable than anyone might think, a matter of being photographed at nearly every event he attended. Whereas Mia was like Nikki and Very, and he wasn't sure about going there, despite their intense attraction. Maybe it was too late for him to break his pattern.

"I'm sure *your* home is quite the swank bachelor pad." Mia paused. "Or did you actually mean you'd bring me home to meet Mother?" She sounded wary.

He mulled that over. She'd given him an out, but he didn't want to take it. Maybe it wasn't too late after all. "Sure. You want to meet my mother? I'll arrange it, as soon as she returns from the summer house."

Mia coughed. "That sounds very nice, but you don't need to trouble yourself. Really. I had a temporary brain twizzle. Must have been the endorphins you riled up in me. What I should have said is that I'm not the kind of girl who *wants* to be taken home to meet Mother."

"Why not?"

"Social graces suffocate me. I could tell you stories—" She broke off. "Let's cut this short. I'm supposed to be tortoise-shelling a fireplace surround."

"Wait. I want to figure this out. Can't have you thinking that you're only a fling."

Silence.

Damn.

"That's generous of you." She spoke archly. "But are you sure that *you're* not the fling?"

He smiled to himself. She was always turning the tables on him and damn if he wasn't starting to like the new perspective. "I didn't look at it that way."

"Of course not. The world revolves around Bachelor Seventeen."

"I don't have an ego problem. Or a confidence problem, either."

"True. That's one of the things I like about you. But there are the control issues…"

"Can I help it if I know best?"

"Father always does."

"Don't, Mia. I can take that criticism from my sister, but not you."

"Oh, Julian." She sighed. "You're so lucky I arrived to put some zing into your life. Without me, you'd go straight from pleasing your family to being pleased by the yes-men in your office and the yes-women in your little black book. And if those worlds ever collided—*kapow!*"

He leaned back in the leather desk chair he'd inherited from his father along with the office. Mia was insightful. She knew he had placed her in one of his boxes. And she'd been right to call him on that, as uncomfortable as the idea of mixing it up might make him.

The usual rules didn't apply to Mia. She was, in a word that defined her, *different*. He flipped open his appointment calendar and scanned the neatly inscribed squares. Saturday night. The Carson Peabody museum benefit he'd been loath to attend.

"Are you busy Saturday?"

"What do you have in mind? Another movie matinee? An afternoon in bed? Maybe get crazy and go out in public among the wannabe wiseguys at Mambo Italiano?"

"Hey, wait. That's not fair. We've gone out—"

"Only in my neighborhood."

"We salvaged the Upper East Side."

She gave a hollow laugh. "That hardly counts. And besides, you became awfully uncomfortable when you were recognized."

"Then prepare for the sequel to Meet the Stuken-villes, Miss Kerrigan. We're going to the museum benefit they mentioned. It's only semiformal, but a very hoity-toity crowd." Too late, he remembered that some of the Silk board of directors would probably attend. If Mia pulled some crazy stunt, he'd be up the proverbial creek. Yet he was willing to take the risk.

Mia kept up the sassy attitude, even though he detected an undertone of skittishness. "Well, my goodness. How exciting. I'll finally get to be a debutante after all these years."

"It's not that important an event," he said, backpedaling. "If you don't want to go…"

"Oh no. I'm looking forward to it. I'll get to see Julian Silk in his native habitat. Should I wear camouflage?"

Anything that would help her blend into the crowd would be fine with him. But he only laughed and rang off, deciding that he'd put off his call to Petra for the time being. If he let Nikki have a little leash, Mia might be impressed with his willingness to compromise.

MIA ENLISTED Cress to help her dress for the museum party, although the preparations didn't actually involve dressing as much as they did a lot of stenciling, painting and gluing. Cress thought she was nuts, but he loved her anyway and so he went along with her plan.

She studied herself in the mirrored folding screen that she'd set up in the middle of the studio. Her dress was absolutely plain. Black, knee-length, with a full skirt and a sleeveless bodice that tied at the shoulders in prissy little black satin bows. Even her hair was tamed, blow-dried into a sedate pouf anchored by a narrow headband of rhinestones.

"What do you think?" she asked Cress, who was dabbing stickum on her behind and attaching fingernail-sized rhinestones to the stenciled lace. "Too boring?"

"Not underneath," he said, but with admiration as his eyes flicked over his work area. "If Julian twirls you while you're dancing, the old geezers will see straight through to China."

"Cress!" She stuck out her lip. "That sounds horrible. Maybe I shouldn't do this."

Mia looked in the mirror again. She bunched the skirt of her dress at her waist while Cress knelt behind her, finishing the final touches of her private surprise for Julian.

"Ignore me. I'm a grouch today. You look very tasteful."

"That's my aim. Julian didn't actually say so, but I think he's worried that I'll embarrass him."

"You're presentable enough, aside from…you know. In fact," Cress added, "I'd send Angelika to you for a honeymoon trousseau, if I gave a good goddamn about it."

"It? What? A trousseau? Who's she marrying?"

"Why not me?" He patted Mia's butt and stood. "All done. You can drop the skirt now, sweet cheeks." He'd adopted the annoying pet name after she'd told him the story of how she'd bumped into Julian at the cover shoot.

Mia rearranged the skirt, then turned and kissed the tip of his nose. "You're a dear, Cress, but you're no more the marrying type than Julian."

"One of us might surprise you." Cress's golden-brown eyes dimmed, and she realized he'd been putting on a good front as they chatted and teased their way as usual through the preparations.

"But it won't be me," he continued, walking to the

kitchen with less swagger than normal. "My angel has a suitor. That's what she calls him—a suitor. He's from N'Awlins. Big in crawdad futures and rich as sin. Not even that old, so there's no hope that he'll get a heart attack on the honeymoon."

"Oh, no. I'm so sorry."

"Let's skip the maudlin sympathy and go straight to the booze." Cress rummaged around under her sink, in the cabinet they called the wine cellar. He stood and tilted a bottle of whiskey to the light, sloshing its contents. "The good news is that she felt so bad after telling me about the engagement that she agreed to pose for the Sweet campaign."

"That's great, but..." Mia chewed off a subtle application of lipstick. "I don't want her if your heart is broken."

"Broken? It's not even bent. Maybe a very small bruise." Cress poured a tumbler half full. "Does that look like two fingers to you?"

"If you hold them upright."

"Damn, you're right. Smart girl." He held up the glass. "Here's to Jim Beam and Crawdaddy Warbucks."

Mia watched with concern as Cress took a big slug of the whiskey, then sputtered as the strong alcohol hit his stomach. For all his talk, Cress was really more mild than wild.

"I can't stand this." She kicked off her classic black pumps. "I won't leave you feeling this way. I'll call Julian and tell him I'm not going."

"The hell you will. I didn't spend my evening playing Fairy Godmother only to see you ditch the ball." Cress poured the remainder of his drink down the sink. "There. All better. Maybe I'll self-prescribe some stripper therapy and go stick dollar bills in the thongs at the Queen Nefertiti's."

Mia wasn't convinced. "Booze and boobs are the only options?"

"Girl, sometimes you forget that I'm a heterosexual male."

"No, I don't."

"Ha! You just let me glue jewels on your cootchie."

"I did not," she said, feeling better now that he'd reverted to their usual sarcasm. "I was wearing paper panties and I *did* stop you when you tried to cootchie-coo me, so there's proof that I know you're a man." They were smiling at each other now, with traces of…not quite sadness. Perhaps a rueful acknowledgement of what might have been. Over the years, there'd been moments when they'd thought of being more than friends. Lonely, horny or bored moments, sometimes all three, but one or the other had always stopped. The only time they'd tried to kiss had been a fiasco. Like kissing a brothah, Mia had teased.

Cress handed her a lipstick. "I'll be okay. Go knock them dead, sweet cheeks."

THE CAR pulled up outside of the Carson Peabody Museum, a classic limestone edifice with tall windows and a banner proclaiming the new exhibit they were previewing tonight. "We're here," Julian said softly as he took Mia's hand. He looked once more at her unexpectedly sedate appearance. He couldn't decide if he was impressed or disappointed by the change in her.

Either way, something wasn't right.

She was checking out the scene in front of the museum. A minor gathering of paparazzi stood around the wide steps, looking bored. Had to be a slow night on the celebrity scene if they were reduced to snapping pix of the museum crowd.

The gathering wasn't so minor to Mia. She gaped. "There are photographers. I can't go out there."

Julian made a sound of dismissal. "They're nothing. We can sail right by without stopping."

She was fussing with the front of her dress where the *V* neckline showed the merest hint of cleavage. It wasn't like her to be worried about modesty. "I'm not used to this lifestyle."

"We're a long way from street salvage."

That drew a smile from her. He patted her hand. "Ready?"

She swallowed. "I guess so," she said, adding, for no good reason that he could think of, "I hope it's not windy."

They exited the car without incident and walked past the photographers, who roused themselves to snap a few shots of the new arrivals. A few of them called Julian's name, but he didn't hesitate or even glance their way. He locked his arm around Mia and kept her moving toward the entrance.

"Hey, girl, gotta name?" one shouted.

Sensing Mia's uncertainty, Julian gave her squeeze. "Don't answer. Trust me, you'd rather stay anonymous."

"Will we make the gossip pages?" she asked somewhat breathlessly as they were ushered into an echoing museum foyer where the cold marble elegance could have passed for a mausoleum.

"It's possible." He shrugged, handing off her cashmere wrap to an attendant. "Do you mind?"

"Kind of weird, but I don't mind if you don't."

He realized he didn't. Not with Mia, someone he really cared about for a change, although to the press and the avid readers she would be an anonymous nobody. *Unnamed date.* No one would be able to tell from looking at her in that proper little dress that she was the one woman who'd knocked him for a loop.

The party was being held in a couple of exhibit rooms at the front of the museum. Waiters circulated with trays of hors d'oeuvres and champagne. A harpist played music that spilled over the murmuring guests like liquid gold. Julian, in a business suit dressed up with a fresh silk shirt and matching pocket square, and Mia, in the cocktail-length black frock, fit right in with the crowd.

So he still wasn't sure why his instincts were on edge. Maybe Nikki or Very…? He scanned the crowd for signs of his sisters. They'd expressed no interest in attending the party until he'd mentioned that he was bringing Mia. But he saw no sign of them. Only the waxed silver pompadour of his most conservative board member, Barron Spear.

"Champagne?" Julian suggested to Mia when a waiter approached them. *In moderation,* he added silently.

She shook her head. Her eyes were wide and her mouth looked pinched. "I need to keep my wits about me, as they say."

They were on the same wavelength, which probably should have worried him.

"Don't be nervous," he whispered. "There's nothing here to scare you."

"I might do or say the wrong thing."

"That wouldn't be the end of the world."

She blinked at him with some of her old spunk, her mouth pulling into a sassy pucker. "You have no idea of the embarrassing spectacles I'm capable of. Stuff that would curl your hair."

"At least you'd put some life into this party." He looked up and saw that Spear was approaching, waddling over to them in a double-breasted jacket with waistcoat, his timid little wife scurrying in his wake.

"Silk," he said. "How do? You know the wife."

"Good evening, Spear," Julian replied. "Mrs. Spear."

Spear's sharp eyes went to Mia. "And the little lady?"

"Mia Kerrigan. Mia, this is Barron and Lorraine Spear. Mr. Spear is on my board of directors."

She blinked. Straightened her shoulders. "Oh. Nice to meet you."

They exchanged pleasantries before Spear zeroed in, looking for flaws, Julian imagined. Spear was that type. Pompous, hypocritical, but greedy. "And what do you do, Miss Kerrigan?"

"I'm a—" She glanced at Julian. "A decorative painter."

"And a body painter," he added. Barron Spear brought out his perverse instincts.

Spear's eyes grew so narrow they disappeared. "What's that?" He huffed. "Portraiture?"

"Not really," Mia said with a tight caution.

Julian put his arm around her. "She doesn't paint bodies; she paints on them."

"On them?"

Mia nodded. "It's an obscure art form."

"Nudes?" piped Mrs. Spear. Her husband scowled, dropping his chin into his collar. The lacquered silver waves of his pompadour caught the light.

"I do a lot of advertising work," Mia said, evading the question. She smiled at Mrs. Spear. "Are you an art connoisseur?"

"Oh yes," said the kind lady, and the two of them launched into a discussion of the current show. Spear listened for a moment with a skeptical expression, then turned his attention toward Julian and a discussion of the projected ad revenues for the next year. Dull, but safe.

Julian wasn't as relieved as he'd expected to be.

"THAT'S MIA Kerrigan?" Veronica Silk said in disbelief. She and Nikki stood near the entrance, ready to make their escape. "That's the woman who's supposed to be—what did you call her? Outlandish? Have to say, I'm really not seeing it."

Nikki sipped her champagne. "I don't understand. Mia's not usually this subdued. She doesn't even look like the same person."

"Yeah, well, she probably dressed to please Julian."

"And she's talking to that horrid man from the board of directors. Look, she got him to smile."

"Julian seems pleased with her performance." Very slid over a step and tucked her empty glass into the base of one of the potted palms that flanked the archway. "I'm going home. You promised me a good time, but this is no fun at all. There's no one here under the age of thirty except you and me."

"And Mia."

"Really? She couldn't be. That's a dress for grownups."

"At least it's not a rag from someone's attic like yours," Nikki said, eyeing her sister's halter-top minidress, a vintage Pucci print in brown and a hot pink that matched the ruff of Very's cockatoo hairstyle. No fashion sense. Punk hair was so out it was almost in again. Almost, but not quite.

Very set her hands on her hips and cocked the heel of one of her knee-high boots. She yawned hugely. "Either I leave now or I set fire to Barron Spear's hair. You make the call."

Nikki giggled. "You'd have to launch a bottle rocket to make a dent in that helmet." She craned her neck. "I think...no, they're still talking. Mia must be a hit."

"Just another standard-issue girlfriend," Very said.

"No, she's really not. I told you about her body painting, and how she's encouraged me with this article."

"What's happening with that?"

"I finished and dropped it off at *Hard Candy*. They're supposed to let me know any day now." Nikki rubbed below her rib cage. "I get butterflies every time I think about it. What if it's really bad, but they won't tell me because I'm Jules's sister?"

"Or what if it's really good and they won't buy it because you're Jules's sister?"

"I can't win," Nikki said glumly.

"Not without our brother's approval. I don't see why you even try."

"I'm not going to drop out like you, Very."

"Don't knock it till you've tried it." Very extended a bony arm and snagged another glass from the tray of a passing waiter. He gave her the eye. She shrugged. "Cute, but too clean-cut."

"At last," Nikki said, paying more attention to Mia and Julian than her sister. The Spears had finally moved on. She grabbed Very's hand. "Come on. Let's go snag 'em before a docent swoops in asking for another donation."

"Whatever," Very said, with a bored expression.

"I'm taking you to Mia's studio," Nikki decided. "I went there for an interview, and she always has these wacky people around, and there's usually music and dancing. They have real conversations, and no one cares about money or fashion. Well, that part is too weird for me, but *you'd* fit right in...."

MIDWAY THROUGH a conversation with Nikki and her raccoon-eyed sister Veronica, Mia noticed that Julian was on the verge of discovering her secret. He'd been standing close beside her, smiling somewhat dotingly, until she'd leaned forward to speak to Very and the neckline of her dress had gapped.

First, he'd blinked. Then he'd frowned. And then he'd widened his eyes and looked closely at her front, as if he was trying to see through her dress.

"Gawd, Jules," Very said. "Could you be any more obvious?"

He snapped back. "What?"

Very hooted. "You were trying to look down the front of Mia's dress."

"No, I wasn't," he insisted. A sheepish grin appeared. "I was trying to figure out what she's wearing underneath it."

Mia felt her face grow warm as all three of the Silks looked at her, then down at her chest. She stood perfectly still so her breasts would give nothing away.

Nikki waved a hand. "No bra. So what?"

"Oh, the scandal," Very said with a dry sarcasm. But she'd perked up.

"This is none of your business," Julian said firmly. He put his hand at the small of Mia's back. "If you'll excuse us?"

Uh-oh. Mia went obediently, even though she suspected the jig was up, tossing a quick wave at the Silk sisters as Julian escorted her into the foyer.

"Mia," he said, looking at her with a serious face. "I should have known that you were being too good to be true."

"I don't know what you're talking about," she said with a flirtatious blink.

His voice lowered to a thrilling octave. "What's under your dress?"

"You know," she purred. "You've seen me naked."

He sighed. "Let me put it this way. If you were naked right now, would you rub off on me?"

She cocked her head to look up at him. "I think I already have."

He glanced down at his suit, misunderstanding, saw it was pristine and then caught her twitch of a grin. "Yes, you're right, you have. I find myself doing these outrageous things—body painting, street scavenging, escorting scandalous ladies to museum parties."

"I've done nothing scandalous," she protested with a light laugh. Oh, this was fun!

He surprised her by suddenly pulling her into his arms. One of his hands dropped to her behind, copping a judicious feel through the rustling layers of her skirt. "You're not wearing any underwear at all." His fingers searched. "Maybe a thong, at most."

"Nope," she said blithely. "But no one else guessed. How is that scandalous?"

"Mia," he said again, trying to sound all stern, but there was a twinkle in his eyes. A very small, very wicked twinkle. "Exactly what do you think you're up to?"

She tossed her head. "Just teaching you a lesson. I want

you to think, next time you see me dressed up in a prim little outfit. I wanted to show you that you're not—"

She drew back to look him in the eyes. "You're not always in control, Julian. Especially not of me. Even if I appear to be absolutely conventional on the outside. Can you live with that?"

Instead of answering, he reached for her hand. "Come with me."

She hesitated, but there was little choice, especially when he started walking away. In one direction were the photographers, waiting outside with their cameras, hoping for a newsworthy shot. Little did they know. She threw a glance over her shoulder at the party and saw the stuffy man from the board of directors watching, along with Nikki and Very, both of them nodding and grinning. Well. What could she do but trip-trap as quickly as she could after Julian, smiling to herself at his bossiness? Oh, yes, this was *so* much fun!

With linked hands, they made their way deeper into the museum, every sound echoing in the stone-paved halls as they left the harpist and party buzz behind. "Are we allowed?" she whispered, glancing into gated exhibit rooms. "Do you know where you're going?"

"Yes." They descended a flight of shallow stone steps. At the bottom, he opened double glass doors that matched the pair at the front of the museum. "This is the courtyard garden. Privacy to talk, and I believe there's a back exit hidden away. I can get you home without the photographers' interference, if we need to."

"Why would we?" she asked, Little Miss Innocence.

He looked at her breasts and sputtered a nonanswer, for once left without any glib words.

She walked past him, out onto a courtyard paved in a checkerboard of alternating squares of grass and pebble. Tall trees in gargantuan clay pots ringed the perimeter, disguising the glass-and-brick building that enclosed three sides of the space. The foliage was still lush and green, with some color remaining from the summer's flower plantings. Benches and a few bistro tables with metal folding chairs were set among the greenery. The focal point of the garden was a sculptural fountain made of twists and arches of copper and steel. Sheets of water cascaded over artfully arranged slabs of slate.

The wet stone and metal gleamed in the low wattage of the security lights. Cold and hard, Mia thought, walking over to touch a fingertip to the sheet of rushing water. Like Spear's watchful eyes and silver hair. She shivered in the cool air.

Not for the first time, she was reminded that she really didn't belong here. Even dressed to blend in, she'd always be different.

"You didn't answer my question," she said.

"Which was?"

She didn't reply. Not yet. She lifted a hand to the bow at one shoulder, first unsnapping the strap beneath it, then tugging on the end of the satin ribbon. The bow came free, separating the strap. She pressed her knuckles to it, holding the front of her dress up.

"If you're trying to prove that I'm not in control..." A warm velvet chuckle tumbled out of Julian. "Oh, Mia. That hasn't been in doubt since the day I met you. I have *no* control with you."

"This isn't only about sex."

"But that's a big part of it." He walked toward her, silent as he stepped from grass square to square, the black knight on a chessboard, come to defend the queen. Defend…or besiege?

"Not the heart of the matter. It's about acceptance." A pebble skittered under her heel as she took a step back. The water rushed in a constant stream. Leaves rustled in the night air. Her heart pounded like a drumbeat in her chest as she undid the other bow.

"What do you think of me," she whispered, "when I look like this?"

She let the bodice fall to her waist, baring her breasts to the cool night air, naked except for the lace pattern she'd painted over herself in the shape of a flirty little bra.

11

FOR A FEW SECONDS, the soft *shush* of the fountain was the only sound.

Julian was thunderstruck. He'd glimpsed the flash of a tiny diamond inside Mia's dress, and he'd *thought* there had been paint, as well. But to see her like this, absolutely bold and unashamed—her beautiful body exposed, lush curves, tight tips, naked but not, ivory skin glowing in the moonlight, the trick of the lace pattern making his head whirl…well….

He couldn't seem to take it all in.

His knees almost buckled as he walked toward her.

With shaking hands, he took the front of her dress and raised it over her incredible nudity. "Cover up—"

She inhaled, catching her lip with her teeth. "Then that's your answer." Crossing her arms over her breasts to hold the bodice in place, she turned away, the hurt evident in the downcast sorrow of her face.

"No," he said. "That's not my answer. I just didn't want anyone to see—"

"That *is* your answer. You don't want anyone to see."

He stepped closer, cupping her elbows, being sure to shield her body. "I'm trying to protect you. There are windows around us—"

"Oh!" Mia glanced up with worried eyes. The few

windows that overlooked the enclosed courtyard were black. "I didn't think."

"It's all right. We should be okay."

"I'm sorry," she said. "As usual, I was too impulsive. Just because I'm falling in love, I shouldn't expect you to—to be ready to throw caution to the winds. Especially in front of ev—your friends and colleagues and—" Her voice was broken, halting. He'd never seen her so unsure. But he could only focus on one thing:

Mia was falling in love.

Julian hadn't expected *that* to come out of her mouth. Baring her breasts seemed conservative by comparison. And he didn't know how to answer. She was right in that the invitation to the museum benefit had been a test, of sorts. For himself more than her. She'd done well, and he'd been less wary of her actions than he'd thought. Hell, he'd even pushed the envelope with Spear.

But he still wasn't entirely comfortable with the idea of making her a part of his everyday life.

Mia had always been separate and unique to him. A rare butterfly—beautiful, but so fragile he had to protect it. Box it up.

No fun for the butterfly, he realized.

When the silence continued to grow, Mia drew in a deep breath and turned her back to him. A slender back, bare to the waist and very vulnerable. She forced a brittle laugh. "Look at me. Falling for Bachelor Seventeen, when I swore I wouldn't. Who has the last laugh now?"

He stroked her smooth shoulder, intending to soothe her, but she shivered under his hand. "I'm not laughing."

"You should be. We both know this can't work. I'll always be wearing paint under my clothes. If I wear clothes."

"But I like that about you. And there's a lot of feeling between us—" He halted with a inward wince. *Feeling?* He couldn't give her more than that?

"This is what we have," she said, uncrossing her arms as she turned and pressed in close against him, her breasts exposed only for an instant before they were shielded again by his chest. She flung her arms around his neck. "And this." Her hand caught the back of his neck, bending him toward her mouth as she rose onto her toes to kiss him.

"Wait," he said, but then she was kissing him. Even though he knew it wasn't a kiss that came from her heart, it was still a kiss. Hot and erotic, and just savage enough to taste a little nasty. He'd wanted to be reassuring, to explain away his hesitation; instead, he reached around and ran his hands over the curves of her bottom through the dress and took a firm hold and pulled her against his growing erection.

"Tell me the truth," she whispered, biting at his neck. Her tongue traced his jawline, slid over the cartilage of his ear. "You're turned on because I'm naked under my dress. All I'm wearing is paint and not a single person at the party knew it except you." She whispered directly into his ear, almost panting with urgency. "Naked under my dress."

He groaned. She was right. He was excited, aroused, especially by the idea that they were putting one over on Spear and the rest of his board of directors—the very people he'd been worried Mia would shock.

She laughed softly. "I can tell." Her hips swayed. "I can *feel*. You want to get freaky with me."

"Maybe."

"Aw, don't get cautious now. Admit it. You know that

if the party guests had any idea, they'd be gasping and moaning about Julian Silk and his outrageous tramp. The women would be appalled and the men would pretend to be, although secretly they'd want me, too. But I'm all yours. Just for you. You're the only guy who gets to touch me—" she rolled her hips under his hands "—and taste me—" a wet, slathering kiss that traveled from his mouth to his throat "—and you're the one who gets to rip off my dress and screw me blind."

She parted his shirt between the studs and opened her mouth on his bare skin, using her teeth and tongue in a sucking kiss.

When he didn't respond, she stopped and looked up at him, shoving her disheveled curls off her face with the back of her wrist. "So come on, what are you waiting for?"

His fingers dug into her tempting flesh. She smiled in triumph and moved sinuously against him; her hands slid across the front of his suit, stroking and squeezing, devilishly inquisitive. He throbbed with wanting her, but the desperate edge in her voice and actions worried him. She would think that their relationship was only about sex. And that would be misleading. He understood that now.

He opened his mouth. "Let's go back—"

"Not to the party. I'm not—I don't fit in—" She stopped, vigorously shaking her head.

"Go back to what you said. About falling in love with me."

Her hands fisted on his lapels. "Can we pretend I didn't say that? I was rash. Premature. Carried away by the moment."

"That's three excuses too many."

She continued to shake her head, looking up at him with suspiciously bright eyes.

He held her chin. "There's nothing wrong with a fast game of slutty sex, but I won't have you thinking that's all that you mean to me. You've got to know better."

Her expression held its stubbornness for a moment and then gave way. She dropped her lashes and admitted, "Oh, all right. We have *feelings* for each other."

"That's better." He pinched her bottom.

Her mouth puckered. "*Now* can we have slutty sex?"

"I should say no, out of principle."

She drew his zipper down and slipped her hand inside his trousers. "The monster has no principles. He's raring to go."

Julian tilted his head back and stared at the smudgy city sky. Damn, he was so weak when it came to Mia. So out of control. She wasn't the kind of woman anyone expected him to choose, but he was coming to understand that she was exactly what he wanted.

She kissed the underside of his jaw. "Julian?"

"Yes." He gave in with a groan and lifted her off her feet, taking two steps to the fountain with her lace-patterned breasts swaying in his face. "This paint's not edible?"

"No-o-o-o."

He splashed a couple of handfuls of the water at her chest. She squealed and wriggled, but he held on, keeping her close even though the white paint was running in rivulets, revealing streaks of pale pink skin. Her nipples poked out, white buttons dotted by a circle of tiny rhinestones. More of the fake diamonds ran in a line from her breasts to her shoulders, making the straps of her provocative fool-the-eye bra. He rubbed one of the little gems with his thumb until it popped off. "God, Mia. You're a trip."

"Mmm-hmm." She nudged his thumb toward the white crest.

He rolled her nipple between his thumb and forefinger, staining them with the trickling paint. "You were right about one thing. Every man at the party wanted you, even without knowing your secret, but I'm the one who gets to do this—"

He bent and stroked her nipple with his tongue. It sprang up even tighter, seeming to beg for more of his attention even when Mia said, rather breathlessly, "The paint. It's not edible…."

"Then I'll clean you." He pulled out his pocket square, snapping it open. "I've always hoped to find a use for one of these."

"Your dry cleaners will wonder."

"They've probably seen it all, including nipple paint." He wet the square in the water and dabbed it on her breasts, carefully sopping up the soluble coloring and prying off some of the jewels as he worked.

After a few seconds of that, she moved, rolling her shoulders, making her breasts shimmy like a burlesque queen's. "Harder," she moaned. "Scrub them clean."

He couldn't wait. The sight of her full round breasts, combined with the knowledge that she'd walked into a fancy party that way, naked and swaying, fully accessible, and yet on the surface clothed most conservatively…

The woman played with his head. She drove him wild. He craved her—constantly.

A *clunk* of a sound from somewhere behind them stopped him inches away from her pouting nipple. "Damn."

Mia folded her arms over her breasts. "Who's there?" she quailed.

There was no answer, except a distant siren in the night. Julian shrugged. "Could have been anything. From the street, or someone in the museum..." He started to lower his head.

"But they might come out here, and we're right out in the open."

"Easy fix." He lifted her again. "Hold on."

"I don't know... Oh dear..." She gripped his shoulders, locking her legs around his waist as he moved away from the fountain. His hands wrapped around her upper thighs, holding her high and tight. The position pressed her hot center against his waist and kept her breasts on a convenient level with his face. He nuzzled into the hollow between them, and she gave a breathy snort of laughter, cradling him with her luscious tits buffeting his cheeks. Almost paradise.

Mia clutched at his head when he staggered, tearing a few hairs out. "Watch what you're doing." She giggled. "Don't drop me."

Indeed. He turned his face a few degrees and was able to pull one her mostly pink nipples into his mouth.

"What are you—oh Julian, that's—oh, you really have to stop—"

He gave no answer, busy trying to see where he was going with his mouth full of her flesh. He played her with his tongue, thinking that he'd really have to insist that she only used edible paints from now on.

"Hrmph," he said, regaining his hold on her thighs as he found a deep doorway that was shadowed by the foliage. The heavy steel door would doubtlessly open into the back ell of the museum, probably a maintenance access point. One caged light bulb burned above the lintel.

Without letting go of her breast, Julian pushed Mia up against the brick wall, easing most of her weight off him. The smell of green plants, moist earth and chalky brick was all around them. The doorway was narrow enough that she was able to brace herself with her sandals leveraged on the opposite wall, pressing her spine into the brick. He angled a thigh under her, providing her more support while he closed his eyes, still suckling at her, harshly inhaling through his nose as his mouth opened to take even more. More sex, more love. More Mia.

She rubbed up and down against him. He put one hand behind her to protect her skin from the rough brick, and reached the other in between her spread thighs. He couldn't see, but he wanted to feel—had she really, truly gone all the way?

Oh yes. She had.

When he touched her naked pussy, she let out an involuntary yelp of surprise—or maybe it was pleasure. Her nipple was yanked out of his mouth. Her heels skidded across the wall, but he caught her before she slipped too far and hoisted her back up again. He stroked the back of her thighs, went higher and found more of the glued-on jewels and the slick texture of the paint, fully aware that she was split open like a ripe fruit inches away from his hands. He reached farther and his fingers played along the enticing crevice, parting her slippery folds to slide deep into her most intimate warmth.

She was tight. Shivering with arousal. Her body rose up and down, riding his fingers. "Are you sure this is private? I don't want to be in the tabloids. Def-definitely not in this position."

"I think we're as private as it gets, considering." He checked for security cameras—cursing himself for not thinking of that earlier—out near the fountain. The glass doors had been left open; the museum personnel must have been aware that guests might drift to the garden.

Mia writhed on his hand. "I can't take this much longer. Tell me that you're prepared."

"As a Scout." But not prepared for the strength of his desire—and his emotions. Mia challenged him at every turn, matched his every move, took him far beyond his safety zone.

He wedged his leg under her more tightly, found the condom in the slim black leather billfold in his inside breast pocket, gave it to her and then dropped his pants. She fumbled with the packet, dropping the lubricated rubber between her breasts when the foil tore. If they'd been in a less precarious position, he'd have investigated the possibilities. Instead he gave each puckered tip a kiss before fishing out the condom. She arched into him, telling him to hurry.

His technique was artless, but no one was scoring style points for this go-round. After somehow managing to reach past her and sheathe himself, he pushed toward her entrance and urged her to take him inside.

She lowered herself with a ragged sigh of satisfaction that raised goose bumps all over his perspiring skin. He hugged her tight, trapping her between his body and the brick wall as he drove the final inch. There was little room to maneuver, not without abrading her tender skin, so he contented himself with grinding their hips in slow circles, giving an extra push with each full rotation. The contact must have felt good because each thrust pulled a quick intake of breath from her, followed by a lower-lip shudder of relief. She locked her ankles at his back, clinging as she rode him home.

As the intensity peaked, their mouths met. They kissed hungrily, all teeth and tongue and hot panting breaths. She became too eager, flinging herself at him on a downward glide and upsetting their delicate balance. They tipped over just as a tremendous climax began to roar through him. He hit the opposite wall with a thud that he'd feel tomorrow, but that was no more than a minor inconvenience tonight. Keeping hold of Mia, plunging inside her as he came—that was all he needed.

She let out a whoop. Her legs slipped off him, but he grabbed hold, keeping her plastered against his length and himself planted deep as the explosive shocks rocked them, one right after the other until he was finally drained. Out of strength.

Slowly, they slid to the cement floor. Tangled, halfway between sitting and complete collapse. He kept his arms around Mia until she stopped vibrating and was down to only the occasional involuntary shudder.

They separated with a squelch. She pushed her hair back. "Whew."

"Yeah. Whew." He looked over at her as she pushed her skirt back down, catching a brief sight of the intricate lace design that had been painted across her bottom.

He reached over, lifting her dress for a better view. "How the hell did you do that to yourself?"

"A stencil and an airbrush." Blushing, she pushed her dress down again.

"You're a contortionist?"

She grinned. "Sometimes. But I had help with the parts I couldn't reach very well. Cress came over."

Cress? Julian decided that he didn't want to know.

Time was wasting. They'd have to move soon, but he still wasn't sure that he could stand. He removed the condom, wondering what had happened to his pocket square. He jerked his trousers up from his ankles and stuffed himself and the tail of his shirt back inside.

Mia sighed. "I can't believe I was all wound up ten minutes ago and now I can't even stand. My muscles are like jelly."

Wound up. He thought back to what she'd said about him having to accept her. It was an important point, for both of them.

He cleared his throat. "About your question—"

"Let's hold off on that." She rested her shoulders against the brick wall, stabbed her heels into the concrete and drew her legs up. "At the moment, I'm too exhausted to face a heavy emotional discussion. Can it keep until tomorrow?"

"Tomorrow," he agreed. Tomorrow, they would talk.

Talk. When had he ever wanted to talk? Was he losing his mind?

Or just his standing as a bachelor?

THE NEXT DAY, Petra Lombardi was enjoying a leisurely morning in bed with a breakfast tray and the newspapers. Everything had been going so well for her lately that she'd allowed herself a buttered croissant *and* a glass of pineapple juice. She'd do an extra thousand feet on the stair climber in penance.

Her latest boy toy was singing in the shower. Troy fancied himself a recording artist, but the only tracks he'd laid so far had been between her expensive linen sheets. The man practically yodeled when he came. Yodeling was horrid on its own, but off-key yodeling was too much for a woman of her taste to put up with. If she kept him around much longer, she'd have to invest in a pair of ear plugs. And a thicker bathroom door.

But there were more important problems to solve. Petra hummed to herself, thinking of how she could persuade Sean Morrissey, the managing editor of *Hard Candy*, to hire Nikki Silk. Shouldn't be too hard, even though Sean was happily married and her usual ploys wouldn't work. Any of the editors in the Silk Publishing empire would be glad to take on their CEO's baby sister, of course. The trick was in making the job offer appear legitimate.

If the girl's article had been publishable, this all would be much easier. But Petra had managed to acquire a photocopy of the submission and it was not up to *Hard Candy* requirements. Who cared about some no-name artist with nothing going for her except that she'd temporarily engaged Julian's undiscriminating libido?

Petra picked up her favorite tabloid, skimmed the headlines, then eagerly turned to the gossip pages. Would offering Nikki a job in her own department be too obvious? Probably so, but that was always an option. Petra didn't know why she hadn't thought of becoming friends with Julian's sisters before this. Unfortunately, she'd believed the hype on him and had underestimated his family devotion.

With a superior air, she scanned the fashion do's-and-don't's photos. Awful.

Petra sniffed. *Honestly.* When she married Julian and gained access to the money and connections these socialites took for granted, she'd put them all to shame. They'd be the most glorious power couple in Manhattan. She could practically taste the accolades.

She skipped down to the society column, and suddenly her world came to a screeching halt. There was a photo of Julian with that dreadful artist. Mia Somebody.

Mia *Nobody*.

It was a sniggly little photo from a museum benefit, too dark to distinguish many details and they hadn't even printed Mia's name, but a hot jealousy surged in Petra nevertheless. That would have been *her* on Julian's arm, if she hadn't jumped the gun on their relationship. She'd let him go without a fight, to sow more of his wild oats. But she'd been biding her time ever since, fully assured that, with her class and style, she'd be the perfect wife for an up-and-coming millionaire CEO. And one day soon, Julian would see the light.

Petra slammed the paper down, rattling the dishes on her breakfast tray. Why hadn't Julian recognized what was so obvious to everyone but him? They'd be perfect together.

Absolutely perfect.

She *knew* she could make him see that, if only she could get cozy with Nikki and move that drab little Mia Nobody out of the way.

THAT EVENING, Mia was busy with her own plotting. Cress and Fred were hanging out; they'd discussed her scheme for the body-painting exhibition over a vegetarian pizza and then moved on to their love lives, both existent and nonexistent. Fred had been mooning over a *Rent* chorus boy for months now, and Cress was in denial about Angelika, which left Mia and Julian as the hot topic of conversation.

"Did he send flowers again?" Cress asked with a touch of pity, once they'd pried it out of her that she and Julian had done the nasty at the museum party and he'd canceled with apologies earlier that day. "I sense a developing pattern."

"No, he did not. Because it was different this time. I think. He had to go to a dinner at his mother's. She returned from their summer house on Martha's Vineyard and wanted to get the entire family together." On the phone, there'd been a moment when she'd wondered if Julian would invite her, but he hadn't. And how could she blame him? She'd made it clear that she did not want to be brought home to do the standard meet-the-parents thing. She had *no* reason to feel disappointed.

Cress nodded. "Uh-huh." He wasn't up to his usual form since Angelika had dumped him.

"I can't decide if I trust that man," Fred said as he paged through Mia's sketches. Fred's lithe, nearly hairless body was the ideal canvas, and he'd gladly accepted her offer of several days' work. "On the one hand, he's gorgeous, but on the other hand, he's gorgeous. My mother always told me—never trust gorgeous men. And she was right. Especially rich gorgeous playboys." His head tilted. "I wonder if there is any other kind of playboy."

Cress, in the armchair with Mrs. Snookums curled up in his lap, snorted. "As if you have experience."

"I do. I was an It Boy in the eighties."

"As in 'Tag, you're it'?"

Mia was spread out among the floor pillows, digesting her pizza while she stared at the gossip page photo that had appeared in the morning's paper. She kicked a foot at Cress to divert his attention from another snipe-fest with Fred.

She balled up the page and lobbed it at him. "I blame this on you, Cress. You're supposed to be my most levelheaded best guy friend. With your experience, couldn't you have guessed that wearing painted underwear to a museum benefit would lead to naked shenanigans in a semiprivate courtyard?"

"You have a problem with naked shenanigans?"

"I'm just lucky that there were no lurking photographers to capture us in flagrante delicto."

"Julian would have a lot of 'splaining to do to his board of directors then," Cress said. She'd told them all about Barron Spear and her cool, restrained performance.

Mia didn't want to think about that too deeply. It only made her sad, knowing that for all their compatibility, she and Julian were still worlds apart.

"Let's go back to talking about the competition," she said abruptly, sitting up. "Now that I've settled on the jungle theme, I have to book the models. Who'd be good for the leopard? I need a long, lean body with muscle definition." Like Julian's, she almost said, but pushed away the image of him, half out of his suit and thrusting hard, before it could get her hot again.

"Maurizio?"

"Way too bulky."

"I'll put out the word at the gym," Fred offered. "I can find the right body."

Cress shifted, prompting the cat to vault over his legs to the floor. "Lots of recruiting going on *there*."

Fred made a shooing motion at him. "Beep, beep, beep. Back in the closet for you."

Mia caught Mrs. Snookums and held the skinny cat up to her face. "Do you believe it? Not that old bone again." As long as she'd known him, Cress had gotten grief from those who believed a neat, handsome, artistic male had to be either gay or in denial. The prejudice hurt, especially when it came from his own dad, and they'd bonded over their mutual failures. She'd always figured that was why he was so visibly interested in the models. Well, that and their fabulous bodies.

She looked for yet another topic. "Hey, guys, did I tell you about this weird thing with Phil Shavers, the photographer who did Angelika's *Hard Candy* cover?"

Cress sat low in the chair, his face dark. He let out a grunt.

"The one who's been recommending you all over town?" Fred said.

"That's the weird part. Turns out I didn't get the Sweet campaign on his recommendation after all. I had sent him a thank-you note with a gift pack of my best edible paints, you know? But this morning he calls to say thanks for the thought, except it wasn't him."

"Then who was it?"

"Could be anyone…I guess." Mia petted Fred's hairless pet, absently wondering if it was possible to paint a cat. "Maybe simple word of mouth. I'll ask someone at the cosmetics company when we have our next preproduction meeting."

"But who do you think?" Cress must have picked up on her vibe; she'd been having suspicious thoughts all day.

"Hmm, well, who do I know who has a penchant for taking charge, doling out favors and fixing other people's lives for their benefit? All out of kindness, of course."

Cress looked at her and nodded silently.

Then Fred said, "I had no idea you knew my mother," and they ended on a good laugh.

12

MIA TRIED to resist. She was a modern New Yorker; she didn't coo over sunsets or cutesy stuffed animals or fall for gushy hearts-and-flowers acts. She certainly never took a man at his word, no matter how buttery smooth and sugary sweet those words were to swallow.

But as the evening wore on and the upscale elegance, rich food, fine wine and constant catering massaged away her defensive edges, she began to weaken. She began to melt.

Had any woman—*particularly* a modern New Yorker—resisted the patented Julian Silk romantic evening of sophistication, seduction and sauterne?

"Château d'Yquem, eighty-nine," the sommelier said, cradling the bottle like the Holy Grail, practically bowing and scraping for Julian's approval.

Who remained James Bond cool. "Excellent. Thank you."

As soon as they were alone, Mia leaned toward him in their horseshoe-shaped banquette. "Isn't this stuff like hundreds and hundreds a bottle?"

He smiled at her awe. "This is an eighty-nine, not a fifty-nine, so you can drop a couple of the hundreds. But the price isn't important. What matters is if you like it."

She sipped, trying to act sophisticated. The golden

wine was very sweet, so rich it was almost sticky. "It's the best thing I've ever tasted."

Julian's hand stroked her leg beneath the tablecloth. "The best?"

She lowered her lashes, hiding a grin in the dainty crystal glass as she took another sip. "Mmm, yes. Better than body paint. You know…" She looked away, searching for distraction in the back room of the very swank, very dark restaurant. "You give me wicked thoughts when you look at me that way."

The dinner had been splendid, the company superb. If there hadn't still been that hard nugget of uneasiness and doubt inside her, she'd have been putty in Julian's hands by now. Instead, she felt like Cinderella, living the enchanted life, charmed by her prince, but also waiting for the other shoe to fall.

She set down the glass and picked up her spoon, digging out the remaining morsel of the lightest soufflé on earth *or* heaven. Like eating a cloud. Stopping the orgasmic moan of pleasure that wanted to slide out of her was extremely difficult. Especially with Julian watching her so attentively, looking good enough to eat for dessert all on his own.

"Technically, you should have only melon or nuts with a sauterne this sweet, but I remembered that you're a chocoholic. I figured you could handle the sugar high."

Thoughtful, too. The man really was perfect.

If only he felt the same way about her.

"Dinner was the absolute best," she said. "And I've dined well before. I've had black truffles. I've had caviar."

Surprise flicked in his eyes. "You have?"

"I'm not a gutter rat, you know."

"Obviously."

She went back in her head over their conversations, trying to remember what she'd said about her family. Did he know that she and Cress had been classmates at one of the country's more exclusive private schools? Had she ever explained that her present style of living was a choice, not a necessity?

It was true that she was relatively poor herself. But there was no need for him to work behind the scenes to secure her a thriving future.

"Julian, who do you think I am?" she asked, licking her spoon as she turned toward him.

His left arm rested along the deeply tufted back of the upholstered booth. Throughout dessert, he'd touched her casually—on the leg, the arm, toying with her hair. Each touch had heightened her anticipation until her body ran with a honeyed arousal as sweet as any sauterne dessert wine.

He brought his hand to his chin, considering the question with the same cool deliberation he'd had all evening. Dinner with the bachelor playboy Julian was as fluid and silky as slipping into a warm bath.

"You're Mia," he said with a small smile. "Incorrigible, independent and unexpected."

"That's very nice." She peered into his soufflé dish. "But aside from that. The actual details."

He lifted a raspberry and popped it in his mouth, then slid the dish in front of her. "Favorite food, color, book, movie?"

"No. I mean, I know about your background—the close family, the Ivy League schooling, la-di-da. But I think you've misunderstood something about mine..."

"I know enough to like you. The rest of it—" He flicked a finger in dismissal.

She devoured his soufflé. "I've mentioned that my father is a minister. Do you think I'm a poor little church mouse who's gone astray?"

Julian's eyes narrowed. "What are you getting at?"

She had another taste of the sauterne. So delicious. Was she getting drunk? No. Maybe a little extra glow; her cheeks were so warm. "I suppose it's true enough that I've gone astray, at least according to my parents. And I suppose I do qualify as poor, to you at least."

"I thought your career was picking up."

"Yes, indeed it is. I've even just signed on with one of the top booking agents, who's very pleased with the level of interest in my work." She blinked at Julian, suppressing an urge to give him a hug. And a sucker punch. "It's so sudden. Almost as if I've been anointed by someone with great power. Isn't that odd?"

He adjusted his blue silk tie. "You're good at what you do. Word was sure to spread among the art directors. There can't be that many body painters to choose from in the city. You were bound to be noticed."

He was repeating himself. Aha. She *knew* her suspicions had been on target.

"Particularly when someone at the top of the industry puts the word out on me," she said softly. "Right, Julian?"

He grimaced. "Okay, what do you know?"

"And when did I know it?" She laughed. "It's mostly suspicion, after I found out that the Sweet job didn't come from Shavers, as I'd believed. Are you ready to admit that it was you?"

"Don't know. Are you going to whine at me about trying to control your life?"

"I've had enough wine for this evening, thank you.

Though I do suddenly have a better understanding of how your sisters must feel."

"Look, I'm sorry if I've butted in, but I just wanted to help you out, after you were talking about having a tight budget for your next project…"

"Promise me it had nothing to do with repayment for sex?"

He stared, beginning to lose his mellow mood, judging by the clench of his jaw. "Of course it didn't. I can't believe you're still thinking that way."

She shook her head. "No, I'm not. I only wanted to hear you say it out loud so I could be sure." But that meant she didn't quite trust him, even if it was only one percent out of a hundred.

There was a short silence. Eventually, he dropped his chin and looked at her sidelong. A half grin lifted one corner his mouth. The look was pure naughty-boy-asking-for-forgiveness. "I suppose now you resent me for interfering?"

"Actually, I thank you. But don't do it again. I'm capable of making my own successes." She took a breath. "Which brings us back to the start of this discussion."

"Now I'm lost. Maybe you'd better come right out with it. Unless you're the secret runaway daughter of the pope…"

"Wrong religion, but that's not so far off. My father is not your average do-gooding Methodist minister. He's a fairly well-known city figure. Some of your friends and neighbors may even be his parishioners." She named her father's church, a large, historic institution with one of the wealthiest congregations in the country. "Have you heard of it?"

"Yes…" Julian began nodding as if he was finally

getting her. "That had to put a lot of pressure on you to conform." He smiled. "But then I've always heard that it's pastor's daughters who are the wildest."

"Hah. I don't know about that. But don't forget my mother—she was even more concerned with propriety. And still is." A note of sadness had crept into Mia's tone and she was determined to lighten it. "My mother is a very refined lady, who has lived a life of privilege and good breeding. She runs a household Martha Stewart can only dream of, works for a half-dozen church committees and has led a book club devoted to French literature for twenty-five years. She is formidable. We can't even begin to communicate." Whoops. Getting serious again. Mia threw in a tinkling laugh. "I, of course, never learned to speak Beaudelaire."

Julian seemed unconcerned that the banquette had become an analyst's couch. "But you've said you're not actually estranged?"

"Oh no. That would be too angry and gritty for them. We simply lead lives that rarely intersect."

"They were strict with you?"

"Tried to be, but as you said, I'm incorrigible. I've never fit into their mold. Cress and I went to school together. We were artistic rebels with far too many causes. For our senior art project, we staged my first body-painting exhibition."

Julian blinked. "I can imagine."

"Oh, I doubt it. It was a complete scandal. I copied popular works by Klee, Cézanne and Van Gogh onto the bodies of the most ordinary models I could find. A middle-aged insurance agent. A high school dropout. A new mother on welfare. Cress built large, overly fancy frames. The models posed stepping out of them to represent the triumph of ordinary man over the commercialization of great art. We were very pleased with ourselves, and even more so when we almost didn't graduate because of the reaction." She chuckled. "Looking back, I kind of get why my parents were so worried."

"What did they do?" Julian said, with a sympathetic laugh.

She pushed back her hair. It was wild tonight, a spiky black halo in contrast to her most conservative dress, a white silk shirtwaist paired with long strands of pearls. Julian had asked with a hopeful curiosity, but she'd assured him that she'd worn real undergarments tonight. "They told me I had to give up the idea of art as my major or they wouldn't pay for college. But they didn't know that I'd already been accepted at Cooper Union, here in Manhattan. Cress, too. We went out on our own and busted our asses to graduate."

"That's impressive." Julian considered. "There are times I wonder if I should have been as stubborn."

"Ah, well, truthfully, it's not easy, knowing I've disappointed my parents. I keep hoping that one day they'll understand me, but—" She frowned. "Not as long as I do what I'm doing."

"Still, you don't let that stop you." He shrugged. "I don't have your staying power. When my dad asked me to take over the family business, I couldn't say no."

She cocked her head at him, finding his self-doubt poignant. So he did have a flaw, other than his need for control. He should let his human side show more often, as she did all the damn time.

"But that's admirable, too," she said. "And you like the work, don't you?"

"Yeah, I do. The corporate life suits me, now that I'm past the fast cars and faster women stage of my life."

"Oh? What about me?"

He grazed the back of his hand over her cheek. "You don't fit in a category. In fact, you blow the mere idea of categories to smithereens."

She cozied up to him. "No more Bachelor Seventeen then, huh?"

"I think we've moved beyond that."

Very promising. Maybe she should stop letting his reputation as a ladies' man color her view of him. Let herself free-fall all the way into love with him.

"Mmm, Jules, you're so good at what you do." The seduction scene was working on her, almost too well. Her defenses were down around her ankles, her panties soon to join them.

"My job?" he said with a smile.

"That, too. But maybe you can name Nikki a vice president someday, to lighten your load."

"Nikki? You're kidding."

"Why not Nikki? *Someday.* She's only in her early twenties. Lots of growing up to do yet. I was waiting tables and doing makeup for off-off-off-Broadway when I was that age. My biggest job was an all-nude *Nutcracker* revue. That was when I started experimenting with edible paint."

He draped his arm around her, nudging her within cuddling distance again. "All right, you can stop the selling. I know it's time for Nikki to fly. My sister's never had a better booster, and I'm sure she appreciates it, but we didn't come here to discuss her."

The soft suede of his voice and the heat from his body were making Mia slip back into warm bath, hot bod territory. "I wasn't aware the evening had an agenda."

"Not an agenda." He plucked her hand off her lap. "I just thought that it was time we explored more of my world, since the party at the museum—"

She nudged him. "Our *private* party at the museum was the best of both worlds, don't you think?"

"We're getting there. But I'm still concerned with— oh, damn, here comes the waiter again."

While the obsequious waiter delivered the check and asked what else he could do for them, Mia left to make a quick trip to the ladies' room. She was returning to the table when a woman who looked familiar stopped her to say hello.

"I saw you were with Julian, so I didn't want to interrupt earlier," the woman said.

Mia couldn't place her, but she held out her hand. "We've been having dinner." Idiot comment. "I'm Mia Kerrigan."

"Yes, I know." There was a long pause as the woman's thin brows crept upward. "Petra Lombardi, *Hard Candy* art director."

Of course. The champagne-cocktail blonde who had spent all her time with the suits while Mia had been treated like hired help. Which she was, but still. "Oh, yes. You'll have to excuse me for not placing your face with your name. I was busy with gumdrops that entire shoot. Didn't notice anyone."

Petra laughed. "Except Julian."

Meow. "He may have noticed me first."

"Yes, he would." Petra seemed amused by Mia's dubious expression. "It's all right. We've all been there." She lowered her voice, getting chummy, and Mia remembered how Petra had been clinging to Julian as the shoot was ending.

"He gave me the fifth-date kiss-off at a dinner just like this one," Petra continued. "It may even have been this very restaurant, now that I think about it. Isn't that funny?" She patted Mia's upper arm. "Eventually, you'll appreciate the irony. Maybe not now, but one day. Welcome to the sisterhood."

"But we're—he's not dumping me."

"Oh." For one instant, Petra's mouth and eyes went hard. Then she trilled a soprano *"Sorry!"* and laughed again. "There's always dessert. Did he order the Château d'Yquem yet? The man does have class, I'll give him that."

Mia stood rooted to the floor, watching as Petra, slinky in a column of black silk, rejoined her party. The airy soufflé now sat in the pit of her stomach like a lead ball. It wasn't that she believed Julian was planning to break up with her. The reminder that he had perpetrated other breakups here was enough. Which, of course, had been Petra's devious intention.

Julian was ready to go when Mia returned to the table. They exited the restaurant and he whisked her to the chauffeured car waiting at the curb.

A minute passed. Mia stared out the window at the glittering city that seemed made for Julian and his moneyed ilk. She wasn't of the ilk, but she did feel slightly ill.

"You seem upset," Julian insisted. "Is it that I'm not Bachelor Number One?"

"You know it's not that." She shrugged, still thinking of Petra and remembering Nikki's comments about her brother's standard operating procedure: the fancy dinner, the romantic seduction. She'd deliberately forced him out of that pattern, but was he reverting to type?

"I'm not sure," she answered. "I suppose I feel more comfortable in my own world."

"I thought you might like to see my apartment, but I can take you home instead...."

Deep breaths, she told herself. *Don't be so easily swayed from what you know is true. Julian cares for you. He may exist in a different stratosphere, but it's a nice place to visit.*

"Your place," she said. "I'd like that." Then, a minute later: "Is this our fifth date?"

"I don't think so, but it depends what counts as a date. Is the fifth significant for you?"

"I just wondered." She was reassured. He probably had nothing on his mind but getting her naked. Which was a funny thing to be reassured about, considering that she was supposed to be wary of his playboy tendencies.

Not so much, when her heart was at stake.

"WHY DID I think you were a conservative old-money kind of guy?" Mia said as she walked around his apartment, an eight-room bachelor pad in a luxury high-rise on the Upper West Side. "This is much hipper than I expected."

"Hip? I don't think so."

She ran a hand over the upholstery of the low Italian sofas. "Maybe *hip* isn't the word. But it's very stylish and contemporary. Not traditional at all."

The mood lighting was on low, making a soft glow from behind the moldings. Recessed spots spilled discreet pools of illumination over the modern but restful artwork, large canvases of subtle color. He'd put on a disk, drawn the drapes and turned on the gas fire, all by remote control.

"Have a seat. Can I get you anything?"

Mia circled the room. "I want to wander."

"Be my guest. Make yourself comfortable."

She stepped out of her shoes, kicking them aside to work her toes into the thickly padded gray carpet. Her gaze lit on him. "How about if I make *you* more comfortable?"

"That sounds promising."

"First, we get rid of this. Ties are a strange fashion, I've always thought. Almost as bad as high heels." She unknotted his tie and yanked it free of his collar with a quick downward whip of her arm.

"You wear high heels."

"Only on special occasions—when I want to feel sexy."

He looked at the shoes she'd abandoned. Pumps with medium heels. *Rats.* On the other hand, they were the same pair she'd worn to the museum.

Her toes wiggled as she undid a couple of his buttons. "But bare is even sexier, don't you think?"

"Oh, absolutely."

She planted a kiss inside the collar of his shirt, but then slipped away before he could wrap his arms around her. "I have to see the rest of the apartment. If it's all as neat and subdued as the living room, I may have to do what I can to mess it up." She looked at him from the doorway and dropped the hot pink sari wrap she had draped around her shoulders. "Know what I mean?"

He swallowed. Kicked off his shoes. "I know what I hope you mean."

Her light laughter drifted from the foyer as she crossed into the dining room, luring him to follow. He got there in time to see her do the panty hose shimmy as she worked her nylons down her thighs. She left them dangling over one of his dining chairs.

She pointed. "Kitchen, this way?"

He managed a nod.

"Not even a banana peel," she called from the other side of the stainless-steel door as he dropped his jacket on his way to join her.

He pushed through and caught her sitting on the granite-topped center island, reaching inside her dress. She pulled out a white lace bra, idly twirling it on her fingertip as she looked around the state-of-the-art kitchen he rarely used.

"Much too sterile," she said, almost regretfully. She hopped down, padding across the tiles, checking out one of the unused stoves before popping the bra into a freezer stocked with pizzas, steaks and a bottle of Stoli. Shaking her head in disapproval, she shifted her pearls to one side and unbuttoned the front of her dress while studying the pristine surfaces and cocoa-colored walls. "This does not bode well for the master bedroom."

He was ready to vault the island in a single bound, but he held himself in check, watching as a wide strip of creamy cleavage appeared. His own fingers forgot how to operate. "I beg to differ."

"We'll see." She picked up her skirt, flashing bare legs as she dashed from the kitchen and into the long mirrored hallway. "No ego problems here," she laughed, sticking her tongue out at his reflection when he appeared behind her, his shirt unbuttoned and hanging loose.

Her dress gaped as she stopped at the door to his bedroom and bent to slip out of her bikini underpants. He didn't know where to look—at the curve of her buttock, the pink crest of the breast that had swung into view, the provocative garment puddled around her ankles…or her face, filled with a carefree joy so different from her mercurial moodiness in the car.

The dress was sliding off her shoulders as she stepped into the bedroom. He unstuck his tongue from the roof of his mouth and hurried after her, unbuckling his belt as he went.

In the center of the bedroom, she stood entirely nude with her white silk dress foaming at her feet. Venus on the half shell.

"Very dark, ver-r-ry sexy," she said, apparently admiring the decor of dark woods and smoky blue walls, though his brain couldn't wrap around the concept with her naked body in the room. "Very you."

He stalked her. His palms itched to be filled with her curves. "*You're* very me."

She put out a hand, holding him off. "Not so fast. I want the full effect. Firelight, please." She spotted the row of votives along a credenza. "Oh, and candles."

The fireplace lighted with a soft *whoosh* of gas. The flames flickered tamely. The candles took longer; he fumbled with a matchbook, singeing his fingers and sending silent curses at the stubborn wicks. He was as awkward and randy as a schoolboy. One would think it was their first time.

First time since you realized this might be love, he told himself. The reminder was not the calming effect he needed, if Mia was expecting perfectly orchestrated lovemaking.

He was too far gone for that.

She had folded back the suede duvet on the contemporary four-poster. Her heart-shaped bottom posed too great a temptation and he came up behind her to grab it, seething with lust as he kneaded the pert cheeks, parting them at the joining of her thighs to find the swollen pink center of her, the one place he wanted to be more than any other. Dew had collected on the ripe lips. His gut clenched and his balls tightened up at the thought of how tight she would feel. But how accommodating.

He tickled her with a fingertip, then found the tight bud and teased it with a flick. Then another. He'd intended to withdraw, but her throaty moan made his hackles rise. So deep and soulful, filled with a desire beyond words. He rolled her clit beneath his finger, pressing firmly.

"Ahhhh." A tremor went through her. She arched and pressed herself back against him, staying bent over the bed with her arms braced on the mattress. "Please." She tossed her head. "Please, don't…don't stop…." The sheet wrinkled in her clenched fists.

He stopped, wanting to be inside her when she came.

"Don't move." He unzipped and thrust his trousers and shorts down in one motion, keeping a hand on her waving butt.

She made a sound of frustration. She twitched his hand away, like a mare swishing her tail at a stallion. "You stopped. You're a tease. Now you have to come and get me."

"With pleasure."

"Mmm, yeah. You want me?" she taunted lightly, tossing her head and stretching forward, sliding her hands along the sheets. He tried to grip her, but she pulled away as soon as she felt him prodding between her legs.

Crawling away on all fours, she glanced back over her shoulder. He stood there with his penis in his hand, like a baseball player who'd just struck out. She giggled. "Uh-uh, big boy. It's not going to be that easy."

"Aw, c'mon." He went down on his knees on the bed, reaching for her again, but she turned onto her backside and slithered farther away. He snagged her pearls. The long strands made a zipping sound as they tightened around her neck.

He tugged gently. "Gotcha."

"Okay, then." She let him reel her in. When she was snugged up against him, he loosened the pearls, freeing the strands so they hung across her breasts. He played with the necklace, crisscrossing it until the pearls outlined her breasts like a harness, lifting them higher, her nipples pointing up when he pulled the strands taut again.

She ran her hands over her spread thighs, rising up to her knees as he tugged and offering her breasts. Naked, silent and obedient. Too obedient. Her eyes were blue flames, luminescent with intense heat and emotion.

The same surged in him—blazing heat, a rush of strong emotion. She was his. Forever his woman, and they both knew it even without the words being said.

With the pearl necklace wound around his hand, he drew her closer. Her distended nipples teased his chest with pinpoints of fire. He thumbed one of them, feeling her breath catch short when he put his face near hers.

"Now," he said wetly in her ear, and without ceremony, flipped her over so she was on all fours again. He bent over her, using his weight to hold her down as he nibbled along her shoulder blades and reached for her dangling breasts. "Now we see…"

Yes, we'll see, Mia said silently. The man did not want to give up control. At least, not until he was inside her.

She wagged her backside. He answered by rocking against her, holding her by the hips; his hot erection was pressed between her legs, almost where she wanted it.

But not quite. She dropped forward onto her elbows, rolling her head to one side. The room was alive with shadows that danced on the opposite wall. "Look there. Shadow puppets." She cocked her head, awed by the eroticism of their shadow image.

Julian chuckled softly. He drew back from her, his shadow elongating in a skewed perspective as he ran his hands along her body, positioning her just so, making her ready for his first thrust.

The edgy playfulness stirred a deep excitement in Mia. She was tempted to succumb, but she wouldn't. While part of her wanted to go all the way and back again with Julian leading the way, this wasn't the position she'd intended to be in this evening. She had to show him that although he may have perfected the art of seduction, he'd never run up against the likes of her.

She was *not* just another conquest.

Even so, her intentions were cut short when she looked again at their shadows and clearly saw the outline of his penis like the prow of a ship, seeming to cleave into her from behind. She was so riveted by the shadow pictures that she forgot to move away until the hot, moist head of his erection touched between her thighs like a shock and jolted her forward.

She rose up, twisting around to push at him. "Not so fast, Jules," she said with a shaky laugh, her palms pressed to his chest. Though she wanted to caress his smooth muscles, instead she batted at him, playfully fighting his embrace until they'd fallen to the bed in a breathless snarl.

He let out a groan. "Contrary woman."

"Stubborn man."

She pushed up to one elbow and slung an arm across

his chest, resting her chin on her hand. Their mood quieted as they looked at each other in silence. The candlelight danced on his tawny skin, illuminating a face so handsome it hurt her heart to look at him.

I'm not wrong. I'm not deluding myself. This is something special.

The expression in his eyes became more serious as he ran his fingers along her arm. His thumb touched her chin and strummed her lower lip. "Mia, sweetheart, I want you to know that you've changed my life. I have a new perspective. But it's—that is, I've begun to realize that my future has to include you. I can't imagine one without you."

Oh yes. "Me, too."

They kissed, very tenderly. "I wonder, though…"

Oh no.

"Now that you've told me about your upbringing…" He leaned back on the pillow, reaching out to tuck a curl of hair behind her ear. "It seems that in many ways I lead the kind of lifestyle that you rejected, so how can we—" He cleared his throat. "You know, be a couple?"

She'd wondered the same. The possibility that they wouldn't find a way, regardless of their bond, was too overwhelming to dwell on.

"That depends on how willing you are to give and bend." She batted her lashes, falling back on humor to ease the moment. "I've already demonstrated how skilled I am at bending."

He slapped her butt. "You bend like that for me and I'll do anything you want."

"Men," she said, shifting position. Her fingers curled around his erection. "So easily led."

She flung the ropes of pearls over her shoulder and

climbed on top of him, settling her thighs over his. On the wall, her shadow wavered, stretching halfway to the ceiling when she reached her hands high overhead and slowly, slowly brought them down onto Julian's chest. Fingers spread, she massaged his muscles, gradually working lower until she'd reached the ridges on his stomach. She traced the line of hair that bisected the flat plane of his groin before spreading into the thatch that framed his jutting penis. A few strokes and he'd grown harder, larger, making his shadow even more impressive when she glanced at it, still entranced by the erotic picture they made.

He tried to sit up, and she dropped him with one pointed finger. "Down, boy. I'm in charge this time."

"All right, but where do you intend to lead me?"

"Into temptation, of course."

"We're way past temptation." He handed her a condom from a low shelf near the bed.

She rolled it onto him, wishing that she could feel the true heat of him, skin on skin. When they committed…

If they committed.

No one would ever expect it—Julian the rogue playboy with *her*, a nobody in the eyes of the world—not stylish or famous, just a kooky artist who loved him with all her heart.

She lifted up, pausing to slip out of the pearls. He caught one end of the necklace, and she wrapped the other twice around his erection. A question showed in his face, along with a stark need, duly restrained. Not for long, she suspected, so she said, "Be still. Don't move, don't talk," as she captured his penis in one hand and steered him where she needed him so badly. "Let me love you."

His eyes burned as she lowered herself. He was big, solid. Her thigh muscles quivered with tension. The most exquisite sensation rolled through her at the first contact of hot piercing flesh ridged by the circlets of hard pearls. She sizzled under the heat of Julian's stare and suddenly she wanted to see what she felt, what he saw, as her body stretched to receive him. She wanted to watch as they joined. As they became one.

She tilted forward, one hand flat on her belly, straining to watch as his shaft slid inch by inch into her, taking the pearls with him. It was dirty and exciting; it was raw and it was beautiful. Her heartbeat was banging; her lungs had drawn so tight she could hardly breathe. And when she looked up, Julian was there. Watching her face. Holding the pearl tether that connected them.

He didn't say a word, but she read everything she needed to know in his eyes.

Swallowing hard, she sank as far as she could go and sat astride him for a moment, her mind expanding to accept the newness. This was about making love with every inch of her body, her mind, her heart. When she rocked a little and squeezed her inner muscles, the sensations shot through her like a skyrocket. She lifted up and then down, impaling herself. Moisture flowed, helping his pearl-ridged cock glide in and out of her. And when she thought it couldn't get any better, he pulled on the tether and the double strand of pearls rolled against her pleasure point, jerking a harsh cry of ecstasy from her throat.

Her bones melted to pudding and she slithered against him, her belly pressed to his, her breasts pillowed on his chest, the pearls strung taut down the center. Their lips met and the kiss slipped through her like warm milk, adding a few more degrees of heat to the flame that burned between her thighs. "Help me," she whispered, and Julian put his hands on her hips, thrusting his hips off the bed. Together, entwined, they rode the pleasure higher, hotter, brighter...until they were consumed.

13

"NIKKI, IT'S Petra Lombardi."

"Oh. Hi! I'm so excited!"

"Then you've already been told you got the job. Fantastic. I'm quite pleased for you."

"Yes, I'm going to be a *Hard Candy* staff writer!" Nikki squealed into her cell phone. "And they're rushing my article and Mia's painted-fashions layout into publication as soon as possible—to build on the excitement after the December issue with her cover. That was a surprise, because at first the editor wasn't sure they'd use more than a paragraph. I guess it helped that Julian pushed the idea. Mia's his girlfriend, you know."

"Fantastic. I have nothing against nepotism."

Petra's subsequent pause was long enough for Nikki to speculate on the woman's sincerity. *Zip,* she decided, before saying with a giggle, "Me, neither."

Finally the art director went on. "*Hard Candy* usually only profiles celebrities. But the editor does love sexy gossip and scandal. Plus, I put in a good word for you, the way I said I would. Since I'll be in charge of that—of Mia's layout—I do have an influence."

"Thank you," Nikki said with scrupulous etiquette, even if she wasn't sure that Petra deserved it despite the advice she'd dispensed at their lunch. "I owe you big-time."

Petra laughed. "Not at all."

Nikki squirmed, her suspicions about the art director's motives deepening. Although they'd barely mentioned Julian when they'd met, there had been something in Petra's voice—a brittle edge when she said his name—that had made Nikki wonder. She'd told herself that she was only networking. And it wasn't as if Petra had even hinted at an exchange of favors.

Besides, what could Nikki do? No more was she a schoolgirl bringing home friends who only wanted to goggle over her brother. Petra was much more sophisticated than that.

"I'll take you out for drinks, my first day on the job," Nikki offered. "I'm starting next week."

"I'm sure we can think of something more exciting than drinks."

Nikki stopped outside of Bendel's window, not even looking at the shoes. "Such as?"

"We will see." Petra sounded like a cream-fed cat. "As they say, what goes around comes around."

A city work crew had set up on the street nearby and a man with neck-to-wrist tattoos was vibrating behind a jackhammer. Nikki held out her phone and shouted at it from an arm's length away. "There's a huge racket here. Sorry, gotta go!"

She snapped the phone shut and stowed it in her bag. Either Petra was maneuvering for the sake of office politics, or she was up to a more personal game. Nikki didn't want to speak to Julian about it. He'd only tell her that she was in over her head and she should have listened to him and written about decorating a country kitchen with ginghams and plaid.

Yuck.

Sex and celebrity were the hot trends. *Hard Candy* was where Nikki wanted to be, even if it did seem as if she'd unexpectedly pulled a plum out of the Silk Publishing pie. Oh well. She'd work so diligently that no one would be able to say she didn't deserve her good fortune.

And she'd steer clear of Petra Lombardi.

IF GREAT SEX really gave a woman that certain glow, Mia figured that she must be lit up like a Christmas tree. Either men could smell it on her or they were responding to her irrepressible grin, because every other guy she passed on the street had a comment, a whistle, a wink or leer. And all of them made her laugh.

She had stayed the night at Julian's apartment. Around 3:00 a.m., she'd been belly down over a raw silk ottoman, watching a late movie on the plasma screen TV while he made love to her from behind. He'd pushed deep, leaned over and whispered in her ear—some variation of Bacall's famous line about putting her lips together—and soon she'd been coming for the third time. Bogart and Bacall were a good inspiration.

They'd slept late and then Julian had raced off to work, leaving her to his apartment. She'd thought about doing the new-girlfriend closet search, looking for clues to his inner life, especially because the place was so spartan. But there just hadn't been time, after a long hot bath, a call from her new booking agent, another call from Nikki and a last-minute wardrobe panic.

"Hot frickin' mama!" yelled a guy from behind as she ran to beat the light at a cross street. Maybe she should have worn the white dress again, even though it had been a crumpled mess.

Nikki was standing outside of their meeting point, talking on her cell. She waved at Mia, eyes widening.

Mia arrived out of breath. "Hi. Sorry I'm late."

"Is that an I-boffed-your-brother-all-night-long ensemble?"

"You might call it that." She'd worn her sari shawl like a sarong skirt, with a pale blue dress shirt of Julian's tucked into it, the knee-length tail peeping out where the makeshift skirt gathered to knot at her waist. The sleeves were rolled up past her elbow and underneath was a pair of biking shorts, but no one could tell that. She looked half-dressed and thoroughly rogered.

"Ew." Nikki shuddered. "Don't you know I'm an impressionable youngster?"

Mia put a hand over her silly smiling mouth. "Sorry. I didn't have time to go home and change."

"But it's noon." Nikki checked her watch. "Past noon. We'd better go in and grab our table instead of waiting for Very."

"Very's coming?"

"Is that okay? She wanted to help celebrate my new job, and I think she's also hoping to get to know you better. Great fodder for teasing Julian." Nikki acknowledged the hostess with a tiny nod and moved with strutting élan through the crowded restaurant. She walked like a runway model; Mia scurried like a bunny rabbit.

The walls were chocolate-brown and chalkboard-black. Pendant lights with a thirties' glam hung over small square tables set mere inches apart. It was the kind of place that made Mia feel chubby and underdressed, even when she wore her best. In a man's dress shirt, she was a lost cause. Fodder, for sure.

She sucked in her stomach and edged toward the long bench that lined the wall, trying not to drag the linen tablecloth with her. "Do you think I can pass my look off as a new trend?" she said under her breath to Nikki from behind oversized menus, aware of amused glances from the next table over, where two women with locked jaws and stretched skin nibbled at raw greens.

Nikki sent the server away with an order for a round of champagne cocktails. "Sure. Just tilt your chin up."

Mia and Nikki tilted, side by side.

"Lower your eyelids. Do a little pout with your lower lip…"

They lowered and pouted.

"And when anyone speaks to you, give them a shoulder nudge and a short pause, lifting your eyebrows if they've been terribly presumptuous…"

Mia nudged, paused and lifted, feeling like a street mime.

Veronica Silk appeared at the table. "What's with the facial ticks?" She air-kissed their cheeks and plopped into a chair, ripping off her shiny satin baseball jacket as if she hadn't a care in the world.

"I'm teaching Mia to be supercilious," Nikki explained.

"Ha! You both look like Mom when Frodo has left a gift on the rug."

The adjacent women were appalled, but also fascinated.

"Exactly." Nikki winked at Mia. "Practice. It'll come in handy when Jules brings you home to meet our mother. Not that I'm comparing you to a dog turd!"

"Perish the thought," Mia said. She wasn't looking forward to the meet-the-parents step, on either side.

"Jules hasn't brought a girl home in years, but it could happen with Mia." Nikki leaned toward Very. "She made Jules late for work, if you can believe that."

Very blinked. "Wow. Then it must be serious. Or you're really, really good in bed."

"Both," Mia said with a modest smile.

The sisters looked at each other and laughed. "Isn't she perfect?" Nikki said. "Jules has finally found a woman with pizzazz instead of the social climbers and fame whores who are usually panting after him." She leaned forward to address the neighboring table. "You know the type."

The eavesdroppers twitched snooty noses and pretended great interest in their salads.

Very nodded. "Now *there's* supercilious."

Mia cast the women a glum look. "That'll never be me. I can't be…cool."

"Thank God," said Nikki. "I couldn't take it if Jules wanted to marry the Petra Lombardi type."

Mia's ears perked up, but it was Very who jumped in. "What? I thought Petra was your new best friend, getting you the job and all."

"She's just sucking up because of my name. Her eyes are on either Julian or a better position within the company, I'm not sure which." Nikki turned to Mia. "Do you know Petra?"

"I've worked with her…"

"Oh yeah. I forgot about the cover shoot. How did she treat you?"

"Um, well, I don't think she paid a lot of attention to me." Not until Petra had seen her out with Julian. "But there's something there. I don't know exactly what." Although her instinct said Petra wanted Mia's man.

The drinks arrived. "I realize that it's kind of early for alcohol," Nikki said as they lifted their glasses.

"Says who? I could use some hair of the dog." Very clinked rims. "To Nik's new job. Her *first* job. Cheers!"

"Cheers." Mia took only a small sip. "Congratulations, Nikki. Am I going to get an advance peek at your first article?"

"I brought a copy with me. But I should warn you, the editor said that I should expect a heavy edit to suit the painted-fashion layout you'll be doing for them. I'm just happy that the piece will be printed at all, in any form. From what Petra said, even Julian's approval wasn't enough."

"I'm sure you did a wonderful job," Mia said. She'd booked the *Hard Candy* layout that very morning. "If it wasn't Julian, what happened to change the editor's mind?"

"Well…Petra hinted that it was her good word that turned the trick. She said something about how the magazine was only interested in stories about celebrities having sex, or whatever, and I got the feeling I was supposed to be very grateful to her for convincing them to take on my article."

"Do you believe that?"

Nikki shrugged. "I have no reason not to. To tell the truth, I thought I'd either be offered a position just because of my connection to Silk Publishing, or else I'd be turned down flat because Jules had learned about my intentions and laid down the law at *Hard Candy*. He swears he rarely interferes with editorial decisions, but…" She shrugged.

"I think you'll find that Julian's becoming more flexible," Mia said. "He does want you to be happy, Nikki. I don't see him *forcing* them into this layout and article, though."

Very took a big swallow of her drink. "I believe I can shed some light on the puzzle." She reached down to shuffle through an overstuffed gym bag. "I was on the train and picked up a paper that had been left on the seat…" She lifted out a pair of boxing gloves and set them on her empty plate. "Ah, here we go." She popped back up, opening the folded tabloid with a rattle. Her gaze went to Mia as she folded the paper over. "You haven't seen this, I'm guessing."

Instinct gave Mia goose bumps. Her mouth went to cotton. The pink ruffle of Very's retro-punk hair flopped over onto her forehead as she passed the paper across the table, looking sort of…wary.

Nikki and Mia huddled over the page of newsprint. The top half of the page was devoted to a premiere of a new movie, but below that was a photo of Mia and Julian leaving the restaurant the previous night. Beside it was a reproduction of the Peachy Keen ad that had caused so much controversy. Mia's eyes went to the headline: "Silk Mystery Date Laid Bare."

"Oh shit," she said.

Very shrugged. "No big deal. You're a celebrity now, for at least fifteen minutes."

"I don't want to be a celebrity." Mia glanced over the paragraphs about Julian's latest conquest, big on innuendo, but also packed with gossipy tidbits about her "sexy" career in body painting, all made to sound as titillating as possible. There was even mention of the upcoming *Hard Candy* cover. "And I *really* don't want to be famous for getting schtupped by Julian Silk. No offense to Julian." She'd never considered herself one of the crowd. Not to mention how appalled her parents would be.

Very swirled her drink. "None taken, I'm sure."

Nikki was noticeably quiet. Eventually she set the paper down and looked up at them, her expression bleak. "What does this mean?"

"Just the usual gossip," Very said.

"No." Nikki gulped. "The timing, and—and—"

Assuming that the girl referred to her new job, Mia reassured her. "I'm sure they wanted to hire you regardless."

"Petra must have known about this article. That was why she made the reference to celebrity sex gossip. But that's not the worst of it." Nikki gulped, looking at Mia with apology. "I never meant for this to happen, but I have to tell you. A lot of these details—" She waved a hand at the paper. "They're straight from my article, after I sexed it up on Petra's advice."

"Oh, I see." Mia frowned, but she couldn't blame Nikki for being manipulated. "It's okay."

"But how did the paper get a hold of your article?" Very said, outraged. "You should sue them!"

Mia shook her head. "Most of this stuff is public knowledge. It's just that no one was ever interested enough in me to dig it all up."

"I'm so sorry," wailed Nikki.

Mia gave her a one-armed hug. "Hey, stop that. It's only a trashy newspaper. I'll survive." Her parents were another matter. "*You* didn't do anything wrong."

"But *Hard Candy* is a national publication," Very pointed out.

"My love life isn't that interesting," Mia said. "Even

Julian—he's not famous like JFK Jr. was, or, I don't know, some celebrity athlete or actor—"

Nikki interrupted. "You underestimate the power of being named one of *Celebrity Gossip*'s hottest bachelors. I saw the huge volume of fan mail he got after that. And the media has been after him ever since."

"In today's world, a person doesn't have to do anything special to be a celebrity," Very said. "Jules is famous for being rich, handsome and successful."

"And for schtupping a lot of gorgeous women," Nikki added with another apologetic smile for Mia. "On the other hand, maybe that was what the editor meant about heavy editing. There definitely won't be any mention of your dating Julian. That part wasn't in *my* article." She tapped the newspaper thoughtfully. "I wonder…"

Mia leaned closer, curious about Nikki's suspicions. The women at the next table did, too, obviously hoping not to miss a word.

Nikki dropped her voice. "Do you think *Petra* is involved?"

"What would she have to gain by embarrassing me?" Mia asked, mystified. "For all she knows, I love the extra publicity."

"But Julian doesn't."

"There's nothing to sweat over. If the *Hard Candy* article isn't appropriate, Jules can nix it—" Very snapped her fingers "—like that."

"Sure, and if I have to go to him to clean up the mess, I'll be right back where I started." Nikki sat back with crossed arms. "After this fiasco, he'll return to threatening to make me the mail-room girl at *Knitting Pretty*."

Mia felt bad for Nikki. She knew a little about beating expectations. "Don't let him blame you on my account. I made my own bed—I'll live through this gossip. Maybe it'll die down quickly." And it wasn't as if this was the first time she'd disgraced the family name.

"You might even benefit," Very pointed out. "You'll be the most famous body painter in the world now."

That was not how Mia had planned to procure the position. With some dread, she thought of the upcoming expo, only a week away. *Maybe* the notoriety would fade by then, particularly if she stayed away from Julian in public. The body-painting exhibition would turn into a circus if she didn't.

Nikki had brightened. Mia didn't want to bring her down again, so she nodded as if she were seeing benefits to the situation.

"I just don't know anymore if I want to work at a magazine that didn't really want *me*, only my family connections. Especially if someone there was responsible for releasing my article to create buzz." Nikki sighed.

"Take the job," urged Mia. "Show them how valuable you are. Make a real name for yourself."

"Just stay away from Petra," Very put in, although her scowl made her look more like the fighting type.

Nikki looked at Mia with admiration. "You're so sure of yourself."

"I guess I am. But it didn't come easily. I had my own inner demons and doubts to overcome."

Ones that had seemingly popped up again. She looked at the newspaper again before crumpling it in her fists. Her parents wouldn't like her appearing in *Hard Candy* either, but the tabloids seemed worse. Maybe because it was happening right now, in bold print. Julian would understand if she stepped away from their involvement.

A temporary reprieve. A cooling-off time.

Her pride hurt to admit it, but perhaps he'd even welcome a little distance. Deep down, she knew that was unfair. But it was easier to accept than the possibility that theirs was only a short-term fling—a superhot flash fire that had been suddenly doused with a hard cold bucket of reality.

SEVERAL DAYS later, Mia bit the bullet and called her mother. The conversation didn't go well, not when she tried to explain her tabloid appearance, nor how Jules was different than his public persona, and especially when she refused once more to give up her career in body painting. She'd thought of offering her parents a couple of tickets to the expo so they could see she was making art, not lewd soft porn. But when her mother could only speak of how disappointed she was in Mia's continued obstinacy, Mia decided there was no point. The funny thing was that for the first time, She was actually involved with a man who could provide what the Kerrigans wanted for their daughter—marriage, children, a solid home, even extreme wealth—but Mia couldn't share that. Not now.

Thus far, Julian was accepting her brush-offs. She'd told him that she was busy with work. When he called again, her excuse was that she had to devote every moment of spare time to her tableau for the expo, which was looming near. The third time, she admitted that perhaps it would be better for them both to stay out of the limelight for the time being.

He apologized about the gossip and the photos, as if that had been his fault. For Nikki's sake, Mia neglected to mention the *Hard Candy* connection, although she worried about what Petra Lombardi might attempt next.

Nikki, meanwhile, had sworn she would conduct a reconnaissance from her new staff position at the magazine. Mia had surprising confidence in her. Nikki was brash and optimistic, blessed with a happy-go-lucky confidence that she could conquer the world if she had the time to spare in between shopping, clubbing and decorating her new office cubicle. If Mia's relationship with Julian hadn't been so up in the air, she would have embraced Nikki as her new little sister. Even Very, who'd dropped by Mia's apartment one day out of curiosity, had returned for pizza-and-board-game night, and now seemed almost like one of the crowd.

Other than for Very and Nikki and Cress and Fred and Leslie asking when she'd see Julian again—so far Stefan and Mrs. Snookums were silent—Mia made it past her fifteen minutes of fame just fine. She stayed in when she could, working at home, giving up salvage night and an invitation to a club opening in favor of tea with Miss Delaney and Edmund Flax. No paparazzi showed up at her door, so after a week she guessed that she was safe. She ventured out for lunch at her favorite Greek diner, stopped to buy groceries at the bodega and was passing a magazine kiosk when some instinct made her buy a copy of the tabloid that had printed her pictures.

She flipped through the pages right there on the street.

And there it was: a photo of Julian, arriving at a premiere party for a movie or a book or designer handbags, she didn't care. What mattered was that there was a stylish new accessory on his arm and her name was Petra Lombardi.

AT APPROXIMATELY the same moment, in the offices of *Hard Candy*, Julian sat on the floor of Nikki's cubicle and moped. "I will never listen to you again," he said to his sister's fishnet kneecaps. "Mia couldn't give a damn about who I escort to which party. And now I'm stuck down here, among your debris—" he pried a candy bar wrapper off his palm and dropped it into the trash can "—hiding from Petra." He started to get up. "This is not dignified."

"Stay down," Nikki hissed. "Petra's still prowling."

"Look. I'll tell her that I went with her only as a professional courtesy. Again. She'll understand. This time. I can't hide from her forev—"

Nikki gave his head a shove, then popped up from her chair. "Petra." She grabbed papers off her desk and hustled out from behind her partitions. "I could use your input on this new idea of mine…"

Julian listened as Nikki rattled on about a girl-talk column, walking toward the door to draw Petra out of the cubicle area of the office. He climbed into her desk chair and sat with his head in his hands, staring at the flower bouquet he'd dropped off on Nikki's first day of work. That was when Petra had cornered him, claimed her current boyfriend was out of town and asked if he wouldn't fill in as her escort to a movie premiere sponsored by the magazine. Initially he'd said no, but after days of Mia's stonewalling, he was at a loss for what to try next. When Nikki had come up with the idea that being seen with a different woman would take the pressure off Mia…

Bad idea, in retrospect. He must have been desperate to try it in the first place.

All day he'd only been able to reach Mia's answering machine, and he'd left increasingly idiotic messages. She'd probably been listening with Fred or Cress and making sport of him, angry now instead of only leery. To top it off, Petra had clawed at him in the back of the limo after the premiere, ready to strip him down and give him a tongue bath. His skin had crawled at the idea, when before he'd found her to be rather sexy in that poised feline way of hers. After he'd turned her down, she'd been less than her usual cool self, talking about how he needed a woman who fit into his lifestyle and how good they looked together. He hadn't been able to get away fast enough.

Life had been less complicated as Bachelor Seventeen, that was for sure.

Nikki returned to the cubicle. "She's gone."

"Then I have to go. I'm supposed to be somewhere else anyway."

"Hold it." Nikki sat on the edge of her desk and gripped the arms of the desk chair, keeping him in place. "You have no perspective. I'm a girl. I understand how Mia is feeling."

He snorted. "Not likely. You love to be mentioned in the gossip columns. Mia's not like that—she's a minister's daughter."

"Really? Wow. I didn't know." Nikki paused. "It doesn't exactly show."

"That's not the point."

"All right. The point is, you have to trust me, Julian. I know what I'm doing, and I swear to you that Mia is not going to stay mad for long once you explain. Just don't be all dominating about it. None of that for-your-own-good crap, okay?"

He thought of the messages he'd left on Mia's answering machine. "Too late."

Nikki sighed. "What did you do?"

He explained.

She threw up her hands. "Then there's only one way to go. Now you have to grovel."

"MIA, THIS IS Julian. It's been eight days since we last saw each other. Call me."

Beep.

"Mia, are you there? Did you go out? That's good. There's really no reason for you to worry about the tabloids. Not now. I've, uh, fixed it. But I have to explain, because you might get the wrong idea if you hear from someone else. So call me."

Beep.

"Don't buy a newspaper until I talk to you."

Beep.

"I meant to say please. This is, er, Julian, by the way."

Beep.

"Hey, Mia. Nikki. I had this brilliant idea for how to draw Petra out. I'm at work—ooh, I love saying that! Anyway, I'm at work, so I'll tell you all about it later. Call me."

Beep.

"Julian again. It's been a couple of hours. Aren't you home yet? I'm at my office, but I'm about to go into a meeting. Call me anyway—Shep is under orders to interrupt if it's you. Not an important meeting anyway. Nothing is important without—oh hell. I sound like an idiot."

Beep.

"Hi, this is Angelika. Do you still need a model for that jungle thing? Call me at my agency."

Beep.

"Mia, Jules again. You can't still be out. I think you're

avoiding me, and if you're avoiding me it's because you've seen the photo in the paper. Listen, it wasn't my—damn it. Now I've turned into a weasel. A week without you and I'm losing it. *Argh,* get ahold of yourself, Silk. So, um, maybe I'll go to the gym and run off some of this energy. Call you la—"

Beep.

"I got cut off. Have you seen the paper? I know it looks bad, but it was strictly professional. I did it for your sake. Honest to God, I was thinking of you the entire time. Okay, maybe not the *entire* time, but you know what I mean…"

Beep.

"It was Nikki. Her idea. Not to make you jealous, just to throw off the gossip hounds. You see? No lie—I did it for you."

Beep.

"This is ridiculous. I'm sick of explaining myself. If you can accept that I had your best interests at heart—"

Beep.

"Julian here. What we have—it's too special to be thrown away over some stupid newspaper that will be in the trash tomorrow. If you don't call me soon, I'm coming over to knock down your door. That's it."

Beep.

Mia pressed a button to shut off the machine. She looked at Cress, who'd been listening with an increasingly dazed look about him. "That's Julian in a nutshell, my bossy beloved. What should I do?"

Cress didn't hesitate. "Call Angelika back."

14

EVEN A BURGLAR wouldn't have to knock down the door to Mia's apartment. He could waltz right in, blend with the crowd and steal her blind. Julian made a mental note to speak to her about using her locks, but for now he was grateful, because he was there to steal Mia's heart.

Grovel, he thought. *Don't forget to grovel.*

Not his style, but sometimes a man had to redo what a man had done wrong.

"We're looking at an all-night session," Mia said to the group. She stood beside her paint table, ready for action in her overalls with a brush in hand. She hadn't noticed Julian. "I'll finish Angelika first so she can go home, then Leslie and Fred, then whoever I get to fill in for our fourth spot."

"How about the guy who lives downstairs?" someone suggested.

"Lance Wheatley." Mia paused, considering. "He has the right body type, but, no, he'd never go for it. Too uptight. I need someone who's not self-conscious. The leopard is the most important key to the scene."

Angelika's head lifted off the posing table. "Did you say the most important?"

Cress petted her forehead, one of the few spots on her

magnificent body that was left bare of paint. "After you, of course, angel."

She smiled and relaxed back into position. "Thanks, devil."

"Can I get you anything? Socks? A scalp massage?"

"Water. I'm parched."

"Here you go." Cress held a sports bottle near her face and squirted water between her open lips. "Better?"

"Perfect." They exchanged adoring looks.

"What's going on?" Julian whispered to Fred, who'd come over with Mrs. Snookums sprawled over his kimono-clad shoulder.

"Angelika dumped her southern gentleman billionaire. She says she can earn her own money, but only one man can give her a perfect bikini wax."

"Let's see some action," Mia announced, clapping her hands for attention. "Cress, can you do the underpainting on Leslie while I finish Angelika's stripes? The gazelle paint is already mixed—the medium brown in the bucket over there."

"I'm on it."

"Fred, you might as well go home for now. Come back about—" Mia turned to look at the wall clock and saw Julian. Her eyes widened and she didn't say a word. But she didn't break out into a banshee scream or chase after him with a mat cutter, either, so he supposed he could consider that a welcome. "About 3 a.m."

"Hi." Julian tried to look humble and apologetic. "I didn't realize you'd be this busy."

"Tomorrow is only the most important day of my career."

"I know. I didn't forget. I bought tickets for my sisters and myself. *Hard Candy* has a booth at the exhibition—playing up your cover, from what I hear."

"Great." Her eyes avoided his.

He dropped his voice. "Can you spare a few minutes for me?"

"Actually, no. I'm pressed for time. I have three bodies to paint and I'm stressing over finding a new leopard. The guy that Fred recommended just phoned—he's in the hospital with appendicitis. So, as you can see, now's not the time."

"Then how can I help?"

She shrugged. "Just stay out of my way."

"I could be the leopard," said a voice Julian recognized. He hadn't noticed his sister among the noise and confusion. What in the world was she doing here?

Very bounded up from the bed in the alcove. She peeled off a thick sweater and struck a pose in slim jeans and a camisole undershirt, showing off her lithe frame. "What do you think? I'm tall and skinny like a model."

"You are *not* taking part in this circus," Julian blurted. "And that's an order. Mom would die."

Mia grimaced before addressing Very. "Thanks anyway, but I prefer a male model for the leopard. I may have to compromise if we can't find the right guy, but for now I'm not ready to change the plan."

She gestured to the table, where Angelika was nude beneath a complicated pattern of black-and-white zebra stripes that followed the curves of her body like a contour map. "When I finish the zebra, Angelika's going to get on the phone to her agency and see if they can come up with a last-minute replacement. Someone without hang-ups about—" Mia's gaze flicked over Julian "—body art."

He felt her disdain like a blow. His command to Very had come instinctively, after six years of worrying over his sisters' safety and well-being and the sanctity of the family name. But, really, what was he protecting? Participating in a revealing art project was no worse than being splashed on the pages of the city's scandal sheets.

Then there was Mia. Perhaps she hadn't yet forgiven him about the outing with Petra, but she wasn't going off on it, either. That was the kind of open, accepting person she was. Open to reason, accepting of his mistakes.

He realized that he couldn't steal Mia's generous heart. He had to earn it.

"Ah…*ahem.*" Julian cleared his throat loud enough to get the group's attention.

Mia stopped with her paintbrush poised over Angelika's striped arm. "What now?" she asked with a tinge of annoyance.

"I'll do it," he said, and watched her eyes widen. "*I'll* be the leopard."

BY 5:00 A.M., when Julian returned, Mia's studio had cleared out. She'd sent her models home in protective sheeting to get what rest they could before they reconvened at the exhibition center where the body-painting competition would be held. Each competitor had an assigned space in which to stage their tableau. Mia had entered in the most prestigious category, where the entrants were allowed to employ multiple models and background features. Cress was in charge of that area— he'd been haunting florists and experimenting with pebbles and water features for days.

She'd been running on adrenaline and Red Bull for the past several hours, but her butt was starting to drag.

Even the sight of Julian's bod as he stripped down to his birthday suit couldn't rouse much energy.

A reluctant smile tugged at her lips. "You're looking very sleek."

He aimed a black look at her. She'd tested his commitment as a model by sending him into the bathroom to be waxed by Cress. Except for several plaintive yelps as his chest hair was ripped out by the roots, he'd done so without complaint.

She looked him up and down beneath tired lids and saw that he'd halted the wax job at a certain point, for modesty. The thong she handed him would cover that, but she couldn't resist needling him. She glanced over the supplies. "Remember my threat about the tweezers?"

Julian got into the thong in record time. "What now?"

"I spray you." She directed him to an area of the studio where she'd taped plastic tarps to the walls and floor. Her airbrush was at the ready, loaded with the tawny gold that would be the background color of the leopard's fur. "Last chance," she said, adjusting her goggles, then his. "You're sure you want to do this?"

"Too late to back out now."

"Not really, but there is good news. Your face will be painted, too. No one should recognize you."

He seemed relieved. Enough to manage a grin. "This is going to be quite an experience. Bachelor Seventeen standing nearly naked in front of crowds of people—"

"And photographers," she put in, to give him fair warning.

"Photographers?" He looked a bit sick. She supposed he was thinking about the reaction of his board of directors if they knew what their CEO was up to. "You're sure no one will recognize me?"

"Ninety-nine percent. You'll look like a leopard, not Julian Silk. And I can pose you so that you're not facing the crowd head-on." She gave an experimental squirt with the gun's nozzle. "Ready?"

He put his hands on his head. "As I'll ever be."

In minutes, he was coated head to toe. She used a hair dryer to hurry the drying time and soon he was able to drop his arms and move around. "Next step," she said, and spread a clean sheet of paper across the padded table. "Hop up here and I'll start on the shading, and then the spots. I'm completing the body work now, then doing faces and touch-ups right before the competition begins."

"Only for you," Julian said as he gingerly climbed into position. He stretched out on his stomach first, as she'd indicated. "Just so you know, I'm never groveling again."

"Groveling?" She slapped a thick brush against the back of his thigh. Many body painters worked strictly with the airbrush, but she liked the detail of painting by hand, even though the work was painstaking. "This is groveling?"

"It's my way of apologizing."

"Is that the sole reason you volunteered? Did Nikki tell you to do it?"

"Being your model was my idea. Nikki only advised me to grovel." He shook his head. "I should know better than to listen to her, after the fiasco with Petra…"

Mia stiffened. "I listened to your messages," she said, rolling her shoulders to get herself to loosen up. Using the airbrush first, she worked quickly to spray on the shadows and highlights along his backside and torso. "You claim you were photographed with Petra for my own good, huh? I don't own any Arizona beachfront, so I hope you don't think you can convince me of that steaming pile of bull crap."

"It seemed like it would work when Nikki suggested it. Throw the paparazzi off the trail, you know?"

"At the risk of hurting me?" Earlier, Nikki had explained to Mia that she'd pushed Julian's outing with Petra so that the woman would lose her cool and they could expose her as the source of the leak to the tabloids. So far, there was no proof.

"I didn't mean to hurt you. I tried to get in touch with you, beforehand, remember? You were already avoiding my calls. Cooling off, you called it. Which hurt *me*, if you want to know."

Mia's heart dropped into her stomach. "What do you mean? I was thinking of you when I suggested we be more discreet. Specifically, of harming your image with the board of directors. I'm not like the socialites who always know how to dress and what to say, how to be the perfect corporate wife—"

"Nope. I don't buy it. Maybe that was part of your reasoning, but you were also thinking about your own family. And that's okay. I understand. Your gut reaction was to believe that you'd disgraced them, wasn't it?"

She winced. He was on target. Even though she tried not to worry about her parents' approval, which was pretty much a lost cause, there was still a part of herself that wanted to please them. "Yeah, you're right…"

"Are you over that now?"

"I guess I am, or all this body painting will be wasted."

"So then…?"

"What?"

"Are we okay?"

"Maybe." She tested the paint on his backside, pressing a finger into the firm muscle with only a small twinge of longing. "You can turn over now."

She clicked off the hair dryer. There was just one thing she had to know. "Did Petra try anything with you?"

Julian hesitated, delaying the answer while he flipped sides. *If he doesn't tell the truth here,* Mia thought, *it would be a sign.*

He rubbed his chin, unthinkingly smearing the paint around. "She claimed that we were making the outing on a professional basis. Her regular escort was out of town."

"Uh-huh."

"But I've never had a colleague who talked business with her tongue stuck in my ear."

Jealousy gnawed áway the last of Mia's sleepiness. Every nerve ending in her body awoke with a snap. "Hey! That's *my* job."

"Even though we were on temporary hold?"

"The operative word being *temporary*."

"Don't worry. I set Petra straight. From now on, no one sticks their tongue in my ear except Mia Kerrigan."

"Gee, I feel so special," she said, but the funny thing was that she really did. Agreeing to be Petra's escort had been incredibly dense of Julian since he didn't know about Nikki's reasoning, but he'd also been well-intentioned. And the fact that he'd actually taken his baby sister's advice told Mia a lot about how far he'd come, even if he didn't realize it.

As did his unexpected patience with lying nude on her table, scarcely moving a muscle while she worked him over with a loaded airbrush. He was completely at her mercy, in a way, and there hadn't been a peep of protest.

"I'm afraid you'll have to get used to being photographed with me," he said. "Can you manage? I realize that you don't relish the publicity any more than I do. Eventually, another pop star or football player will be arrested for something despicable and the media will move on to fresh kill."

Contemplatively, Mia shaded in a long swath of orangey-brown over his flank, giving the muscle even more definition. "Logically, I know that the only way I'll ever please my parents is if I compromise. Compromise can be good. But it can also mean selling out."

"I know you're also worried about my expectations, but I'll never ask you to compromise what's important to you."

"We all compromise," she said softly. Her brush dabbed along his inner thigh and he shifted a little. "I've already done it, by turning body painting into a career. Advertising work, especially, can be one compromise after the other. But then there are the times that I get to be free. Like when I did the peach. *That* was a true work of art."

Julian closed his eyes and moaned. "The peach." After a moment of reverie, he opened an eye and peered at her, poised over him with her derriere stuck in the air. "Maybe we shouldn't talk about the peach."

She glanced at his burgeoning thong. "Good idea."

"Back to compromises…"

"Yes. Those. Umm…right. What I've realized is that I won't ever again be the perfect little girl in Sunday school class, and certainly not the perfect little wife and mother in the front pew, but maybe someday, now that I've found you, I might come close enough that I can go to visit my parents and be accepted for who I am."

"Meaning?"

She blushed, not ready to admit that she was thinking about marriage and motherhood. She and Julian had to be a couple before they could be a family. "Let's wait and see on that, okay? I haven't decided to forgive you about Petra yet."

He nudged her with his foot. "Yes, you have."

"You don't know how stubborn I can be. I hold a mean grudge."

"Not on your life."

She sighed. He'd found her out. She tried to be cynical, but inside she was just one big ball of mush. Of course, it was very likely that everyone knew that—look at her friends, every one of them aware of what an easy touch she was. But romantic feelings were different. Those were reserved only for Julian, who'd helped her to see that falling in love was just the start of actually being in love. And staying that way.

She'd come a long way from the woman who'd craved a mere taste of Bachelor Seventeen. Now she wanted all of him. To be filled forever.

They fell silent. She continued painting, still working on the background shading before she could start on the leopard's spots. After a while she checked the clock. A few more hours until she had to be at the exhibition hall. She'd hoped to get some sleep, but there was so much to do. At least she was wide awake now.

Her gaze traveled up and down Julian's supine body. He was totally at ease, except for…

"Hmm." Her paintbrush hovered above the bulging thong. A ridiculous garment. Not many men could pull the look off, and here she was, asking Julian to appear before a crowd in nothing but paint and a swatch of matching fabric. It was possible that he'd hoped she'd turn down his offer to model. She'd thought about it, especially after he'd proved his mettle with the waxing and the stripping and the submitting to her every direction. But if she let him off the hook now, she'd never know if he'd really have gone all the way for her.

She'd been using a light shade on his chest and stomach to simulate a leopard's snowy chest. There was nowhere else left to go, so she feathered the edges along his hip bones, blending them into the tawny undercoat.

Finally, her brush stopped.

Julian's head was raised, watching her.

She coughed. "This has never happened before," she said, trying to keep a professional tone and failing abysmally. She could not avoid his erection any longer. He'd stretched the thong to the breaking point. The head of his penis stuck out over the top, swollen and ready, welling with one glistening droplet that seemed to beckon her.

"Really?" he said.

"Well, no. Come to think of it, a few of the male models have become a little excited. But this is the first time that I…you know, *cared*." She licked her lips, the heat that kindled between her thighs telling her that she cared much too much. She was supposed to be exhausted, not aroused.

"What can we do?" Julian asked. "Paint around it?"

"Kind of distracting."

He lifted a hand, but she told him no. "You'll smudge the paint if you move too soon."

He grinned wickedly. "There's bound to be a mess one way or the other."

She took a deep breath, then set her brush aside.

"Spread your legs. Scooch down a little. Try not to drag your butt."

"Wha-at—" His voice cracked and broke off entirely when she stood at the end of the table, reached past his thighs and slid her fingertips under the thong. Carefully she worked the pouch lower, allowing his erection to spring free. A strange sight, considering how the rest of his body was painted golden brown.

She stroked him between her palms. His eyes were wide, depthless black, except for the rim of white showing all around. "Wait," he said. "Let me—"

"No. Every other inch of your skin is painted. I have to leave it until it dries. This is the only part of your body that I can touch."

His chest heaved for breath, sucking a hollow beneath his ribs. *"Mia..."*

"Lie back and enjoy it. There's nothing else you can do." She put her elbows on the table between his thighs and leaned forward, avoiding contact with his painted skin. Her tongue licked across her lips, wetting them. Her mouth opened.

At the last second, she stopped and looked up at Julian, narrowing her eyes to a menacing stare. "If you ever tell *anyone* I did this..."

"Never," he said, and then stiffened and jerked as if he'd been shocked by electricity when she lowered her head and swallowed him whole.

LIKE HER BROTHER, Nikki had the best of intentions. She always did. All she'd wanted to do was fix the mess that she'd had a hand in creating. It wasn't her fault that no one had bothered to keep her informed of the developments regarding Mia's jungle tableau. If she'd had any idea that Julian was about to appear stark-screaming naked in front of the world, she wouldn't have invited Petra over to see the unveiling.

The expo center was bustling with an enormous crowd visiting the wide variety of vendors and exhibits, set up in booths arranged at the outer edges of the vast hall. At the center was a stage of raised exhibit areas, each one partitioned off from the other, with curtained dressing rooms behind. A number of the more elaborate displays were already in place. Strange creatures populated each tableaux, frozen in posed positions for the inspection of the audience. Each appeared to be wearing a skin-tight body suit at first glance. It was only on second or third that the viewer realized...

"These people are nude," Petra said distastefully. She stared at a muscle-bound man in a telephone booth, painted red and blue with a large *S* on his chest. His supersized package was on prominent display.

"Of course they are," Nikki said, although she was agog herself. "What did you expect?"

"A bit more class, but I don't know why." Petra shook her head. "Where's the *Hard Candy* booth? This place is bedlam."

"We're down at the other end of the hall, but let's find Mia's space first." Nikki checked her watch. Her plan was for Petra to see firsthand that Julian was accepting—even proud—of Mia's work. Then Petra would know that her attempt to embarrass Mia through the press hadn't worked. Subtle maneuvering had been a waste of time. Sometimes you had to go the pie-in-face routine.

"I can't believe that Julian would lower himself to be involved in this—this—" Petra waved as a large man painted with chain mail and armor walked past as if he were strolling through Central Park.

"It's an art form," Nikki said, disgusted. Petra's aim seemed to be to elevate herself and put down Mia at every opportunity. If this was only about the rivalry for Julian, Petra had already lost and she would soon know it.

Petra snorted. "Sure it is."

"I'm surprised you don't appreciate the creativity, especially since you'll be featuring Mia's work in that layout and all."

"That wasn't *my* choice," Petra muttered.

Nikki had been scanning the crowd. She spotted Mia's buddy Cress heading toward the center booths with his arms wrapped around a giant potted palm.

Ready or not, here we come.

"Let's head this way." She led Petra into the surging traffic as the spectators began to congregate at the middle of the hall. A small knot of people with clipboards and sashes were making their way from one display to the next. "Looks like the judging has begun. Maybe we can get a glimpse of Mia's entry."

Petra tilted her chin high. "Is Julian here?"

"He should be."

A covetous gleam appeared in the blonde's eyes. "I suspect that seeing Mia in this milieu will give him a new perspective." Petra pulled in her shoulders to avoid contact with a woman painted in S&M style. "So…unconventional. Julian can't possibly enjoy this type of crowd."

"Actually, he's probably helping out behind the scenes." Nikki smiled wickedly, unable to resist needling Petra. "He's devoted to Mia, you know. Would do anything for her."

Petra frowned. "I'm sure there are limits."

"We'll see about that." Nikki had no idea how right she was.

CRESS DUMPED the final potted palm on the stage and levered himself up. Mia came out from behind the curtain and helped him slide it into place behind a fake boulder and a waist-high swatch of ornamental grass. "That's it," he said, dusting off his hands. "Call the models into place. The judges are only a couple of spaces away."

Mia took a rag out of the front pocket of her overalls and rubbed at the streaks of paint on her face. She'd been in overdrive since early that morning, what with finishing Julian's spots, grabbing a catnap, carting all her gear to the expo center while trying to maintain her cool for Julian's sake and then putting in several more hours of work on details and smudge repair.

She was so jittery that she no longer cared about winning. She just wanted it to be over, to finally know that Julian had forgiven her for putting him through this. He'd been quiet in the cab on the way over, swathed in a protective covering under his regular clothing and a droopy old raincoat. He'd worn a hood and sunglasses to disguise his identity, and she'd experienced more than a few pangs of regret. Despite his status as a most eligible bachelor, he was a private person. It was very possible that she'd asked too much of him.

"I'll get them," Cress said, giving her a pat when she was too stricken to move.

She looked out over the crowd. Most of the attention was focused on the judges, who were studying a staging area nearby. She had maybe ten minutes to get the models into position. Ten minutes before Julian exposed himself, just for her.

He won't be recognized. She'd applied an elaborate face makeup—coal-rimmed eyes, feline nose, special contouring around the mouth so he seemed to have a muzzle and whiskers. A person would have had to look very closely to distinguish any of the models' features.

"Hi, Mia!" A voice carried from the crowd of spectators.

Mia tried to focus her bleary eyes. Nikki. With a friend. No, not a friend. Petra Lombardi.

Smiling grimly, Mia returned Nikki's wave. Why had Julian's sister brought Petra over? There was no telling what the woman might do if she realized that Julian was taking part in Mia's tableau.

Mia decided that she had to warn Julian, but Cress was herding the models out from behind the curtain and suddenly there was no room to maneuver on their small square of stage.

Angelika took the prime position, bending over with her hands placed on one of the fake rocks so that she appeared to be on all fours. She cocked one leg and lifted her head high, assuming her zebra pose. Her dark hair had been sprayed and teased to make a stiff fringe down the middle of her head, a modified Mohawk that gave the effect of a zebra's mane.

Leslie took the right side, poised like a gazelle frozen in midflight. Behind her, squatting on a platform Cress had hidden behind the greenery, Fred the lemur struck his pose, one monkeylike arm raised to curl around the branch of a tree.

The crowd had grown as the judges approached. There was a buzz even before Julian stepped out from behind the curtain. His eyes connected with Mia's and he must have mistaken her panic for stage fright, because he gave her a quick smile and a nod before dropping down onto all fours. She'd worked on his stance earlier, and after he'd overcome the self-consciousness, he'd made an excellent leopard.

For a moment, she was frozen, watching as he elongated his body in a feline stretch, every muscle long and lean, his back curved, his shoulders bunched. There was something so primal and sexy about him that even without the spotted makeup he was pure *animal*.

She looked over the tableau, complete except for the drawn-back curtain, where Cress was motioning to her to join him. The scene was better than she'd imagined it and she was tempted to slip away with Cress, certain that she had an excellent chance of winning.

But at what cost to Julian?

Mia whirled to face the crowd. Yes, Petra was still there with Nikki, who'd been joined by an animated Very, whispering frantically in her sister's ear.

Even worse, several photographers had gathered around, getting ready to shoot the scene. Suddenly, Petra appeared among them, sleek and cool, studying Mia's setup with intense interest. Her eyes widened and she grabbed a photographer by the arm, pushing him off to the side where Julian was positioned, gesturing at the stage while she issued commands.

Had she recognized Julian?

Mia knew that she had to make her move, and fast. The judges had finished marking their scorecards at the adjacent exhibit and were on the way. She turned to reach for Julian, blocking him from the crowd as she urged him up to his feet.

"Mia!" he said. "What are you doing?"

"Don't argue. Just come with me." She shoved hard to get him moving, both of them lunging through the jungle greenery that Cress had arranged with such care. An exotic bird of paradise plant tipped over, but she wasn't about to stop to right it.

Cress yanked the curtain closed behind them. "You just cost yourself the top prize."

"I don't give a damn about winning the gold medal." Mia was panting as if she'd run a race. She kept her hands on Julian's shoulders, scared that he might try to rejoin the models. "Stay here, okay? Trust me. You don't want to be out there."

He was baffled. "Mia—why...?"

"I just, uh, decided that you weren't that necessary to the scene after all."

Behind them, Cress peeped through a narrow crack in the curtains while the judges evaluated their exhibit.

"What's going on?" Julian demanded, trying to catch a glimpse.

Mia squeezed her hands into fists. "All right. If you must know. Petra Lombardi is out there with a photographer. I think he's from *Hard Candy*. She may have recognized you."

"Petra," he echoed. He took a step back. "Okay, thanks for the warning. But it doesn't matter. I'm still willing to follow through. I promised you I would."

"I know, but *I'm* pulling the plug, Julian. It's not your choice."

"But—"

"There are other photographers, too. If Petra gives anything away, if they get even a whiff of your identity, it'll be a melee. That just suddenly seemed like too much of a risk. I don't want to see your photo splashed all over the papers, you know? Not like this." She gestured at his spots, then patted his bare chest for reassurance. "It's okay. Really. The prize isn't as important to me as you are. I don't want to be the cause of your embarrassment, or any grief from your board of directors."

After a moment, Julian let out a deep sigh. "I can't say that I'm not relieved."

She bear-hugged him, unmindful of his painted skin. "I'll never forget that you were willing to do this for me. I love you for that, Jules."

He pressed a kiss onto her cheek. "And I love you for getting me out of there, even if that means you lost the prize."

A bolt of pleasure went through her at his words, but she didn't dare pin him down to exact specifics of how and why and in what other ways he loved her. Instead she nuzzled his throat, letting her relief and joy percolate into giddy laughter. "One of us has to have dignity. You know it's not gonna be me."

"Don't forget, you're telling that to a man who's wearing a leopard-print thong."

"No leopard has ever filled one out better." She gave him a squeeze, then left his arms to rummage through her supplies. She found a bottle of nontoxic solvent and tipped it over a cloth. "We'd better get you cleaned up before any of the press realize what I did to Bachelor Seventeen."

"You did a lot for me," he said quietly.

She gave him a quick smile and began cleaning his face, rubbing away the painted-on whiskers and tufts and spots, finding a clean area on the rag and continuing on to his ears and throat, then his hands. He could put on his regular clothes and even if Petra made her way backstage, she'd never know for sure. No one would be the wiser except his sisters, who'd never tell. If only because there'd be no fun in torturing him after the beans were spilled.

"The judges have moved on," Cress announced from near the curtains. "Man, Angelika looks gorgeous. The photographers are still there. They can't get enough of her."

Julian's eyes glinted at Mia. "Whew," he whispered. "You saved my neck."

She nodded, wondering about Petra. Julian was her boss, in effect. What would she have done with the revealing photos? Probably arranged to have them leaked to the press so that there'd be no doubt that Mia was a bad influence on Silk Publishing's CEO. How desperate and sad. And how hugely Petra had underestimated Julian's courage.

Mia gave him a light kiss, having no doubt that he would face down his board of directors for her, if it came to that. "Did I hear right, or did you say something about love a few minutes ago? I've been waiting to hear that from you, but I want to be sure I got it right."

"You did." He put his arms around her, speaking softly for her alone. "I love you, crazy woman. I love every undignified bone in your body."

She smiled. "That's what I thought you meant."

Cress interrupted. "Hey, Mia. It wouldn't surprise me if you still won, even without a leopard. Wouldn't that be something?"

"I really don't care," she said, as Julian held her snugly against his nearly nude body. The cleaning rag dropped away as she put both of her paint-stained hands on his face. Her heart sang with the love she had for this man, the kind of love that was too exalting not to last, despite their foibles and flaws and outrageous mistakes. "I'll be happy even with seventeenth place."

"I think I can offer better than that," he said. "If you're willing to accept."

Mia kissed him. "I accept."

"Wait," he said with a laugh. "I haven't asked yet. You're always jumping the gun."

"So we'll slow down. We have lots of time. All I need for now is this." With loving hands, she stroked his paint-streaked face. "You love me as much as I love you. I have plenty of proof."

And so it was that while the judges awarded the prizes, and Nikki and Very discussed how much fun it would be to have a kooky artist in the family, and Cress worshipped his zebra-striped angel with adoring eyes, and Petra fumed over how close she'd come to getting the goods on Julian that would prove once and for all how he and the trampy body painter didn't belong together, Mia and Julian simply held each other and kissed. Slowly, sweetly, telling each other with each caress how good it was to know that together they made *one*.